Praise for
THE SON OF ABRAHAM
and Kathleen Kaufman

"*The Son of Abraham* is an immersive, haunting, touching story about family, love, and the supernatural. Kathleen Kaufman has woven a tapestry of original entities, visceral setting, and dark magical wonder that is equally unsettling and hopeful. A powerful read."

–**Richard Thomas**,
author of *Disintegration* and
the Thriller Award nominee *Breaker*

"Beautifully conceived, genuinely chilling and a brilliant culmination to Kathleen Kaufman's horror saga!"

–**Jennifer Brody / Vera Strange**,
award-winning author of *the 13th Continuum* trilogy
and the *Disney Chills* series

THE SON OF ABRAHAM

THE SON OF ABRAHAM

KATHLEEN KAUFMAN

+ KEYLIGHT
BOOKS
AN IMPRINT
OF TURNER
PUBLISHING

Keylight Books
an imprint of Turner Publishing Company
Nashville, Tennessee
www.turnerpublishing.com

The Son of Abraham
Copyright © 2021 Kathleen Kaufman

Library of Congress Cataloging-in-Publication Data

Names: Kaufman, Kathleen, author.
Title: The son of Abraham : a novel / Kathleen Kaufman.
Description: First edition.
Nashville, Tennessee : Turner Publishing Company, [2021]
Identifiers: LCCN 2021021832 (print) | LCCN 2021021833 (ebook) | ISBN 9781684425389 (paperback) | ISBN 9781684425396 (hardback) | ISBN 9781684425402 (ebook)
Subjects: GSAFD: Occult fiction.
Classification: LCC PS3611.A8284 S66 2021 (print) | LCC PS3611.A8284 (ebook) | DDC 813/.6—dc23

LC record available at https://lccn.loc.gov/2021021832
LC ebook record available at https://lccn.loc.gov/2021021833

Text Design by Meg Reid
Cover Design and illustrations by by M.S. Corley

Printed in the United States of America

To my husband and son, I love you both till the moon's upside down.

This World is not Conclusion.
A Species stands beyond -
Invisible, as Music -
But positive, as Sound -

—*from* "This World is not Conclusion" by Emily Dickinson

THE SON OF ABRAHAM

PROLOGUE

THE SUN WAS RISING JUST OVER THE CAP OF THE bungalows on Sinder Avenue. *Sunrise. An odd time to choose*, Ceit thought as she brushed the messy hair off Alan's face. His eyes caught the light, which made them glow. He turned his head and grinned at her. His two front teeth were growing in. A dusting of freckles lined his nose and cheeks; those would disappear in the next year or so, and Ceit would miss them forever. Inside, she could hear her mother in the kitchen, the sound of water running, a frying pan on the metal stove.

"What have you done, Alan?" Ceit asked gently.

He shook his head. "I had to." His voice sounded hollow and thin.

"You didn't. And you can't undo it," Ceit whispered while tucking a wisp of his soft hair behind his ear.

"This was the last time I felt safe," he said, looking past her at the rising sun and then turning his gaze to Ceit. "Momma will get sick tomorrow. But today she made pancakes and walked us to the bus stop, do you remember?"

Ceit nodded. "I do."

"Do you miss her?" Alan asked, his nose scrunching up, as though he were trying to riddle a problem too big for him.

"Yes," Ceit said. "I miss you too."

"I'm coming with you though. Now you have to take me with you." Alan's plea turned into a whine.

Ceit shook her head. "No, darling, not after what you've done. You cannot come with me."

Alan stamped his feet. The sun stopped its upward movement, and the sky took on a greenish tint. "You *have* to."

Ceit took his hand, stroking the soft skin of his fingers. He felt so warm, so alive. "It's too late, my love. You cannot come with me."

"It should have been me," Alan growled, snatching his hand back.

"It never would have been," Ceit answered simply.

"I am more than you think I am," Alan muttered, shifting his gaze back to the skyline, where a storm was now building, blocking out the rising sun.

"You'll stay here, little brother—not in memories, but in your body. You'll walk with the restless ones until your physical form becomes as insubstantial as smoke." Ceit watched the little boy's face contort with anger and then grief.

"No! It doesn't work like that. You *have* to take me with you. You *have* to. It's the *rules.*" His face was growing red, and tears were sprouting at the corners of his pale eyes. He turned and looked at her, his skin dewy with emotion. "I'm *sorry*, okay! *I'm sorry!*"

"I hope so, but I'm not sure I believe you, little brother. This is the last time we will talk. I will not hold an audience with you again." Ceit felt human emotion she had not felt in many years well up in her throat.

"It's not *fair*! It should have been *me*!" Alan rose to his feet and towered over her; his little boy form seemed to stretch to the sky. A streak of lightning sizzled through storm clouds behind him.

"Goodbye, Alan."

PART I
LOS ANGELES
NOVEMBER 2012

1

KARA

KARA GLANCED AT THE CLOCK: 5:45 P.M. THE BRIGHT green neon flashed, pulsing in the wake of the power outage. In the kitchen, the coffeepot flashed similarly, as did the timer on the stove. Absently, the woman reminded herself to reset the timer so the casserole wouldn't burn. She discarded the thought easily, staring at the blank face of the television. Fifteen minutes, that's what they'd said—the president with dull horror on his face, the news anchors with numb reactions. Fifteen minutes. Then everything had gone black, only to flash back a moment later. *Maybe they're wrong*, the woman thought. *Maybe they said it wrong. The power wouldn't come back if there was only fifteen minutes.* As if in answer, the blinking lights again went black, the smell of half-cooked casserole filling the room.

From his place on the floor, the child turned his startled brown eyes up to her. This time of year, the sky was already approaching darkness. Without the light it was too dark to see where he was driving his blue plastic bus.

"Mommom?" he asked hesitantly, his toddler voice faltering, on the verge of tears. The woman was frozen. She looked at the child blankly, unable to help him. On uncertain legs, he pulled himself up and lunged toward her, wrapping his tiny hands around her calves, burying his face in her knees. Her hands instinctively buried themselves in his wispy blond hair. The curls were uncombed; she felt the remains of fall leaves between her fingers.

How much time had passed? Five minutes? How much time had she wasted standing there? Suddenly panicked, she bent down to meet the child's arms, pulling him to her. He wiped his nose on her shirt and settled his weight on her thigh, knocking her off-balance. The woman landed against the low-lying coffee table, the child on her lap. He giggled at the motion, a soft noise muffled in the crook of her neck. In the fading light, she looked around the room helplessly. The boy's books lay scattered, never to be read again. His toys were precariously stacked in plastic coffee buckets.

The woman pulled him closer, feeling tears in her eyes. The boy looked up at her confused and repeated his question. "Mommom?"

She pulled him tight, too tight, and he wiggled out of her arms, standing to grab the bright lidded plastic cup full of Goldfish crackers from the table. Without asking, he pulled the top off. Instinctually she moved to stop him, but with a shriek of laughter he threw the cup into the air, scattering Goldfish to the corners of the room. A moment of frustration filled her and then dissolved instantly as a roar of impact shook the house—the sound of metal ripping, the crack of wood, no screams. The boy's face crumbled from the shock, and he started bawling. The woman pulled him to her, lifting him off the floor while clumsily standing and then crossing to the window.

A small white car was embedded into the magnolia tree on the front lawn. Smoke from the collision engulfed the scene, and the woman squinted to see in the windows. She made out two heads, both motionless, thick blood dripping. A still hand gripped the steering wheel.

The woman stroked the boy's head, his cries quieting. She should call someone. She glanced at the phone on the table. Who? The news anchor had said all emergency services were disengaged. That had been at least ten minutes ago. How long did they have left?

A shudder rocked the house, throwing the woman backward into the wall. Through the window she saw a small plane—one of the prop planes they flew tourists around in—weaving back and forth, trying to take off from the airport across the field from the house.

Her husband wasn't going to make it back; the realization hit the woman suddenly. He never got home before six thirty. She wasn't going to see him before time was up. She held the boy to her, his wet face buried in her chest. He tucked his small hands in, warming them on her stomach. Another quake rocked the house, knocking the woman to the floor. She landed painfully on her tailbone, trying to keep the boy upright. He clung to her, frightened. A framed picture slid off its hook and crashed to the ground, barely missing her head. The prop plane dropped out of view, weaving precariously. From her vantage point on the floor, the woman didn't see it go down, only the plume of smoke and fire that accompanied the tremor.

How long did they have? Had it been fifteen minutes already? The sky was almost completely dark now, the absence of the artificial light previously offered by the streetlights making it seem darker still. The boy lurched out of her arms suddenly and lunged for the couch, where he grabbed his yellow stuffed bear. The fuzz had been worn off by countless naps, and the soft cloth tag was in tatters from the boy's habit of rubbing it between his fingers. He turned to her triumphantly, his smiling face hard to see in the darkness. The woman fell forward as a quake—stronger, more resonant than its predecessors—rocked through the house. Frantically she flailed through the motion, reaching forward for the boy. His panicked cry gave her a direction in which to move in the now pitch-blackness. She pushed aside the furniture that lay askew, moving closer to his high-pitched scream.

"Mommom!" he screamed in pain as she pressed on toward him, ignoring the wet pain that dripped into her eye, ignoring the growing numbness spreading down her legs. Blindly, she reached forward and grabbed at the sound. She felt his soft, tangled curls and his baby silk hands reaching up to grab her hand. With the last burst of strength in her, she pulled the boy to her, his screams deafening. She curled around his tiny body, madly stroking his hair, kissing his forehead. Outside the roar of destruction continued, louder and closer with every passing moment. The house groaned in protest, debris from above crashing down, painfully slamming into the woman's back and legs. She curled tighter around the boy and closed her eyes.

2

MIRIAM

"MIRIAM! TURN ON THE TELEVISION!" THE DEEP VOICE rocked the house and disturbed Miriam from her nap. She'd fallen asleep watching *Dr. Phil*. Her husband had turned the set off sometime later. She sat up, rubbing her eyes, confused by the urgency.

"Miriam! You hear me? Turn on the TV!" Miriam grumbled her displeasure and felt around for the remote. *If it's so damn important, why don't you come in here and turn it on your damn self?* she thought. After thirty-five years of marriage, she was used to his tirades, his demands, his general crankiness. Now that they were both retired, she was bombarded with it every day, no break, no job to go to, no place to be. She heard his footsteps from the kitchen; he was running from the sound of it. Miriam found the remote and squinted to see the buttons. She reached for the lamp, but it just clicked—no light.

"David! The power's out again! You need to check the fuse box." She pushed the power button on the remote just to be sure. Nothing. David's footsteps came to a halt. The low pulse of the radio she'd been hearing from the other room abruptly stopped and turned to static. It ran on batteries. *Odd*, she thought. *No reason that shouldn't work.*

David appeared in the doorway. Even in the growing dark, she could see the fear on his face.

"Hon? What's—"

Before she could finish her sentence, she caught out of the corner of her eye a white car go flying past, weaving crazily. As she turned her head in alarm, it collided with the magnolia tree in the yard next to theirs.

"Jesus God!" David exclaimed. He ran to the sofa, roughly grabbing Miriam's hand and pulling her to her feet. Before she could object, he was pulling her to the door, grabbing her fuzzy pink sweater from the coatrack as they went.

"Hon? What's going on? What's happening?" Miriam's head was aswim. All she could think about was the car rocking slightly on its axle on the neighbor's lawn. *The little boy must be terrified*, she thought. He was only two, not old enough to understand what had caused the noise.

Without answering, David pulled her outside and toward their car.

"David!" she demanded. "We need to call someone!"

"It's too late," he said, his voice breaking. "There's no one to call. We've got to get out of here!"

"No!" Miriam planted her feet, straining against his urgency. "We need to help Kara and the baby! They must be terrified. And we need to get an ambulance out here!" She shifted her gaze to the smoking car and swallowed her gag reflex.

David started to answer but was thrown back by a violent quake. The sidewalk split in front of her eyes, rising up and ripping her hand from her husband's. Miriam felt herself falling backward, flailing for something to break the fall. Her back landed hard on the sidewalk, her ankle twisting underneath her. Miriam heard herself scream, but the sensation was washed away with pain as the back of her head smacked against the concrete. Her vision clouded and then became clear again.

Miriam struggled to sit up, shaking off the panic that was steadily overtaking her. She could see David lying half under their blue Toyota. It looked as though he'd been knocked down and thrown back. His head was dangerously lodged against the right rear tire. She tried to shout his name, but no noise came. Miriam tried to clamber to her feet, but her strength betrayed her. David wasn't moving. His head lolled to one side as though asleep. Miriam looked up, around, silently begging for someone to help them. She saw a cloud of fiery smoke rising from the airport runway. Numb, she realized what must have caused it. As she pulled herself toward her still husband, a second quake ripped the concrete apart beneath her. Miriam felt herself roll into the crevice created by the space. The darkness was overwhelming. As she reached for the edge, a sharp and sudden pain echoed through her neck and down her spine.

With a dim realization, she felt her hand release and the twitch that accompanies sleep overtake her consciousness. As the numb darkness spread, she gave in to the blackness, closing her eyes, letting go of the moment.

3

LYNN

EDGAR PURRED CONTENTEDLY IN HER LAP, UNAWARE that anything was different. Lynn continued to pet him with long, even strokes, not changing the rhythm or pressure.

"This is the way the world ends, this is the way the world ends, this is the way the world ends..." she repeated to herself. With a wave of overwhelming relief, she thought of the stack of collection notices on her kitchen counter. She thought of the eviction letter that she'd thrown in the trash. She thought of the checkbook, her constant source of panic, soon to be nevermore. She breathed deeply, exhaling the anxiety of the last year. A weight had been lifted. She smiled—a strange, small gesture. Her watch read 5:48. Three minutes since the announcement. *What if they're wrong?* She frowned a little, letting the weight resettle a bit. Abruptly she shook her head. This wasn't wrong; this was the end, finally the end.

"I'm coming, baby, I'm coming..." she said softly to the framed picture on the coffee table. Victor's face smiled back at her. *Waiting for you, babe, waiting.* She hugged Edgar to her chest, tears forming in her eyes. Edgar nuzzled her chin, cuddled in—5:49. She was suddenly racked with mundane thoughts: Would it hurt? Would she survive despite herself? Would Edgar be left behind? She thought of the paring knife in the kitchen. It would take one small cut, that's all, if you knew where to do it. Make the slit right on the artery under your chin, where the blood pulsed, and you bleed out in twenty seconds. She could do Edgar first, then herself, and then no one would be left behind.

Her thoughts were interrupted by the sound of screeching brakes outside. She twisted her head to the right, barely making out the outline of a light-colored car flying past the Markowitz's house next door and into a tree on the corner. The impact shook her house a little. *That's the house with the toddler*, she thought suddenly. The boy was responsible for the yellow sidewalk chalk scribbles that decorated her walk and steps. His mother—a thin, nervous woman—always apologized and offered to come and wash them away. Lynn had always felt inexplicably sorry for them both.

Lynn watched the outline of the willow tree in her front yard against the darkening sky. The cloth ribbon wrapped around one of the branches was tattered, flapping in the wind. *The flag of my disposition*, Lynn thought wryly as she watched it. Weird that she'd never asked why it was there. A man in a Cubs baseball hat with two teenagers had put it there one Saturday. They'd stood around the tree, an air of sadness surrounding them. Lynn hadn't even considered removing it, nor had she thought of asking them why it was there. She understood loss and the inexplicable things it made you do.

She slid off the couch and onto the beige carpet, still hugging Edgar, who had now wrapped his paws around her neck—as he was apt to do—and was clinging to her T-shirt. Victor's face was dim in the darkness. He'd been gone for a little over a year now, and still she swore she could smell him in the pillow she'd been unable to move from their shared bed. His clothes lay scattered on the floor in the same order as they'd fallen on the last day he'd left for work.

A distant impact sent a tremor through the house. *Must be from the airport.* She thought again of the paring knife. It was the smartest way that she could assure they both would go painlessly, quickly. But what if the report was wrong? What if this wasn't the end? What if it passed and she was just another suicide, another damned soul? Surely God would understand. Surely it wasn't suicide if you were going to die anyway. She reprimanded herself immediately. "We do not know His plan," she whispered on the edge of silence.

Lynn stroked Edgar's thick fur, slowly, methodically—5:52. The out-of-place smile returned to her lips. No, God would spare her this time. He wouldn't make her continue in this life anymore, surely. He would take them both, take them home. She thought of her mother, and the uncertain discontent returned. She'd never call her again, never hug her. Her mother lived alone outside of Sacramento, too far away.

The quake knocked Victor's picture to the ground and threw Lynn to her side. Edgar, still hanging on, raked his claws across her chest in panic. Lynn screamed and felt the blood begin to pulse to the surface. The cat jumped away and scurried under the sofa. Lynn rubbed the wounds, feeling the sticky damp between her fingers. The bookshelf teetered and swayed, and she watched with horror as it began to tip forward, spilling its contents. Lynn held up her hands as books began bombing her from above. The heavy oak shelves lost their battle with gravity as the unit tipped forward and came crashing down.

Lynn didn't know how to react. She had never felt that kind of pain before. She tried to pull herself forward, but the oak shelves had pinned her legs. The pulsing radiation threatened to take her breath entirely. She tried to analyze it. It bordered on intense nonfeeling and escalated into a sensation so severe she felt like screaming. No one would answer, she knew that. The television had been right; this was the end.

Lynn thought of the paring knife. She wished she'd had the courage. The second quake hit just as hard, and for a bright moment time slowed and she seemed to pass out of herself and into total numbness. *No—not numbness,* she thought dully. *It's like an embrace...a thousand embraces.* Lynn looked down and watched the still body below, pinned underneath the oak bookshelves. She waited for him, but she was alone here. She waited to leave this place, but instead she stayed. She waited for the pain to stop, but it grew to an unbearable decibel, threatening to break her. The wall caved in, and plaster flew over the still body below her, snowing tiny white flecks. As she watched, the white began to reflect against the pitch-black of the street, growing thicker and thicker. As her internal ache finally began to fade, she felt a hand reach through the darkness and wrap around her own. Calloused palms, familiar warmth—she was home.

DEA

THE FUCKING CAR WON'T START. JESUS CHRIST, THE *fucking car won't start.* Dea slammed her head into the steering wheel and then reeled back from the pain.

"Jesus, what the fuck are you doing?" Next to her, Brian's voice was inordinately high in his panic. She bit her tongue on the smart-ass comment that made its way up and almost out of her mouth. Without answering him, she turned the key again. The engine growled and died.

"Let me try!" Brian pushed her against the door, smashing her rib cage in his attempt to wrestle the keys out of her hands. She slammed her elbow back, catching him in his pelvis.

"Fuck! Ow!" Brian fell back into his seat, looking hurt. Dea glared in his direction and tried the keys again. This time the engine sputtered and reluctantly caught, heaving a ragged sigh of submission. Next to her, her brother sighed with relief. *Idiot,* she thought. *He's relieved, and we have less than fifteen minutes to try to make it to San Jose. What a fucking joke.* Still, her dad's voice rang in her ears.

"Get to the airfield. I have a plane, just get here. We have to get out—now."

Dea backed out the driveway, ignoring the caution she usually used. The car screeched into place, facing south, the airfield three minutes away. Brian was breathing heavily next to her. She glanced over at him. He was a baby, only fifteen. She was the responsible one in the house; she was the one who needed to get them there. The clock in the dash read 5:47. Thirteen minutes—three to get to the field, five to get into the air, five minutes left to escape the blast zone.

Dea hit the gas, and sudden motion rocked them forward. She'd gotten her license last month. She hated driving a stick. Her dad had told her to get used to it. "Even in LA," he'd said, "you need to drive a manual." The car lurched and threatened to die again. Brian whimpered, a low, desperate sound that made Dea want to smack him.

It was 5:48. Fuck. Dea hit the clutch and tried to shift into second gear. The car groaned and the gears ground together, but the car moved forward. Dea hit the gas and the car flew, the low gear screaming in protest. She didn't have time to care. They just needed to get there—three minutes to the field, five to get into the air, five minutes to escape the blast zone.

"Lights! Lights!" Brian shrieked in a desperate half whisper. Dea hadn't even noticed she was driving in near blackness. She fumbled with a knob, flipping it this way and that. Finally the lights blared the street, startling them both. Dea pressed her foot on the gas and forced the car forward past the houses she'd grown up next to. Past the tree that her mother had planted in the neighbor's yard to make up for Dea and Brian yanking up their spring flowers when Brian had been five and she had been six. A sad white ribbon hung on a branch, a reminder of the anniversary of her mom's death last week. Her dad insisted on tying the ribbon on the willow, even though the house had changed owners three times since she'd died and the woman who lived there had looked at him like he was nuts. Still, she'd left it. Dea guessed she was afraid to question the sad man with his two nearly grown kids standing in her yard holding hands.

The car screamed in frustration, begging to be shifted into third gear. Dea ignored the roar of the engine—5:49. As they neared the end of the block, she saw the old couple who lived in the stucco house looking out the window, their faces reflected in the headlights. The moment seemed to stretch and hold. At the same time, a dark figure darted into the street. It was too low to be a person. Before Dea could identify the shape, she swerved to avoid it. The car veered crazily to the side. Brian let out a terrified shriek. *Fuck*— 5:50. Dea tried to regain control, tried to hit the brake, but in her terror, her foot found the gas. The car roared and flew forward, across the lawn where the old couple fell out of view and into the yard littered with toddler cars and giant bouncy balls.

Dea didn't feel the impact, just the emptiness that preempted the pain. She twitched uselessly, left arm still gripping the steering wheel, frozen in place. Next to her, Brian was silent. She tried to yell, but even as the sound raged in her head, her body grew stiff and still. Her head felt like it was wrapped in a thousand layers of marshmallow padding. Her right arm ignored the command to move; instead of reaching toward her silent brother, she felt a paralytic numbness wash over her almost as though she were underwater.

She felt the car shudder, the remains of iron and oil emitting a tinny death rattle. Miraculously, the clock on the dash still glowed in the darkness—5:51. In the distance, she heard the whir of a prop plane gearing up for takeoff. A torn cry escaped from her mouth as she realized that she would die here. She wouldn't escape. She would die here in this car, with her baby brother's body still and quiet beside her. A wave of impact rocked the car and Dea slammed again into the steering wheel, her body perfectly numb. The darkness began growing in the corners of her eyes, the languid stillness that comes before sleep catching her breath. She felt a release, a pull from the metal prison that trapped her body. With a feeling of inordinate lightness, she flew upward from the car to the top of the magnolia tree, staring down without judgment.

5

DAN

THE PHONE RANG THREE TIMES AND THEN WENT TO voice mail. *Dammit.* Dan called the number again. *What is the point of giving the kids cell phones if they never turn them on?* Clumsily, he squinted at the tiny buttons and tried to find the redial. *Dammit.* As if by a miracle, the phone in his hand buzzed. Dea's smiling face appeared on the screen, dressed in a silly reindeer sweater that she'd worn for three straight days last Christmas. Dan fumbled with the big green button. He took a deep breath as he heard her voice on the other end.

"What's up, Dad? Sorry, ringer was off." Dea sounded distracted. Dan cleared his throat.

"Hey, honey, listen. I need you and your brother to get out here as soon as possible. Can you do that? Don't pack anything, just get in the car. You can get here in three minutes, just...honey? You there?" There was a cautious silence on the other end of the phone.

"Dad? But...why? What's happening? Are you alright?" Her voice cracked a little, her panic seeping in. Dan looked anxiously at the clock. Any minute the president would be on television, telling everyone what he had just learned from the air traffic controller at the Santa Monica Airport. If Dea panicked, she'd never get to the airport in time to get out of the blast zone. He had to stay calm despite the urge to vomit that he was fighting.

"Baby, I'm fine. Look, hon, something's happened. I just need...I really need you and Brian to jump into the car. You need to get here as soon as possible. Drive to Airport Road, go past the park. I'm in the hangar behind the café. The gates are all unlocked. You need to hurry. You have three minutes to get here. I can get us up in the air in five, and then we need to get away."

"But..." Dea sounded panicked and bewildered. "But I can't drive the stick, Dad, I can't..."

"You can do it, honey, you can. Trust me. Just get it into second gear, that's all you have to do. You can get here in second gear. It doesn't matter if it hurts the car, just drive. Will you do that? Just drive." The television screen latched to the wall above Dan's head flickered, then revived, revealing the live feed of the presidential podium, waiting for the weight of the news it would bear. The emergency warning tone began to wail. He lost the control he'd been struggling to maintain.

"Drive! Just get here! You have three minutes to get here, five to get in the air. We have five more to get out of the blast zone!" Dan's voice sounded frantic, too loud.

"Daddy?" Dea sounded like she was crying. "What's happening? The TV—"

"Dammit! Just get in the car!" Dan fought the urge to slam the phone into the metal wall of the airport hangar. "I have a plane. We have to hurry! C'mon, baby, you can do this. Just get here!"

With a click, the phone abruptly cut out. Dan couldn't tell if they'd been disconnected or if Dea had hung up and done what he'd told her to do. The dial tone cut back and forth. Above his head, Dan looked up to see the president's mouth moving soundlessly. Behind him, someone pushed the volume. Dan wished he hadn't. He didn't need volume to know what was being said. The president's stoic face ashen. The normally polished man had a loosened tie and top two buttons undone on his dress shirt. For whatever reason, that scared Dan more than the words the man was saying. The first sign of damage, the first thing to crumble is the president's wardrobe.

He had spent too much time getting the prop plane ready to get them to San Jose. *Dammit—why didn't I call first? They'd be here by now.* But he knew the answer; he'd been waiting for someone to say it wasn't happening, someone to say it was all a joke. If he told the kids, that meant it was real, and it couldn't be real. *Please, please, please, please say they've left. Please say they're driving.* Nervously, Dan watched the clock. Two minutes had passed, still he didn't hear anyone pulling up.

"Our sources tell us the epicenter of the blast will be downtown Los Angeles. Anyone who is on the ground within one hundred miles of the blast zone is unlikely to survive. We need you, *I* need you to go underground, cover your faces. Rescue services in Los Angeles County have been disbanded, as they will be rendered useless." The president paused, bone weary and out of words.

"I was advised not to go on air tonight with this warning. It was said that there was no point in warning people of a tragedy that they cannot prevent, nor can they run from. I ask us now to pray, for all those in the line of attack, for all those who will perish tonight. You will not die in vain."

Dan pushed past the dozen or so stunned faces and ran out onto the darkening field. *Dammit, where are they? They should be here by now.* Behind him, the room lit only by the flickering television went dark. A stifled scream escaped from one of the other pilots. Still there was no movement from the road, no headlights, no roar of a car stuck in second gear by a teenager who had just gotten her license.

Dan ran up the grass hill to the side road, looking in the direction where his kids, his life, should be arriving. He found himself shaking his hands uselessly, an old habit that used to drive Sarah nuts. She used to say he looked like a palsy victim. She had been right; she had been right about most things.

Standing in the darkness, he felt time slow and speed up. How long had it been? At least five minutes since he'd run out of the hangar. They'd estimated fifteen minutes. *How do they know?* he suddenly wondered. Had the president said anything about fifteen minutes? All Dan could hear was the panicked voice of the air traffic controller on the radio with DC earlier that evening.

"Dan! C'mon, man! We've got to go! This is it, buddy, c'mon!"

Dan spun around in the darkness to see another pilot pushing the small plane out onto the runway with the help of another dark figure.

"C'mon! We can't wait!"

Dan stuttered. "I can't... The kids are coming..." Even as he said it, he knew it wasn't true. They'd be here already. They weren't going to make it out, and neither was he. In the dark, the other pilot yelled in his direction, yelled that he needed to go, that he couldn't do anything to save them. Dan ignored him. Instead, he walked down the sidewalk toward the sand-filled park on the edge of the runway. Behind him, he heard the roar of the engine as it caught and began to taxi into the blackness.

Dan found himself standing in the cold sand, the tiny pellets climbing into his socks uncomfortably.

"I'm sorry," he whispered.

Behind him the sound of the plane cut out, sputtering midair. Dan turned around just in time to see a flash of white metal bearing down on him. In a moment that seemed to last a lifetime, he saw an incredible lightness spread over the field. The blackness was erased and replaced with the green fields in Clover Park, his kids, his babies running ahead of him, finding treasures from yesterday's picnics—bottle caps, bright-colored twist ties. A plane takes off in the distance, and the kids stop, their creamy faces aimed skyward to watch as the plane climbs into the sky. "It's always been us," he whispers to himself. The sun warms his shoulders as Dea looks up to his face. He reaches to take Brian's hand, the boy too distracted to react except by instinct. *It's always been just us.*

6

AARON

"CAN YOU HEAR ME? I REPEAT, CAN YOU HEAR ME? Am I coming through?" A low pause, then a desperate "Will someone say something? Are you there?"

Aaron sat back and stared at the radio. He reached hesitantly for the radio mic, holding it in his hand, staring at the black button he would have to press if he were to respond. In his hand the radio continued to plead for attention.

"I will repeat. At seventeen forty-five, approximately twenty minutes from now, the president will address the nation. You need to evacuate now, do you copy? Evacuate. Do not wait for the president's address. Evacuate by air. You need to be as far from downtown Los Angeles as possible by eighteen hundred hours. Do you copy?"

"Why?" Aaron asked no one. He didn't press the black button; he didn't appease the desperate voice. Instead he looked over his shoulder at the small crowd of men standing behind him. Some were crop dusters; most were small-time pilots who owned biplanes, prop planes, charged money to fly tourists over the ocean.

"What...what does she mean? Evacuate?" Aaron looked at the stout fifty-year-old man wearing a Cubs cap. Dan. His name was Dan. He looked like a soccer dad, a weekend Little League coach. Aaron felt numb.

"I don't know," Aaron said simply. He stared at the mic in his hand. "We've got to go. Guess it doesn't much matter why." The radio continued on.

"Please, someone copy. You need to evacuate now. If you are within one hundred miles of downtown Los Angeles, you will not survive the blast or the aftershocks that will accompany it. You need to evacuate by air. Do you copy?"

Aaron reached over and numbly switched off the control panel, silencing the voice. He looked at the stunned pilots. "Okay, who has a plane?"

The action broke their silence. The men closest to the door raced to the runway. Aaron stood uncomfortably, staring at the remaining pilots. Dan in the Cubs cap wiped his stubbled face with his hand and started for the door.

"Who will take me?" Aaron asked quietly. The remaining men looked stunned. They all stared at the silent radio.

"Maybe you should turn that thing back on," a man near the door started. "We might need to know—"

"Who will take me?" Aaron repeated, ignoring him. He thought of his small apartment off National Boulevard, the traffic outside his kitchen window, the ginger tabby cat that dug holes in the small potted lemon tree on his patio. He shook his head. "Well?"

Finally, a man in a flannel shirt who looked too young to be a pilot waved a hand at him. "C'mon, you can come with me. I'm not waiting around for some speech. Let's get the hell out of here. Fuck clearance, we're going."

Aaron followed him out the door, past the others who seemed frozen in place, unsure of how to proceed. The lights flickered and dimmed, then came back full strength. Aaron glanced around nervously. He should call someone, warn someone, but who? At twenty-three, this was the only job he'd ever had, and he'd been pretty sure he was going to get canned in a week or so anyway. *Fuckers*, he thought angrily as he followed the pilot into the darkening runway. If they paid him more than thirty grand a year, he wouldn't have to do all the extra stuff he'd been doing. *Not like it's that bad anyway, seriously*, he thought as the pilot made a beeline for a black-and-silver prop plane. *Selling fuel isn't hurting anyone.* He'd done it for a year before the assholes in the head office had even noticed it was missing. All he'd had to do is mark the inventory sheet and input the amount into the computer spreadsheet; no one ever noticed it wasn't the right numbers.

"C'mon, grab the other block!" the pilot shouted. Already Aaron could hear the other planes starting up. He leaned over and pulled the heavy metal brake block out from under the landing gear. The pilot was pulling a ladder from the side. He started to climb up into the cabin.

"You coming or what? I'm going now—I mean *now*."

Aaron nodded and followed the pilot into the cramped cabin.

"Sit back there. We'll be up in a sec," the pilot barked, slamming the cabin door and indicating the four tiny seats behind the control panel. Aaron sat down cautiously and reached for the seat belt out of habit. Not that it mattered anymore. They crashed, they were dead; they stayed, they were dead.

"Alright, hold on."

The plane started with a cough. Aaron jumped back in his seat. He wasn't religious, but he found himself muttering the Lord's Prayer. He couldn't remember all the words, so he just repeated "Our Father, who art in heaven" over and over. As the plane taxied down the dim runway, the pilot snorted.

"Good luck with that shit. Never did me any good."

Aaron looked out the tiny window and saw another small plane taking off in the distance. He wondered if the people in the houses were going to get wise to the fact that something was up. *Probably not*, he thought dully. They'd be so used to planes by now that they wouldn't really notice if there were a bunch in a row.

The plane picked up speed, pressing Aaron back into his seat. As the landing gear lifted and the wings caught the air, Aaron breathed a sigh of relief. He looked at his watch—5:40 p.m. They had at least fifteen minutes to get the hell away from here. The plane seemed to be flying straight up. Aaron held his breath, fighting the panic that was rising in his gut. As they sped out over the houses and toward the marina, the pilot let out an audible sigh.

"I'm Gus. I've seen you around the hangar but never introduced myself."

Aaron leaned forward slightly, his voice cracking.

"Aaron...thanks for this, thanks." He felt awkward.

"Yeah well, don't thank me yet. Thank me if we get out of this thing. I'm heading out over the water. The radio's all static, no way to check flight patterns, so we're winging it. Guess the FAA can't get on my ass if this thing's for real. If it isn't, well, we'll see."

Aaron hadn't even considered that the warning might be a hoax. Below him he saw a flood of blackness engulf the land. It started in a wave. Whole neighborhood, business towers, everything—a rolling wave of blackness.

"The lights are gone. Jesus, the lights are all out," Aaron whispered, the panic of what was about to happen finally settling in.

"All the more reason we need to be the hell out of there." Gus sounded unnaturally calm.

Aaron thought of his tiny apartment again. He had nothing there. A mattress on the floor, no bed frame; he'd never gotten around to getting one. Sparse kitchen, no food in the fridge. He usually ate at the McDonald's or KFC down the street. They knew him there. The employees always tried to smile, but he ignored them. He ignored everyone. In front of him, Gus indicated to him while keeping his eyes peeled on the sky.

"Hey, can I ask you a question, since we might be the last two men escaping from LA?"

"What?" Aaron responded cautiously.

"It is true? About the fuel and the cash box? Did you do it? The guys have been talking for weeks. They said you were getting axed in a few days. Is it true?"

Aaron felt anger welling up. He dug his fingernails into the tiny armrests next to him. His silence rolled out in impatient waves.

"Listen, buddy, like I care. I'm not the cops. I'm just curious, is it true?"

Aaron dug his fingernail into the palm of his hand, seeking blood.

"Yeah, it's true," he replied steadily. "I . . . it's true."

"Huh. Well, I lost that bet." Gus chuckled darkly. "The guys said you did it. I said, 'That guy? No way. Too much of a pussy.' No offense. Didn't know you then. You just always seemed kind of like a pussy to me."

"Is there a point to this?" Aaron asked quietly, barely containing his urge to grab the man from behind and twist his neck until it snapped.

"Not really," Gus replied as he stared forward. Aaron looked at his watch—5:50 p.m. People would be panicking. The president's speech would be long over, and people would be trying to get out. It was impossible to tell out the window what was below him. Without the light of the houses as a marker, Aaron had no idea if they were over water or land.

"How much did you get for it?" Gus asked with a hint of a

taunt in his voice. "Was it worth it? One of the guys said they were planning on pressing charges. That woulda sucked for you. That's what? Thirty years? Theft, falsifying documents, lying to a government agency or some shit like that—whoo, I got you out of there right in time."

Aaron was about to respond when a flash of red fire rippled out from the land below them. He jumped back in his seat, his fingernail making its mark and ripping his palm open. An eternity passed in silence while Aaron looked at the long red ripple making its way across the black.

"It started early," Aaron whispered.

"Early? Fuck that. Bet that's just the warm-up act," Gus responded. He sounded almost giddy. "They probably planted a fuckload of bombs. That was just one of the little ones. Wait till the biggie blows, that'll be some fireworks."

Aaron shifted in his seat, notably uncomfortable. He was suddenly wishing he was back on the ground, back where he knew what was going to happen. As he watched in dull horror, a wave of red gold lapped the darkness like a wave on the ocean, chasing the first red streak. Aaron could tell they were over the water now; the red gold stopped before it reached them.

"See! That was nothing! That one probably took out downtown proper. Now just wait. The one that's coming, that'll be the killer, that'll be the big dog." Gus pulled back on the controls, pulling the plane higher in the air, circling sharply so they were facing the darkening wave of red gold.

"What, where are you going?" Aaron asked in horror as he realized that this nutbag planned on taking them right into the blast zone.

"I'm not going to miss this! We have three minutes till the end of the world—I'm not missing that shit! Calm the fuck down.

Nothing's getting us up here." Gus's voice was high with excitement. Aaron felt like he was going to barf.

"You sell those assholes our fuel, huh?" Gus turned around and glared at Aaron, his face glowing in the pool of artificial light created by the control panel. "You do this, you little pussy prick you?"

Aaron pressed himself as far back against the seat as he could. Gus stared him down and then burst into laughter and turned back around.

"Jesus, jumpy little fucker. I'm just giving you shit. You really are a pussy, aren't you?" He chuckled at his own joke. "Like I care. I'm not the cops. In the here to come, pussy pricks like you will be useful. Glad to have you on my team. You are on my team, aren't you, little fucker?"

Aaron vomited onto the floor of the silver-and-black prop plane as the land below them exploded in flames. The impact shook the tiny plane. The weight of the rising screams rocked them off course. All the while, the man at the controls laughed on and flew into the heart of the horror.

7

LEVI

"I LEFT MY PURSE IN MY DESK ON THE EIGHTH FLOOR. I just need to run back up there real quick and—" The woman in the gray skirt set was cut off by a twentysomething business kid wearing a black suit jacket, tailored jeans, and Converse sneakers. It was all Jacobs could do not to snort a laugh.

"Look, buddy, I need to get to my car. I have an extremely important appointment in the valley at six, and you know Friday traffic. I've got to hit the road, if you know what I mean."

Gray Skirt Set began to protest the interruption when Officer Levi Jacobs cut both of them off.

"No one's going anywhere. This is an evacuation, and you all have to stay out here beyond the safety line until the building is cleared." When Gray Skirt Set began forming a word that looked a lot like "but," Jacobs held up his hand, silencing her.

"Everyone is important, everyone has a place to be tonight— god knows I do—and no one is going anywhere until the building is cleared. So relax and be patient."

Converse Sneakers stared at him, trying to find an angle. Jacobs's radio crackled; a man had threatened an officer a block down, and they were hauling him to the precinct office.

"Hear that?" Jacobs asked both of them. "That's what happens when people aren't patient."

Gray Skirt Set wandered back into the crowd, visibly frustrated. Converse Sneakers paced back and forth angrily, madly punching buttons on his fancy cell phone.

Jacobs looked up and down the street warily. Across Hope Place, the US Bank building was lined with another layer of LAPD. Jacobs had been given crowd control—keep the people across the street until the building was clear. Why he'd been given this shit, he couldn't figure. It was a crap assignment. No one ever seemed to understand that it was a mother lovin' bomb threat, not a firework demonstration, not a police training exercise. Granted, Jacobs had never seen one that wasn't a hoax. Well, once maybe, but that was five years ago when a kid had tied a handful of roman candles to his calculus book and left it in his high school locker room. Jacobs guessed that it could have potentially blown up, although the calculus book would have sustained the bulk of the damage.

But this crap, man, always on a Friday, always in the last hour of the day. *Mother lovin' freak of nature—probably off his or her meds, mad at their husband or wife—calls in some dumbass threat, ruins everyone's night.* Jacobs glanced at his watch; it was 4:45 p.m. He was supposed to be off fifteen minutes ago. Instead, here he was, standing on Fifth Street, listening to a businessman young enough to be his son tell him how important it was he gets his BMW out of the garage. Jacobs's wife, Rachel, called it "pretty girl syndrome": everyone's pretty, everyone's special—especially twentysomething pricks in sneakers and jeans.

Downtown was a goddamn mess, that's what it was. The former

inhabitants of the US Bank Tower were lined up for three blocks. Some had defected from the wait and were in the bar on the next block. Jacobs wished they'd all find a place to go. The sky was starting to get dark. *Daylight savings time is a waste of goddamn time*, he thought. *We should be like Arizona. They don't do this nonsense every year.*

"Officer, I need to use a phone. Is there one on your truck?" asked a plumpish woman in her late forties carrying a gigantic leopard-print purse and wearing a too-tight black miniskirt. Jacobs thought she looked like a sausage about to pop its casing. He just stared at her, as was his way when people asked him ridiculous shit.

"My cell just died, and I need to call my son's nanny, tell him I'll be late. Are you listening?" She tapped her foot, which was bursting out of a pointed heel that looked like she'd hacked off most of her toes to fit into.

"Lady," Jacobs began wearily, "we're not a phone company. You need a phone, use the pay phone on the next block."

Her nostrils flared, and her round cheek twitched in annoyance. She looked ready for a fight when another officer came up behind Jacobs. The woman took a deep breath, her voice a model of controlled outrage.

"I pay your salary. I have a right to use whatever equipment you have. If I have to pay late childcare fees, I'm sending the bill to your supervisor with a full report." With that she stomped off, walking unsteadily on her spiked heels.

"Give me some good news, buddy," Jacobs said over his shoulder to the officer who was standing there grinning.

"I see you still have your charm intact. Good to know," Officer Lee Stans said, walking to Jacobs's side.

"Yeah, well, it's not easy being me. I'm a magnet for the ladies. Jeez, did you see how old that lady was? And she's worried about a nanny? I bet she was one of those wonder-egg ladies, you know the ones who froze their lady parts and then had them implanted by a doctor. Saw it on *Oprah*. Crazy shit." Jacobs shook his head.

"I'm not sure that's exactly the way it works. And to be fair, forty is the new thirty—don't you watch television?" Stans said with a steady voice and a straight face. Jacobs glanced over at the sandy-haired man, gray beginning to show around his temples, and chuckled.

"It's not my fault. It's the stress. When you going to move me off babysitting duty? I've been here since four o'clock. Any time estimate coming from the bomb squad?" Jacobs asked.

"They found something on the thirty-second floor, no word on what or how long. But I do have good news—you're being moved down to city hall. I'm taking your spot here. Some wacko called in another threat. They're evacuating now. Go jump on the bus, get out of here." Stans nodded, a slight movement of his chin in the direction of the big black LAPD bus. He kept his eyes on the sidewalk full of people.

Jacobs glanced at his watch—4:50 p.m. "I don't see me getting home before eight o'clock."

"Nope," Stans said simply. "Go. Babysit a whole different crowd for a while. Try not to get us sued." He raised his eyebrows at Jacobs and then turned his attention back to the sidewalk.

Jacobs chuckled and set off across the street for the bus. He needed to call Rachel. She'd be off in about fifteen minutes. She'd be ticked off too. They were supposed to meet Sarah at some fancy Santa Monica restaurant tonight. She was introducing them to her new boyfriend. Rachel kept telling him to be nice, that this was a nice boy. Sarah had met him in her chemistry class up at Northridge. Jacobs grunted to himself as he thought of what Rachel was going to say to him when he did finally get out of this mess.

As Jacobs climbed onto the bus, he nodded in the direction of the other men. A couple of officers followed him on before the commander on the sidewalk waved the bus closed and down the street. City hall was about seven blocks away. There would already be a crowd of cops down there, Jacobs knew. He was just backup. Maybe he'd get a spot at the door, away from the freakin' whiny people. It was already 5:00—no way he was getting out of there in time for dinner. Even if he did make it, he'd have to show up in full uniform, gun and all. Sarah always accused him of trying to scare off her boyfriends in this way. He'd never hear the end of it.

The crowd outside city hall was larger than even that back at the US Bank Tower. Jacobs wrinkled his forehead in confusion. It was a smaller building; the crowd should be about half that of the other. Over his radio, he heard a crackle.

"Attention all units, a third Code 29 has been reported at the Disney Concert Hall. It's being evacuated now."

Jacobs groaned. *Jesus.* As he exited the bus, the commander on the ground pointed him to the far sidewalk, away from the crowd. At least that was a relief. He marched to the building entrance where the bomb squad was readying to enter. The commander nodded at him and the others.

"I need you men on the entrance. No one in or out without my clearance, clear?" he barked, obviously stressed.

"Yes, sir," Jacobs answered, standing on one side of the glass door. The other officers lined up accordingly. Across the street, the business men and women milled about on the darkening sidewalk. Jacobs watched as two or three at a time approached the officers. He knew what they were asking—can I just go get my wallet out of my desk, can I just go get my car, can't I just run up and grab my sweater, how long is this going to take, don't you know I have to be somewhere?

Jacobs felt his phone vibrate in his pocket. Fancy thing. Sarah had bought it for him last Christmas so she could text him at work. *Text.* Jacobs wondered what had happened to calling someone. The bomb squad charged through the open doors, spreading out, some with dogs, sniffing for a trail. Several men streamed straight for the stairwell. They would go floor by floor, checking every nook and corner. Jacobs's radio crackled. The sound was muffled by a news helicopter flying low over the scene. The camera crews would be blocked from the scene; they'd be ticked off too.

"Attention all units, a fourth Code 29 has been called in to the Concert Hall. We are currently evacuating the site." Jacobs felt funny; this wasn't right. The threats never came in sequence like this. This wasn't right at all. He watched two big black LAPD buses pass on the street. The people on the sidewalk were beginning to shout. Jacobs could hear their voices rising up across the space. A pregnant woman in a black skirt and button-up top was trying to convince an officer to let her back in to use the restroom. Jacobs couldn't hear her, but she kept pointing to her belly, her face strained. He could just guess what she was asking. The radio crackled again.

"Attention all units, attention all units. Due to increased safety concerns, we will be evacuating all buildings in a ten-block radius. The occupants will be bused to the Staples Center until further notice. Crews on the ground, buses will be arriving momentarily."

All of a sudden, downtown seemed to shift into high gear. The already tense atmosphere exploded with energy. People began streaming down from the adjoining buildings, their inter-com services alerting them to the new action. The commander approached, walking hurriedly. He stopped before Jacobs and the others standing in front of city hall.

"Alright, men, I need you loading people on those buses. We have fifteen minutes to do this thing—let's go."

Jacobs took off in a run toward the row of black buses that was pulling up on the street. *Fifteen minutes? Are they nuts?* This was going to take hours. People were already beginning to storm the police lines, trying to flood back into the building, trying to get to their cars. Jacobs nearly collided with a wall of well-dressed businessmen. They stopped as Jacobs and the other officers on either side of him held their arms out, herding them back. Jacobs cleared his throat.

"Alright, everyone, calm down. We need you on the bus. The sooner we get you out of here, the sooner we can secure the area and you'll be able to return home. We need you on the bus."

A thousand different arguments rose up as loudspeakers began sharing the plan with the growing crowd. A few cars that were parking on the street were being overrun. Jacobs glanced over to see two men in white button-ups trying to break a window with a briefcase. They were interrupted by an officer, who pulled his nightstick out to stop them.

Jesus, Jacobs thought, *they're going to riot.* As if on cue, the SWAT officers appeared in the light of the streetlamps, marching in a line like a row of malevolent black beetles. Jacobs knew that there were probably a hundred more SWAT officers that he didn't see. They were like cockroaches; you see one, there's fifty hiding.

Men and women were stumbling onto the buses. A full bus pulled out into the street, stopped abruptly by the crowd that refused to budge out of its way. It blared the horn, somewhat dismantling the pack. Jacobs stood his ground as another group of men and women attempted to storm past him and into the building.

"On the bus people, on the bus! The bomb squad is working as fast as they can. You have to turn around and get on the bus!" Jacobs barked. A man tried to muscle past the officer to his left. The officer took him down, pinning him to the sidewalk.

"Sir! Stop!" the officer yelled.

"Motherfuckers, let us get our cars! Let us get out of here!" the man yelled.

"Listen, asshole, you get your butt on the bus. That's how you get out of here," the officer growled.

Jacobs ran toward the crowd when he saw a woman fall down in the mass of people. She was trying to get up, but feet kept moving over her. She was screaming. He made it to her just as a man in overpriced leather loafers was about to stomp her hand. Jacobs hauled her up by her arm and pulled her from the flow of people. She was bawling, her face bloody.

"Miss, are you alright? Can you breathe?" Jacobs heard the wail of sirens, police and ambulance, from every direction. "Help is on the way. Just sit tight."

A fire truck pulled through the crowd, the firemen flooding off carrying red medical kits. Jacobs waved one of the men over to where the woman lay propped against his legs, gasping for breath through her sobs. As the firemen took over, Jacobs moved back toward the crowd. *Jesus*, he thought. There were too many people to see where they were all coming from. The radio crackled. Jacobs held it to his ear, barely able to hear the voice.

"Evacuation time for downtown is ten minutes. We have transport helicopters landing in the following locations—" The radio crackled, hiding the addresses. The bomb squad abruptly came flooding out the doors of city hall. Their faces were a mask of controlled panic.

They streamed past Jacobs and into the crowd, beelining for the building across the street. Jacobs held his ground as people surged around him, trying to make a break for the parking garages. Suddenly, the radio crackled again.

"Attention all units, in order to expedite the evacuation process, you are to allow all civilians access to the garages. We need to move people fast. Let them get to the garages." The voice was ragged, unprofessional, torn between the illogic of the command and frantic energy.

Jacobs heard the loudspeaker announce the new directive. He waved people on to the building entrance. The men closest to the doors were already inside the lobby, trying to make sure the people went down to the garage and not up to the offices. *Not that it matters now*, Jacobs thought numbly. Whatever had caused this clusterfuck wasn't going to be made any worse by a few people getting their purses out of their desks.

Jacobs followed the crowd inside the building. The cell phone in his pocket buzzed impatiently. Outside the glass barrier, bedlam reigned. The streetlamps flickered, threatening to throw the crowd into blackness. A communal scream rose from the masses. The motion never stopped, people running every direction. More streamed into city hall, running for the stairwells, ignoring the slow elevators. Already a few cars were starting to make their appearances from the garage exits. *Not that it is going to do much good*, Jacobs thought cynically. The streets were at a standstill. A few cops still tried to usher people out of the way, their efforts useless. Jacobs helped an elderly woman through the glass door. She looked ashen and was breathing hard. As Jacobs waved to a paramedic who began to sprint to the lobby, the woman collapsed onto the floor. The paramedic reached her, and Jacobs ran back to the door, where a cluster of people trying to get in at once was causing a blockage. A woman was crushed against the glass.

"Back up! Back up!" Jacobs barked. They didn't back up exactly, but they moved enough to unwedge the trapped woman. Jacobs led her over to the paramedic as the crowd continued to swell and flood the building. Cars honked madly outside, trying to drive through the chaos. The big black buses continued to herd people on board. A few were trying to pull out into the street. As Jacobs watched, a bus sideswiped a white BMW with several occupants inside. The force of the blow knocked the car off-balance; it swerved and crashed head-on into a parked motorcycle. The driver and his passengers were leaning out the window, shouting in vain. The bus was already half a block away, easing its way through the flood of people.

Jacobs staggered back, his cell phone repeating its frantic buzzing. He reached for it and stared at the tiny screen. It was Rachel. She knew he couldn't answer; what was she thinking? Rachel had worked in dispatch the same amount of time he'd been on the streets. She knew what would happen to a cop who decided to answer his cell phone in a crisis.

Jacobs tried to swallow the hopelessness he was feeling. He ran back outside, trying to avoid the crowd. A loudspeaker was shouting instructions again. Jacobs had no idea what it was saying. He pulled a businessman off the ground as he stumbled forward. He looked stunned. Without a word, the man ran on into the lobby. Jacobs stood on the steps of the building helplessly. There was nothing he could do. He watched as the white BMW that had collided with the motorcycle pulled back into traffic, nearly hitting three other vehicles. Engine steaming, it pushed forward, moving through the sea of people at a snail's pace.

All of a sudden, Jacobs felt an arm on his shoulder. Lee Stans stood behind him, looking uncharacteristically ruffled.

"C'mon, we're out of here. They landed a copter on the roof. C'mon. They're trying to evacuate as many people as possible, and we'll need officers at the Staples Center for the buses. I need you on that copter." His voice was firm, without argument.

Jacobs nodded. He looked at his radio. It was on, but in the noise of the scene, he hadn't heard the order. Without speaking, he started toward city hall. As they got into the glass lobby, Jacobs and Stans headed for an elevator that was being held open by three other officers, all looking frazzled. Jacobs breathed a sigh of relief as the elevator doors closed. For a moment, it was normal, calm, nothing was wrong.

"Look here, men," Stans began. "I've been privy to some information that isn't exactly public knowledge. I have some buddies on bomb squad, and I need to tell you exactly what I heard."

The men looked at each other hesitantly as the elevator crept up the floors.

Stans took a deep breath. "There's enough explosives down here to blow up the entire city. In addition to the Code 29s that they announced, there were explosives found in five other buildings. The timers are all set for six o'clock. There's more than can be disarmed."

One of the younger officers shook his head. "What does that mean?"

Stans nodded his chin in the young man's direction. "What it means is that anything or anyone within one hundred miles of downtown will be in the blast zone. The Staples Center isn't safe. San Diego is the next safe place."

Jacobs head was reeling. His wife, his daughter and her new boyfriend—he was meeting them. They were going to a fancy restaurant in Santa Monica. This couldn't be happening.

"Look, men..." Stans began slowly as the elevator stopped on the top floor and the doors opened. The men stepped out onto the dingy brown carpet. It was obvious that this top floor was storage and not offices. As they all stepped out and the doors shut behind them, Stans continued. "My source has told me that at a quarter to six, the government is going to make some kind of statement on the situation. There's been news copters covering this thing up and down out there. We can go to the Staples Center as planned, but I don't blame a one of you if you'd rather try to get as far as we can from the blast zone."

The men looked stunned. Jacobs's mind was racing. The opportunity to run was so appealing. He knew Stans was right; it was suicide to do anything but try to get away. The Staples Center would be flattened. All those people who were stuck on the freeway in their cars and in the buses, they were all dead, and they didn't even know it. Jacobs also knew that Stans had told him they were being moved to the Staples Center just to get him up here, to try to get him to run. Jacobs thought of his wife—her wild hair, her caustic laugh. He thought of how she always smelled like cookies, no matter what she was making. His little girl, her soft baby hands, her beautiful smile, so like her mother. He couldn't run and leave them behind.

Jacobs spoke first, his voice small and hard. "It doesn't matter. If you are going to run, I'm going back down to the street. My wife is out there, my daughter. They can't get one hundred miles away, not now. I've got nothing to run for. So if I can be of use for a little while longer, I will be." He made eye contact with Officer Lee Stans. The other men looked at each other.

"Okay then," Stans declared. "Anyone coming with me, let's go. Jacobs, good luck." With that, Stans nodded his chin in Jacobs's direction, his version of a salute. The younger officers trailed after him uncertainly. Jacobs didn't blame them. Their lives were still stretched out before them; they should run. So should he, for that matter. Instead he turned toward the elevator and then punched the button, waiting for the door to reopen. He took out his cell phone, hit the redial button, and waited for Rachel to pick up.

"Levi! Oh Jesus, Levi! Is that you?" Her voice was frantic.

"Yeah, hon, it's me." He slumped against the wall. He'd be useful in a minute. Right now he needed to do this.

"Honey, I've been worried sick. I got the first call, you know, the threat? I meant to tell you tonight over dinner, but I'm guessing you're not going to make it." Her voice was lightening. Jacobs smiled a little.

"I should have known. You always have a knack for finding more work for me to do." He paused, unsure how much he should say. Did it do any good to know your fate when you can't change it? The clock on the wall read 5:20 p.m. Jacobs heard the roar of the helicopters taking off from the roof. "Sweetie, I need to tell you some stuff, and I need you to listen."

"Hon? Everything okay?" her usually calm voice cracked.

"Not really, not really. I need you to know that I've always known you were right. That time, right after Sarah was born and you jumped all over me for going out with my buddies instead of staying home with you, and I yelled and slammed the door...remember?"

"Levi, that must have been twenty years ago, but yes, I remember. When you have only one fight a marriage, you tend to remember it."

"Yeah, well, I knew I was wrong. I knew it then. I was too proud to say it, but every minute I ever spent away from you and Sarah...I was an idiot. I'm sorry."

"Hon, why are you doing this now? Can we talk about it later? I haven't been mad about that since the late eighties." Rachel's voice held the edge of a joke.

Jacobs broke down, his voice trembling. "Baby, listen, downtown is going to be leveled. Anything within one hundred miles is going to be leveled. I'm not going to get out. There's no way to warn Sarah, there's no way to get you to safety. I just—just can't stand the idea of it all happening so fast..." Great heaving sobs shook his stout body. For the first time in his life, he wasn't self-conscious of the burst of emotion. What did it matter anymore?

On the other end of the phone, Rachel was silent.

"Sweetie, you there?" Jacobs whispered.

"Oh, hon, I'm here. Baby, I've got to do something. When is this supposed to happen?" Her voice was strangely businesslike.

"It's set to blow at six o'clock. There's supposed to be some kind of statement from the mayor or governor or somebody," he replied, puzzled.

"The president, they said he was speaking at a quarter to six. I thought it was just about the multiple bomb threats. I had no idea..." Her voice sounded as if she was calculating the odds. "Hon, I don't want to, but I can do something, try something. I'm still at my station. The power's still working. Don't move, don't go anywhere, don't hang up."

With that, Jacobs heard the muffled clunk of her cell phone being dropped onto the hard plastic shelving of her dispatcher station. He heard her deep voice, muffled but still clear.

"Can you hear me? I repeat, can you hear me? Am I coming through?" A low pause, then a desperate "Will someone say something—are you there?"

He heard a clicking and quiet "dammit." After some more adjustments, he heard her voice again.

"I will repeat. At seventeen forty-five, approximately twenty minutes from now, the president will address the nation. You need to evacuate now, do you copy? Evacuate. Do not wait for the president's address. Evacuate by air. You need to be as far from downtown Los Angeles as possible by eighteen hundred hours. Do you copy?"

More fidgeting with her control panel and then "Please, someone copy. You need to evacuate now. If you are within one hundred miles of downtown Los Angeles, you will not survive the blast or the aftershocks that will accompany it. You need to evacuate by air, do you copy?"

Jesus, Jacobs thought as she continued her warning. *She radioed the airports. Of course,* he thought with amazement. *Of course that would be the thing to do.* People could still get in the air; people could still get away. The cell phone clunked and banged, and finally her voice came back into focus.

"Okay, well, I've pretty much just got myself fired if you're wrong about this thing. So if you are, I hope you're prepared to take care of me in my old age." Her light tone belied the darkness of her comment.

"Rach, look, I need you to know how much I love you. I need to say that. I need you to hear me." Jacobs ignored the open elevator door. The clock said 5:35 p.m.

8

RACHEL

RACHEL JACOBS CRADLED THE PHONE ON HER SHOULDER. Her hands were shaking too hard to hold it steady. She couldn't believe what she had just done. Every bit of her training, her thirty years in police dispatch had been defied. Yet something in her husband's voice told her that he wasn't kidding. The breaking news was nonstop. She was watching from the small television mounted on the wall above her work station, the sound muted. Downtown was in chaos. The news copter showed people running every which way, the traffic cam flashing at the dead stop on the 110 freeway that leads in and out of downtown. On the other end of the phone, she could hear Levi breathing.

"Hon, I love you too, but don't talk like that... Please don't talk like that." Her voice shook. She needed him to say he was kidding. She needed him to be alright.

"I have to. I'm not getting out of this, Rach, I'm not. None of us are. I'm so sorry...so sorry," he said softly. Suddenly his voice raised a little. "Oh god—Sarah—have you talked to her? Where is she? I need to talk to her. I need to hear her voice..." His voice was ragged, desperate.

Rachel looked at the control panel in front of her. Technically she was off work. No one was in this wing of the building right now. The dispatch call center in the next room was a model of masked panic. The call she put through to the airports was the least of the problems in there right now.

"Hon, I can get her on the line. We can talk to her together." Rachel began dialing the number, connecting them on a conference call line usually used when police dispatch needed to talk to different services like fire or medical at once. She was a little ashamed that it hadn't occurred to her to do this in the first place. The clock read 5:45 p.m. The president interrupted the silent image above her head. For a moment, her fingers froze, mid-dial. The reality of the situation sank in. This was really happening.

"Mom?" Sarah's voice was teary, shaky.

"I'm here, baby. We're both here," Rachel said soothingly.

"Dad too?" Sarah asked hesitantly, the fear in her voice belying her twenty-one years.

"Yeah, baby, I'm here. I'm on the line," Levi said from the other end, his voice stronger now. Rachel knew he was going to try to be strong for his girl.

"Daddy? Where are you?" Sarah's voice was unsteady.

"I'm downtown, honey. Are you watching the news, sweetie?" Levi asked.

"Yeah…I don't understand…" Sarah started hiccupping, her nervous habit. It always made Rachel's heart warm a little. It reminded her of Sarah's baby hiccups—so tiny, so sweet.

"Baby," Rachel started, "baby, I just need you to not worry so much. We're all together right now. We love you, do you hear me? Your dad and I love you more than anything." Rachel felt the lump in her throat begin to choke her.

"Mom…I love you both too. Why is this happening?" Sarah was crying softly. It was hard to understand her.

"Sweetie, don't cry. It's going to be okay. I promise, honey, I promise..." Rachel kept repeating the words although she didn't believe them herself.

"Sarah, babygirl," Levi said softly. "No matter what happens tonight, we'll all be together. You don't need to be scared. I love you...I love you both."

In the next room, all hell was breaking loose. Rachel realized the other dispatchers and staff were running down the steps, evacuating the building. The line crackled, and Sarah let out a frightened squeal. The clock read 5:51 p.m. The president was long gone, leaving only the blank, dead screen. The lights flickered and then went black. Rachel guessed that they had probably been out in most of the city for a few minutes. The dispatch stations had a pretty serious backup system; they were the last to go in the event of an emergency.

"Mom! Daddy!" Sarah half screamed. "Are you still there! Mom!"

"Sweetiepie, I'm here, we're both still here. The line broke up a little, but don't worry, baby. Don't worry..." Rachel chanted over and over. Levi joined her, and Sarah continued to whimper quietly. There was nothing really left to say. They'd had a good life, with none of the drama that infested so many lives. They loved each other. No one kept any secrets beyond a few broken curfews. No one had any dark things to confess in the last moments. Hearing one another's voices was enough. Rachel sunk to the floor, leaning against the pressed wood of the cubicle wall.

When the first blast hit, the line went dead. Rachel hugged the phone, watching with a dull numbness as the objects around her propelled to the ground. The ceiling began to crack down the middle, and Rachel knew she should crawl under the heavy desk. She, instead, pictured Sarah's sweet head in her lap, her infant curls still wet from the bath. She remembered Sarah's first pair of big girl pants that she wore to kindergarten; they'd had an embroidered walrus on the pocket. Sarah had been so proud. And Levi, his quiet manner, his rough hand on her cheek.

The second explosion brought the ceiling down. Rachel held her arms up to the rapidly approaching sky, mercifully unafraid.

*

Cooper Carlson

CBS Breaking News Report

*

At 6:00 p.m. this evening, a horrific and cowardly act of terrorism destroyed the greater part of Los Angeles. What we know is multiple bombs were detected in multiple buildings in downtown Los Angeles. The SWAT teams, despite their best efforts, were unable to diffuse all the explosives in time. The destruction reached over a hundred miles from the epicenter. Thousands of lives have been lost. This is what we know.

What we do not know is who perpetrated this act, who assisted, and who collaborated. We do not know the extent of the damage, and we do not know when the area will be safe for reentry or rebuilding. We do not know the names of all the victims, and we will not know for some time. Thousands more are homeless tonight, grieving tonight, without basic necessities tonight. This is, without a doubt, the worst act of terrorism ever perpetrated against the American continent, perhaps in the world, in history.

If you survived, stay where you are. Rescue teams are looking for you. If you can, light a fire. If you have flares, use them. If you have water, be sparing. We do not know how long services will be out. If you have a radio, if you can hear this broadcast, you know that rescue stations are being formed all over the city. We will find you. You are safest staying where you are. Wireless services are down throughout the city, as are telephone and satellite services. You may feel you are alone, but you are not. We are stronger than those who would destroy us.

Good night and Godspeed.

PART II
NOVEMBER 2022

9

ESTHER

"TODAY IS THE TENTH ANNIVERSARY OF THE SON OF Abraham bombings, the single worst domestic terrorist attack in the history of mankind. In the years since Los Angeles was destroyed, we have come to understand a great many things about the dynamics of the Son of Abraham cult. We have talked to the followers who left before the bombings, the men and women who knew what was about to occur and ran from the city in the last moments. Many of these ex-followers are in prison now as accomplices to the crime. Many are still awaiting trial. With us tonight is a young woman who has remained an outspoken advocate for the victims and their families. Please welcome Esther Robertson."

The lights went black. The stiff leather chair made it difficult to sit up properly; Esther kept wanting to slide forward. A small, thin girl carrying a foot-long makeup brush and a pallet of colors swept forward and began madly patting her face. Across from her, Cooper Carlson—CBS anchor, nighttime news god—was getting the same treatment. He grew impatient and shooed the girl away. The makeup brush that was assaulting Esther's face abruptly stopped its attack and disappeared.

On the monitors that hung from the black wall of the small studio, Esther could see the opening titles of the show still running. Shots of her father, some that contained her sister, flashed across the screen at a dizzying speed. Cooper Carlson's pretaped voice narrated the sequence, defining her innocence, identifying Esther Robertson as a child incapable of stopping the evil, therefore blameless for the 15,789 deaths that occurred within the span of fifteen minutes ten years ago.

Esther said the number to herself often—15,789. There were officially 4,285 people still missing. They were presumed dead, but without any evidence the police kept alive the hope that they were merely wiped clean of their memories, wandering the country, and could still be found. *We should all be so lucky*, Esther thought bitterly.

The promo slowed, the pictures passing by slower, until it faded into a montage of explosions, even a picture from space, taken by the Soviet research station. The bright red and yellow, the color of the grief, gave way to grainy photos of a barren landscape that used to be Exposition Park, a pile of bricks and mortar that used to be the Disney Concert Hall. Bodies lay strewn on the beach, drug there by the survivors in hopes that someone might identify them. Then another image appeared, the photo that had haunted all, the one that now hung in the Smithsonian: A little girl wearing an ill-fitting, torn dress, her face marked with blood like the ancient Celts, lay curled up in the crook of her dead mother's arm. The child stared down the camera. In her lap was her mother's hand, her soul long flown. The girl seemed to dare the camera to do the same. She had become the very image of grief, of devastation.

The images faded, and the lights in the studio burned Esther's skin. Cooper Carlson, Pulitzer Prize–winning journalist whose career had been made by his coverage of the bombings, sat across from her, his face stony. She had refused to read the prep material, refused to come up with prefabricated answers for their questions. Esther refused to hide. Like the little girl in the photo, she dared the camera to steal her essence, dared them to try.

A man in a black baseball cap counted down silently with his finger—sweeping, exaggerated motions—and pointed at Cooper Carlson as a red light blinked.

"Welcome, and thank you for joining us. For ten years, Alan Robertson evaded capture. This past month, he was finally arrested and is awaiting trial in federal court. With us tonight is his only living daughter, Esther Robertson. Esther, thank you for being here."

Esther stuttered a little, shaking voice betraying her nerves.

"Thank you." She didn't know what else to say.

"Esther, I want to get right to it." This was Cooper Carlson's trademark. Esther had steeled herself for this tactic. He avoided the talk show etiquette and went right for the arteries.

"In fifteen days, your father, Alan Robertson, will face the federal grand jury for crimes against humanity, terrorism, and mass murder. Will you attend the trial?"

She took a deep breath.

"Yes, sir, I am planning on attending. I feel it is my responsibility. I am the only family my father has left."

His gray eyes stared at her unblinking.

"Take us back. You grew up in the Mar Vista neighborhood of West Los Angeles, correct?"

"Yes, by the Santa Monica Airport. I lived there with my parents and my younger sister, Sarai." Esther's voice was uniform. She had answered these questions a thousand times.

"You were born one of ten children, were you not?"

Esther relaxed a bit; her stomach released the knot it was holding, just a little.

"Yes, I'm actually the eldest of ten."

On the monitor, there flashed a water-stained photo. Children mobbed the frame. Apart from Sarai—standing with her head turned to the right, her hair blowing across her cheek—the other faces were strangers.

Esther stared at the photo, not waiting for the next question.

"I didn't grow up in the same household as any of my other siblings. As a result, I didn't know them, and they did not know me. I met them only once."

The photo flashed on the monitor again. Across from her, Cooper Carlson sat calmly, waiting for her to talk.

"Our mother raised us. My father came and went. Most of the time it was just the three of us." Esther felt herself babbling, waiting for someone to stop her.

Cooper Carlson cleared his throat, a pointless gesture. He did it to drive the interview back to him. Esther knew this, and still it worked.

"Esther, in talking to my producers, you described your childhood as 'blessed, perfect.' Can you speak to this? What kind of father was Alan Robertson?"

She smiled a little.

"I never said 'blessed.' I don't know what that is. When I was little, my father was a wonderful dad. He was quiet, he read a lot, and he didn't like to talk to the neighbors much. But with Sarai and I, he was open, loving. It was a very normal childhood, for a time. He was…he was…like a kid. He wasn't always with us, in the same house that is, but every Saturday and many days during the week, he would be there. He was a normal dad. It was a very normal childhood, until it wasn't."

Cooper Carlson narrowed his eyes. Esther could see him calculating.

"Tell us about life with your father," he asked.

She stuttered a little, knowing this was a trap but unable to do anything but fall into it.

"He bought my sister and me ice creams off the truck in the afternoons. My mother would get upset with him for ruining our dinners. It was all very normal. He would walk with us around the neighborhood. We would stop and look at houses, and he would tell us about the plants they were growing in their gardens, about what kind of cars were in their driveways. Everything." Esther felt like she was defending him. *I am,* a voice whispered inside her head. She was eternally defending him.

Cooper cocked his head slightly. "At the time, did you have any idea who lived in these houses? Did anyone ever act suspicious, curious about your father?"

Esther heard herself answering his questions, telling him all the correct information. But how do you categorize a normal dad, a normal childhood, a normal life? She swallowed the answer that almost escaped her lips. *Yes, people did act strangely around my father. And he acted strangely around them. He was nervous, painfully shy, awkward around everyone but us. He took our hands before we walked across the street. He showed us how to make bubble soap from the dishwashing liquid and laughed as we blew bubbles over the yard. I used to love watching him with Mother. He would walk up behind her and place his head on her shoulder, stroke her hair. I always dreamt of finding someone who loved me that much. I still do.*

"No. I never thought to be suspicious. We kept to ourselves, I didn't know my neighbors well. I didn't know a lot of things about my father. I realize that now," Esther answered carefully.

Again, Esther heard the whisper of the answer that welled up inside her, the one Cooper Carlson wanted to hear. But it was too much, too honest, and the worst thing you can be with a man like Cooper Carlson is too honest. *I didn't know that he lived in a house that was walking distance from us. I didn't know that his signature and a dozen fake names were on the leases of two dozen houses in the neighborhood. I didn't know that to fund these houses he had convinced people that he was the messiah, the Son of Abraham, come to save us all. I didn't know that he claimed to have visions of God, that he claimed God spoke through him and had told him to collect an army. I didn't know a lot of things.*

"Tell me about the religious atmosphere in your house as you grew up." Cooper Carlson thought he knew this answer.

"My father treated religion as a joke. He thought it was funny," Esther said bluntly.

Cooper Carlson's face twitched in annoyance; he hadn't wanted that answer. He wanted to hear the traditional response, the standard reply for a man like her father. He wanted to hear about a zealot, a man who made his daughters memorize the psalms, a man who believed in the literal interpretation of the Word. He wanted what had been splashed around the tabloids, what had been written about in *Newsweek* and *TIME*. He wanted a wild-eyed madman, a Charles Manson incarnate, dull, dark eyes staring out from behind a nest of tangled hair.

"When I was seven," Esther said with a small smile on her lips, "he called my school and told them I had the day off because it was 'Moses Day.' When the school secretary questioned him, he pretended to be outraged, insulted that she didn't know his religious holiday. Instead of school that day, he took me to the Santa Monica Pier. We rode the roller coaster and ate hot dogs with lots of mustard. We laughed about Moses Day. For years he would pull Sarai and I out of school on random days in February, telling the staff that it was Jesus's true birthday. The three of us celebrated

'Baby Jesus Day' by going to the movies and eating popcorn and drinking soda." The words came out in a tumble. Cooper Carlson's face was impassive but agitated as he took it in. Since Esther had refused to do the preinterview, this was the first time Cooper Carlson was hearing this information. It was part of the deal she had signed. Esther had spoken to many journalists before, enough to know how to rattle them back, enough to know when to see the snares in the brush waiting to catch a lie or twist a truth.

Religion was a joke to Alan Robertson. That was what Cooper Carlson was struggling to understand as Esther explained about Baby Jesus Day. How could a man who created the most violent religious cult in the history of man not be a believer? How could he possibly not be a raving lunatic, a deranged psychopath? The possibility that he was just like Cooper Carlson, or just like Esther herself, was far scarier.

"You said before that your childhood was normal, until it wasn't. I want to talk about the 'wasn't.' How did you become aware of your father's activities?"

Esther stared at Cooper Carlson, meeting his dark eyes with her pale ones that were said to be the very mirror of her aunt's. This was not a question about her father; it was a question about her. How did she not know? How did she not warn someone? Esther heard the murmuring response to his question ringing in her head, but she knew she must be careful with what she shared. She held the power to create the narrative that would define not only her father but also her future life. If Esther was ever to live in a world that wasn't defined by her father's tragedy, she had to weave a story. Esther had sole ownership of these memories now. She would choose what to set to the light and what would be cast to darkness eternal. Did Cooper Carlson want to hear the story of a man on the edge of philosophy and society, a man who used obscure teachings to control those around him? *Alan Robertson was always busy. He read constantly—at dinner, in the bathroom, while he was walking. We had a home office in the corner of the living room. It was stacked to the ceiling with books on Kabbalah, Ancient Hebrew, Egyptian mysticism, Crowley, Lovecraft, Gnostic Gospels, Plato, Socrates, Pythagoras, and countless others. We had a cat who would knock over the stacks sometimes. It scared all of us out of our minds, shook the house like an earthquake. Mother used to make fun of him, tease him, but you could tell she loved him, even if she didn't understand.*

Esther could see growing frustration in Cooper's face as the seconds ticked by into a full minute and she still had not opened her mouth to answer the question he had asked.

Did Cooper Carlson want to know about her father's temper? The story of a father and husband whose violence traveled in unpredictable waves. The flash-in-the-pan anger that raged and died as quickly as a bolt of lightning. *When I was thirteen, I was caught cheating on a quiz at school. As punishment they sent me home early and suspended me for the next day. My father had picked me up. He didn't speak until we were in the house. His face had been fixed with control. As soon as we entered the house, his fist went through the wall, crumbling the plaster. When he withdrew it, it was bloody and torn. I cried. But Father quietly went to the bathroom to wrap his hand and then began filling the hole, his rage gone. We never talked about it, but there were holes in the walls all over that house. He always meticulously filled them in, careful to blend the paint lines.* Is this what Cooper Carlson wanted to hear?

In lieu of any of these things, Esther finally responded in a calm, level voice, "He got paranoid, stopped coming to the house as often. Sarai and I were scared he'd leave altogether." She spoke quietly, so many unspoken memories behind a simple response.

Esther took a deep breath. "One night he got into an argument with my mother. Sarai and I hid in the closet. All we could hear was her crying and him yelling. We didn't understand."

"Was this the first time he had been violent with your mother?" Cooper Carlson asked pointedly.

Esther nodded her head, although that wasn't entirely true. She had seen bruises on her mother's arms before, five perfect finger marks. The same stain would occasionally appear on her mother's shoulder, the base of her neck. She never discussed it. Esther and Sarai never asked.

Esther continued. "I looked out the door. He had a butcher's knife to my mother's throat. Her face...her face was..."

"Do you need a moment?" Cooper Carlson asked in response to a producer waving madly from behind the camera. Esther shook her head; she wanted to get this out. She was the last one who could give voice to the suffering her mother had endured.

"He left. He still had the knife. My mother dropped to the floor. She was crying. I was thirteen, and Sarai was only ten. Three minutes later he came back in. The knife was gone. His face was...it was different. He was calm, but scared. He said he'd forgotten the last three hours, he couldn't remember." Esther said the last bit so softly the microphone hovering over her head came in closer.

"Did you believe him?" Cooper Carlson's question was straightforward.

"Not at first. But he was so upset, so confused. He thought he had just arrived. He didn't understand why we were so upset. He thought someone had attacked my mother. She screamed at him to leave, to get out of the house. He was shaking, but he did it. My sister ran after him. When she caught up, he was standing in the garage, his hand on the hood of his truck."

Cooper Carlson looked confused. Maybe he didn't understand

why Sarai had tried to stop him from leaving. Maybe he didn't understand that Alan Robertson had just realized that the truck engine was cold, which meant that he hadn't just pulled up, that he'd been there for a good long while and couldn't remember.

"What was life like after that incident?" Cooper Carlson asked.

"Sarai and I were terrified he would disappear. His appearances became less frequent. Suddenly we weren't allowed to leave the house unless it was to go to the backyard. We weren't to talk to any of the neighbors. He became more paranoid. He began bringing boxes of junk to the house. He said they contained files, important documents, things that could not be replaced. Sarai and I looked through them once. They were full of old Christmas cards, car insurance bills, receipts from the grocery store. He moved a storage freezer onto the back landing. Every day, he would bring food—bags of frozen vegetables, bargain packages of hamburger. We weren't to eat it, he said. We were to save it. We would need it later, he told us. The freezer frosted over and freezer burned everything inside, and still he forbade us from touching the contents."

"This was two years before the bombing of Los Angeles," Cooper Carlson stated as fact; there was no question. Esther nodded. "When did you become aware of the Son of Abraham cult?"

Esther took a deep breath. "One night he was working on Mother's computer, and he called me over. I knew what message boards were. I wasn't allowed to use the internet, but I knew from my friends at school. It was titled 'Son of Abraham Speaks.' He told me, 'Look at this. Watch what I can do.'"

"What did he do?" Cooper Carlson leaned in slightly. This was a story he was utterly unprepared for, and he was betraying his cool professionalism in his curiosity.

"He typed a message to the whole group. I don't remember

it exactly, but it said something to the effect that he had seen the Lord's image here on earth and they had to go to the place he had been told of to seek forgiveness—or else the world would come to an end. Then he typed in a series of coordinates. I recognized them as latitude and longitude numbers, which we'd studied in school. 'What is this?' I had asked. 'An egg hunt, a rabbit hole, a game of hide-and-seek. I tell them where to go, and they will do it.' That's what he said. 'We'll call in a day and see how many have shown up. If it's less than one hundred, I'll tell them that God will send an earthquake if they don't hurry.' That's what he told me."

Esther irrationally wanted to laugh. Cooper Carlson paused, letting her story absorb. She knew that behind the scenes the producers were madly trying to fact-check the words. They were pouring through old message board posts, looking for something that would match this account. They would find it easily enough; the internet was harder to destroy than a city.

"Where did he send these people?" Cooper Carlson asked.

"An Exxon station off State Route 58, right outside Barstow," Esther said, the laughter dying in her stomach and an icy nausea replacing it. A producer waved to Cooper Carlson, and he listened to an invisible voice through his earpiece.

"My producers confirm that there really was a posting. In fact, I think we have an image, right?" Cooper looked to the cameraman, who gave him a thumbs-up signal.

The monitors displayed the message that Esther had read that night in the living room, looking over her father's shoulder:

> Attention, children, the great Lord has seen fit to bless me with a vision. I have seen our great Lord's image here on earth. You are to make a pilgrimage and pray for our salvation, pray that the wickedness in the world will end. If you

do not, we will be punished and grace shall not be ours. Go, my children. Travel however you have means. Seek the forgiveness you desperately need for the sins in your heart. Pray for your neighbors who have not accepted Jesus as their personal Lord and Savior.

The cameras were not on Esther as the image lingered. She looked Cooper Carlson in the eyes. "I have no reason to lie," Esther said with an edge to her voice.

He nodded. "We don't think you do, but you were quite young when this happened. It's what we have to do. We dot all the i's and cross all the t's."

Esther nodded, but she knew he was looking for a hole in the story.

With a wave from behind the cameras, the were back on-screen.

"My producers are telling me there was enough of a commotion caused by this—can we call it a prank?—that it was recorded in the *Barstow Gazette* the following day," Cooper said, looking for Esther to add to the voice in his ear.

"I can imagine. He called the Exxon station the next day, made me listen. Father asked how many people were there. The clerk said a couple hundred had shown up in the night. Barstow police had arrived. People were passing out in the heat, and cops were having to remove people from the property, but more just kept showing up. Father had laughed for an entire day after that. 'They're going to get arrested,' I had told him. 'Don't you care if they end up in jail?' Father had just laughed."

"It's impossible to speculate, but if you had to, what do you think his motive was?" Cooper Carlson asked quietly.

"It was a game to him. He wanted to see if they'd really do it. He wanted to know they'd follow his command, do this thing that was weird and nonsensical just because he said so. He didn't believe in Jesus and all that sh...stuff. He said what he needed to to make people react," Esther said firmly. She didn't know many things about her father, but Esther knew this.

10

ESTHER

THE LIGHTS IN THE STUDIO DIMMED, AND THE CREW rushed the stage. Cooper Carlson stood and stretched his legs and then reached for the coffee cup that sat on the low table next to him. A stage manager pointed Esther to the bathroom, telling her to hurry, that they were live again in five minutes.

In the tiny studio restroom, Esther stared at her reflection. Light eyes and pale hair, thin, and a look far younger than her actual age. Her father told her once that she favored his sister and a great-great-grandmother before her, neither of whom Esther had ever met. People said she was attractive, but only until they knew who she was—the only living progeny of the worst criminal known to mankind.

There were many who thought Esther should be sitting next to her father as he faced the grand jury, even though she had done nothing wrong. During the first year after the bombings, she made a collage of the hate mail that she had received. Esther had been at the hospital then, under suicide watch. The idea to let her see the letters had been the psychiatrist's. The doctor said that Esther needed to confront the reaction to her father's actions, to alleviate any responsibility that she felt.

Esther spent hours reading the stacks of letters and postcards during her monthlong stay at the Langley Porter Psychiatric Hospital. She would take the vitriolic letters and carefully crease and tear them until they were perfect squares. Then she would fold them carefully, meticulously into cranes, elephants, long-necked giraffes that wagged their ears if you pulled on their paper tails. Esther left them everywhere, silent scenes that the other inmates/ patients left strangely untouched. Esther hung tiny swans from the ceiling of her room, the words created in their folds mangled and distorted—not directed at her, nothing to do with her.

A knock at the restroom door led Esther back to the bright lights, back to the dark walls. The makeup brush assaulted her face once again. As Cooper Carlson took his seat across from her, he smiled, asked if she was doing alright, if she needed anything. "Coffee?"

"Coffee would be good. Sugary, black coffee to keep my mind focused," Esther responded politely.

He indicated to a crew member. A moment later the hot black liquid was sitting next to her in an official CBS mug. Magic.

The lights swelled. There were no more promos, no more flashing photographs. Cooper Carlson regarded the frail figure—more girl than woman—who sat across from him as if from a distance. No longer did he care if she was too hot or cold, if she wanted coffee. Now Esther Robertson was the daughter of the Son of Abraham, suspect by the very nature of her birth.

"How much did your mother know about Alan Robertson's activities?" The question was loaded. If her mother knew, then Esther must have known, and if Esther had known, why hadn't she told anyone? Why hadn't she told them to get out or when it was going to happen?

Meg Robertson, round hips and face, her form masking her sharp edges. She knew how to be a good mother. But from the very beginning, it had been their father who had held their hands, given them hugs. Their mother had dispensed medicine when they were sick, as efficient as a school nurse, but her eyes were voids. How much had she known? It was an interesting question.

"She knew our father saw other women. We never asked questions as to why he didn't live with us. It wasn't unusual for children in our generation to live with only one parent. We knew we were lucky that he came around at all. Many of my classmates had never met their fathers," Esther answered cautiously, knowing she would not be allowed to let it lie at this.

"That said, your father was in fact the head of a multinational cult that had been planning a massive domestic terrorist act for years before it was perpetrated. Did your mother know?" Cooper was coming in for the attack. Esther could feel him rearing back, a viper about to strike.

"You know their history," Esther said abruptly. Cooper Carlson sat back. He thought she was falling into the trap he was laying. "They grew up in a cult. My mother was taught to not ask questions, to not be curious. I don't know what she knew. She was good at keeping secrets. I found out on my thirteenth birthday that I had brothers and sisters aside from Sarai. The photo you showed, that was the only time I met them."

"What was your reaction? Can you tell us a little about how you found out?" Cooper leaned in slightly, intent.

Esther paused. She remembered clearly the day that photo had been taken. Her mother had told her and Sarai to dress nicely and brush their hair, her nerves showing themselves in her wavering voice. Esther hadn't asked a lot of questions. Her father had been gone for long spells of time back then. She was numb in many senses to what was, in retrospect, clearly off-kilter behavior.

"My sister and I were taken to a house a few blocks away. We weren't told much except that there were people our father wanted us to meet. There were kids everywhere, and they...I think I knew the moment I saw them." Esther stumbled over the words. It was hard to describe how she had felt. A cold chill—not quite fear, not quite dread—had settled over her skin when she entered the room and saw it was full of people who all, in one way or another, reflected her father's face in their own.

"Did the other children and women know about you and your sister?" Cooper asked.

"I don't think so. They looked as surprised as we were." Esther closed her eyes for a moment, watching that strange morning play out silently behind her lids. "We didn't stay very long. My father spoke, but I don't remember what he said. My mother wouldn't come in. The other women...it was like they were ghosts. They didn't say a thing. My father lined us all up for that photograph. I remember talking to a boy, my brother, his name was John. He shook my hand and said he was glad to have a big sister. I never saw him again after that day."

Cooper watched her for a moment, letting the silence settle. "Can you tell us what you were feeling?"

"I felt...nothing. I felt like I was watching a movie, like I was disconnected from everything. Later that night, I remember being angry, and I remember Sarai cried. But I don't think I ever really let it settle in—until November 17, when I realized all of them were dead...like Sarai, like my mother. They were all gone, and my father had killed them. I wish now I had talked to each of them, held the baby, learned anything at all about John. Something."

"Why do you think your father chose to introduce you all on that day?" Cooper looked genuinely curious.

"I don't know. I expect it was a game, just like Barstow. I expect he wanted to see what would happen, if we'd cry or scream or run. My father sees everyone as a pawn in a game he imagines he is running. I don't know why that day happened, or why we were never brought together again."

"You weren't aware of the other houses your father operated in your own neighborhood? Your mother never let on to the extent of his relationships with other women?" Cooper was starting to become impatient.

"Not until I was thirteen. I cannot speak to what my mother knew or didn't know. She died on November 17. Everyone in that photograph is dead except me." Esther's voice cracked as all the air started to drain from her lungs and her heart began to beat erratically. This was a mistake. All the other interviews she'd done had been about the charity, the fund for victims and families, the work she had to do to atone for her father's sins, her own included.

"Alright, let's redirect a bit." Cooper seemed to realize he was pushing too hard.

Behind the cameras, Esther could see worried producers and crew. They had thirty minutes left on this interview, and if she bolted, they'd have to scramble. He'd probably been told to cool it through the little earpiece.

"Let's redirect," Cooper repeated, his brow furrowed. "You were in San Francisco when the bombings occurred."

"Yes," Esther answered simply.

"Can you tell us how, why?" Cooper pushed.

"My father sent me there on November 15, two days before the bombings. He gave me a bus ticket and told me to pack anything I wanted to keep because I was not coming back." Esther closed her eyes as she spoke, knowing how crazy it would look but unable to stop seeing her father's impassive gaze staring back at her as her lips formed words.

"Why did he spare you and no one else?" Cooper asked quietly.

"I don't know. And I've had to learn to accept that I will never know the answer to that question. I don't know if my mother knew why he sent me away. I don't know why me and no one else. I just do not know."

"Tell me about San Francisco. Where did you go when you arrived?" Cooper asked.

Esther took a deep breath and then a swallow of the coffee. "I was met at the bus station by a man named Hector. He said my father was his Ceannaire, and he told me he would take care of me."

"What is a Ceannaire?" Cooper Carlson asked, although he fully knew the answer. The word had been splashed around the media as the trials ensued, as those who still followed Alan Robertson came forward.

"It means leader, or godfather. It's what my father called himself. Hector worshipped my father. He would have done anything for him. Hector took me to his home, and I stayed in a backhouse." She could almost smell the mildew and fertilizer of the converted garden shed that had been her brief home during that time.

"You were fifteen years old, is that right?" Cooper asked, looking down at a card.

Esther nodded. "I was fifteen."

"Did you know why you were there? Why you had to leave Los Angeles?" Cooper asked.

"Did I know he had planted eight weapons of mass destruction all over the downtown area? Did I know that 15,789 people would die in two days' time? Did I know? Is that what you're really asking?" More growl than response. Esther felt her face growing hot.

"Did you?" Cooper Carlson asked directly.

Esther felt the world spinning. The heat of the lights and a cold nausea spread over her entire body. She didn't feel her body hit the studio floor, didn't feel the panicked crew fanning her forehead, didn't hear the medics or Cooper Carlson's booming voice over the din. When she awoke, only a few minutes had passed, but it felt like hours. Esther was lying on a medic's cot with an ice pack on her forehead. A worried face hovered over hers. Too much makeup, hair pulled into a baseball cap—Esther vaguely recognized the production assistant who had shown her around the studio that morning.

"Esther, are you alright?" She looked back and waved someone over. A medic appeared in his tight black uniform. He had a puppy dog sort of look—big eyes, kind eyes.

"Hello and welcome back," he said softly. His breath smelled like mint. He flashed a light into Esther's eyes, making her flinch. "Sorry about that. We took your vitals while you were out. You're perfectly normal. Good for you," he said with a grin.

Esther tried to sit up. Her head began to spin again, and she leaned back against the wall. "Perfectly," she repeated.

"We can take you to the ER, but they'll tell you you're dehydrated and in a very stressful situation," he said, kneeling in front of her. Esther irrationally found herself wondering what it would be like to take his hands in hers, to feel his touch on the small of her back. A stray thought passed through her head and was gone. Sometimes she felt like she fell in love with every man who showed her a kindness; it was a dangerous pastime.

"No. No ER. I want to finish," Esther said firmly, her head already clearing.

The production assistant looked to the medic and then back to Esther. "You don't have to," she said. "Cooper is an asshole, everyone knows it. That question was over the line."

"And if I don't answer it, everyone will think I'm guilty. They already do think that. Cooper just asked what everyone already thinks," Esther said and stood, pausing a moment to get her balance.

"I lost my parents, my girlfriend, my sister, and my brother-in-law on November 17," the medic said, his kind eyes tainted with the pain. "I don't think you're guilty. I never have. I know who is to blame, and it's not you. You were a kid."

Esther paused, looking at both the faces before her. "I'm so sorry for your loss," she murmured. Empty words. Nothing to be said that could fill that grief. She nodded and walked past them to the chaos that had become the set. The producers asked all the usual questions: Was she sure she wanted to finish? What could they bring her? A few minutes later, Esther was rewired, re-make-uped, and ready. Cooper Carlson sat across from her, his face stoic.

"Are you ready?" he asked simply. No apology for the question. Esther was glad. Everything he had been doing in this interview had been leading to it. The viper never apologizes to the mouse.

They were live again, the network schedule thrown into chaos over the delay. But CBS knew this was ratings gold; the more drama the better.

"Did I know what was going to happen on November 17?" Esther cut off Cooper Carlson before he could restate his question. "Did I know?"

He nodded. "Esther, your life has been under intense scrutiny for the last ten years. You were investigated and exonerated. You started what has become the largest charity organization in the country for the attack survivors and their families. But your motivations have been questioned. I think you are owed a chance to respond to that."

"I left Los Angeles and moved into a garden shed, alone, in the San Francisco winter when I was fifteen. I left because my father told me I had to. I begged him not to make me leave, I begged him to let me take my sister. He refused. My father is a monster, but I'm not sure I knew that then. I left because he told me to. After the attacks occurred, I had a nervous breakdown and spent the next year in a psychiatric hospital. I survived, and 15,789 people did not. I will always carry that guilt. I can never raise enough money or do enough charity to make up for that. Do you have another question?" Esther asked him pointedly.

He paused and had just started to speak when the voice in his ear interrupted him. He sat up, alert, the information flooding his earpiece distracting him from this last chance to deliver a killing blow, his last chance to debunk Esther's story, question her motives, unravel the story she had repeated for ten years.

Cooper Carlson shook his head. He said all the exiting language, thanking Esther, the historical society for the photographs and images, the production team. The lights went dim, and he rushed off the set. As he did so, Esther watched the crew behind the camera with interest. Whatever they had relayed to him had the entire studio buzzing. Figures were dashing back and forth. A nervous energy filled the room. Esther sat frozen in the armchair as the production assistant removed her microphone and then hustled around cleaning up the set.

"You did a really good job out here," she said softly from behind Esther.

Esther turned. The PA was disassembling a metal structure of some sort.

"Did I?" Esther stared at her. "What happened? What did they tell him toward the end? I thought there was another segment of this thing." She looked back at the frantic pace at which the studio had shifted away from the interview.

"Something happened in Dallas. They're saying some kind of landslide. They're not sure if it was a natural disaster or a bombing or what. I don't really know the details, I only heard they're getting Cooper on a flight out as soon as they can." The production assistant, in her tidy black jeans and studio T-shirt, looked ill at ease to be the one to deliver this news.

Esther nodded, letting it sink in. "How bad is it?" she asked, knowing the answer already.

"Bad from the initial reports. Maybe the same as Los Angeles." Her face was pale, her voice distant.

"Do they think my father was involved somehow?" Esther asked, pushing the girl, even though she could see the trauma on her face. Esther wondered if she had people in Dallas.

The girl shook her head. "I really don't know."

Esther felt numbness creep up from her toes as she made her way to the dressing room to collect her things. Another city destroyed. The crew paid little attention to her, the breaking news far more important than this interview. Esther could hear bits of news broadcasts and static-filled radio communications echoing all over the studio. Cooper would be heading to the airport by now. He was already late on this story. *He's become the preeminent spokesperson for disaster. How could the masses handle it without him?* Esther thought darkly.

It had been estimated that on November 17, one out of two people had either lost someone in the bombings or known a person who had lost someone. Everyone became defined by their relative distance to the victims. Those who had been in LA at the time and somehow miraculously survived were forgiven anything.

The credit card companies had erased millions of dollars of debt. Cell phone carriers offered free service. People scrambled to do something, anything. First degree of separation victims—those who had lost a spouse, child, mother, father—were next in line for goodwill. They flooded the talk shows in the months following the bombings. They called into the radio stations and were bumped past the callers who had waited for hours. It followed on down the line. At Langley Porter, the psychiatric nurse had lost her daughter and her mother. Her little girl had been seven years old and had gone to Los Angeles with her grandma to visit friends. They hadn't survived the first blast. Just months after the bombings, the nurse who had lost every reason to live brushed Esther's hair, forced her to eat, forced her to sit in the sunshine of the courtyard. She helped Esther hang the paper cranes, composed of strangers' hate. She smoothed Esther's hair back from her face and never blamed her for anything. She was one of very few.

So what good had Esther really done? All she could do now was hide, try not to trigger any more memories, any more anger. And now that cycle would start again—a new city, a new horror. Esther felt as though her insides had been hollowed out.

She shuffled to her car, looking at the traffic as it barreled out along Folsom Street. Esther had lived in San Francisco since that day her father had sent her there. After everything, she'd still hoped for her father to come for her, to find her. He never did. Now he sat in a federal court holding cell in Denver. Esther paused, watching the cars flying past. *You could walk into traffic right now and be done with it*, she thought. *You could take the penknife in the right front pocket of your purse and slit your carotid artery. You could swallow the bottle of Xanax in your medicine cabinet. You could, you could, you could.* Esther was tired, spirit and body numb. She started the car and drove without thinking, away from this studio, away from the questions.

*

Cooper Carlson

CBS Breaking News Report

*

We find ourselves on familiar ground, mired in a familiar grief. At approximately 7:30 p.m. central time, the greater downtown Dallas area suffered catastrophic damage in what is now believed to be a sinkhole that at current measurement stands at 400 kilometers, or roughly 250 miles. It is growing steadily, and the surrounding suburbs are under mandatory evacuation. CBS learned that the horror began with a call to emergency dispatch from the Praetorian Building regarding a series of what was thought to be earthquake tremors. Within moments of that recorded call, an area the size of a football field dropped thirty stories in as many seconds. The sinkhole has been steadily growing since, and the entire Dallas area is considered to be under direct threat. We do not have an estimate for the catastrophic loss of life that has occurred. This horror has yet to be categorized, labeled, counted, and assessed.

This is beyond imagining for a thousand reasons. We will be staying abreast of the US Geological Survey as they release information regarding this unprecedented disaster. CBS will provide continuing coverage of rescue efforts.

Ten years ago, we mourned the loss of our loved ones in a catastrophe that was entirely man-made. Tonight, Dallas was toppled by a force of nature we have yet to understand. But our grief remains the same. I will repeat what I said to you, the American people, ten years ago tonight. We are stronger than those who would destroy us. We do not know what force is behind this, and at the moment of this broadcast we do not have any information on how, why, or if other areas will be affected. We do know this—we need each other right now. We need to help our neighbors and friends. If you survived this horror, if you can hear me, stay where you are. Emergency crews are looking for you. If you can light a flare or have some other way to indicate your position, please do. If you have water, use it sparingly. We do not know how long it might be until you are rescued, but rest assured, you will be. We will find you. Be kind to each other tonight. Hold your loved ones close. We will survive this as we survived ten years ago.

Good night and Godspeed.

11

COOPER CARLSON

"COOP, WE NEED YOU BACK IN THE LIGHT. CAN YOU step to your right? That's it. Hold that." The producer's voice sounded strained, weary. Cooper stood stoically even though his knees were starting to shake and his skin felt clammy. It was 4:00 a.m. Dallas time, marking the twenty-four-hour mark since he'd last slept. *Too old for this shit*, he thought bitterly as the crew adjusted the lights. With a rush of impatience, he glared past the lights to the figures that stood beyond.

"Good?" he said simply. Hearing no reply, Cooper stormed past the lights, past the madness of production, to the makeshift trailer the local Fort Worth news crew had sent over. They had another broadcast in an hour. The damage assessments were rolling in; already it was estimated that over five thousand were dead. Anyone outside the initial drop zone had been evacuated as quickly as could be done, but given a crowded downtown and the rate at which the gaping hole widened, it wasn't enough. He slammed the door to the Airstream trailer behind him and sat back at the cramped booth-like table that folded out from the wall. *People live in these shitholes*, he mused as he reached for the recorder. The mini recorder still took the little tapes, though he had to special order them now. His assistant had tried for years to get him on the apps that ran with the phones. He could speak right into the earpiece, record everything, that's what they said. What they didn't understand was that the tape recorder and its tiny, archaic tapes were the same as a baseball pitcher's lucky socks. Cooper had recorded the entire coverage of LA ten years ago on the little device and transcribed it later. It had been the only solid reminder that he was separate from this horror—reporting it, not living it.

He pressed record and spoke.

"Leaving Fort Worth in two hours, headed to Denver. Alan Robertson is in isolation following a poisoning attempt. I don't expect anything." He clicked the recording device off and laid his head on the tiny table.

These notes were entirely for his sanity now. In the last ten years, things had changed. He had an assistant, an assistant for that assistant, production assistants, producers, caterers, handlers, everything he thought he'd wanted back when he'd been a junior reporter at the *LA Examiner* before the disaster. Now he was the great Cooper Carlson, and didn't even need to do his own reporting.

"Coop?" a voice sounded outside the trailer door.

"C'mon in," Cooper replied, his throat aching. His body was so weary, he thought he might never be able to stand up again.

His assistant, Ross, stood in the doorway holding a paper cup of something steaming. Cooper managed a smile.

"That for me?" he asked gently.

Ross nodded, entering the tiny space and placing the cup down on the table. *Poor kid*, Cooper thought as he took a long gulp.

Barely out of college, they'd assigned him as an intern, but Cooper had insisted they pay him some sort of rate. He hated interns. It sounded like a good idea to the network—free labor and all that—but Cooper had been around long enough to know that you get what you pay for. Free labor usually meant spotty hours, half-done jobs, and gossip spread all over set and even to other networks. Because he had insisted on Ross getting paid, he was now a god among interns on set. Bullshit really; they were giving him a pittance, not half what he was worth. Still, it was a small victory, and he'd bought the kid's loyalty if nothing else.

"They set for the five o'clock broadcast out there?" Cooper asked.

Ross nodded, but his face was distracted. "Coop, can I ask you something?"

Cooper looked up from the coffee. "Nope, no questions. It's in my contract." Seeing Ross' shocked and admonished face, he softened his expression. "I'm kidding. Seriously, you've been up too long, young man. You've forgotten I'm an asshole. What do you want to ask me?"

Ross nodded at the joke but was too deep in worry to react. "I just...I know you have to say you don't know...it's just, I have family in Denver. All my family actually..."

"Where are you going with this, Ross?" Cooper swallowed his impatience and a yawn simultaneously.

A vein in Ross's temple twitched madly. "It sounds nuts given what happened out there, but there's talk that Alan Robertson was involved, like some kind of underground bombing or something. Do you think he's involved?"

Cooper indicated the bench across from him, and Ross sat. "Look, it doesn't sound that nuts. No more nuts than a giant sinkhole opening up under a major city, where sinkholes never happen.

No more nuts than five thousand people suddenly dropping thirty stories without warning. There is nothing about this that makes sense. If you look at the reports coming from the USGS, it makes even less sense. But Robertson has been god knows where for nine and a half years, and sitting in federal holding in Denver for the last six months. I have no earthly idea how he'd be involved in this, but until they find some evidence of explosives or whatever, I just can't say. Neither can you, not until we find something to link him," Cooper spoke soothingly. He needed Ross to clear his head.

Ross nodded.

Cooper swigged the last of the coffee. "They haven't found any of the *Son of Abraham* tags that were left last time. No one has any evidence that this is anything other than a freak act of nature. We have people in Denver right now getting ready for his trial coverage. I can say this, if Robertson is connected in any way, no matter how small, your family is safer there than anywhere else. They won't want to hurt him. Nothing in Denver will be touched so long as he's there."

Ross nodded, but he didn't look convinced.

"Look, I can get set up for the five o'clock on my own. Lie down for a bit." Cooper indicated the little cot in the back. "Seriously, I need you sharp. Use the studio phone to call your folks."

Ross looked uncertain, but Cooper nodded again and then got up from the table, leaving the trailer and Ross alone inside. After the LA bombings, *Son of Abraham* had been tagged all over the wreckage. It had been how they tracked him before LA. And after the disaster, it was how they knew. Now they had to wait until someone else gave them a sign.

He was headed to Denver as soon as the 5:00 a.m. broadcast was done. The network was livid about it, but he had promised to fly back to Fort Worth once he'd spoken with Robertson. Cooper knew it didn't make any sense, but he had a nagging thought that he couldn't shake. The connection between this and Los Angeles was tenuous, if not entirely imagined, but he couldn't unsee the thin threads he saw linking the two. How does a man in federal lockup cause the world's largest natural disaster, a sinkhole that had reached three hundred miles before the growth began to slow? There were perks to being the great Cooper Carlson, and one was that he didn't have to explain why he needed to do this. He wanted the first interview with Robertson. NBC, CNN, FOX—they were all on the scene here in Texas. Cooper couldn't shake the possibility that the real story was thousands of miles away.

Esther Robertson would most certainly be on her way to Denver as well before too long. She gave him the creeps, truth be known. There was something deeply unsettling about her. The eyes and the face were a dead ringer for Alan Robertson's long-missing sister, the one the news had dredged up from old surveillance photos when he'd made his own headlines. The most popular theory was he'd murdered her. Most people assumed she was dead, maybe underground, maybe the mastermind for the whole thing. None of it had ever made much sense. Alan Robertson was a kid who'd barely made it out of high school. No one remembered him, didn't seem to have any friends, nothing. He certainly hadn't been the genius mind that he evidently was now—five languages, and the power to persuade thousands from his damn chat rooms. The network he'd had in West LA before the bombing had been mind-blowing. At least five houses, all leased to him, all housing whatever ragged bits of people he'd picked up along the way. Women, sister wives or whatnot, ten kids, and this insane network of influence that had been tagged in Germany, France, Qatar, New Zealand, Canada, South America . . . every damn where. How'd a kid who'd grown up in a freaky, if harmless, cult that looked more like Mennonites or Amish turn out to be the Son of Abraham?

Cooper poured himself more coffee from the craft service table, passively watching the hustle around him. Of course, it wasn't all that simple. Robertson had been in the news before. He had been ten years old when he was kidnapped from his foster family. But he'd been in the news before that, when that shitshow happened—the trials, the mother dying, then the father going crazy and trying to go after the sister. *Jesus*, thought Cooper. *No wonder the kid grew up to be a psychopath.* And then the sister disappeared entirely. Buried under the house was Cooper's thought, although all that land was unrecognizable. It was Abbot Kinney West now, where a studio apartment went for the price of a five-bedroom mansion in the Midwest; no more bungalows and Sinder Avenue.

"Cooper, you ready for makeup?" a production assistant asked, her voice cracking. The whole team had been on it all night. "They'll brief you while you get prepped."

Cooper nodded and paused to check his madly buzzing phone. New email, marked urgent, and it was driving his phone to distraction. He started to open it and then stopped. He'd get to it after the broadcast. It was time to find out the preliminary numbers, the counting of the dead. Time to tell the world what they had hoped to never hear again.

*

Ashiks@qmail.com via Kqur.ber
to: Cooper_Carlson

Hello.

Happy anniversary, Cooper. We've missed you. Dallas has fallen and soon more will follow. Our Ceannaire will rise from his cell, and a reckoning the likes of which you have never seen will descend upon this plane. The faithful will be rewarded, and those who stood in judgment of our one true father will suffer. Dallas is just the start. Our Ceannaire will topple your cities, will burn your homes. The Son of Abraham will rise from your ashes.

We gave you a present in Dallas—another chance to become a star.

12

ESTHER

THE GIRL AT THE UNITED COUNTER GAVE ESTHER THE slightest look of recognition. *She probably knows exactly who I am*, Esther thought darkly as the tickets were printed and the bag sent on its conveyer belt journey to the plane. The interview had aired hours ago. Esther had changed her flight as soon as she got home. When LA happened, planes were grounded and transportation services went into chaos. It wasn't 9/11, no one flew a plane into a building, but in the midst of trying to figure out what happened—how, why, who—the world froze for a long minute. This time, Esther changed the flight before the world froze. No one was talking about how many died in Dallas; no one needed to. The number 15,789 rang in her head like a bell. Knowing that number hadn't answered shit.

She stumbled through security and headed to the terminal, stopping at a coffee cart. A full hour before boarding, the television overhead was playing Cooper Carlson's coverage from Fort Worth: *Live at 5*. His lips moved while a news ticker ran across the bottom of the screen—estimated mortality numbers. Esther closed her eyes. *Don't want to know, don't want to know.* When she opened them, her father's face filled the screen. It was his ID photo from maybe fifteen years ago, the face Esther remembered.

Esther had no idea if they would even let her see him when she arrived in Denver—and no idea if she really wanted to. Yesterday, Esther had clearance for visitation. Today was a brand-new reality. Esther hadn't been able to express to Cooper Carlson why she needed to be there for her father's trial or why she wanted the hour visit with him before it started. She'd imagined the scene over and over in her head so many times. She dreamt about it most nights. In some, she cussed him out, and he stood with open arms, wanting to hold her. Sometimes she let him. In some, he attacked her, accused her of being a spy, being a murderer, a liar. He accused her of selling him out to the feds, the CIA. He tried to choke her. Sometimes she let him. Sometimes he was quiet and didn't respond to Esther's rages or tears. He sat on a bench as though waiting for a bus, staring across the horizon line. Sometimes Esther sat next to him.

She knew only that she needed to see him this last time, needed to cuss or cry or scream, otherwise she would dream of it the rest of her days.

"Excuse me." Esther looked up to see a man looming over her, staring down with a furrowed brow. He was wearing a rumpled business suit. He looked like someone's dad, someone's terrible husband, and he stank of airport bar and deli meat.

"Yes?" Esther answered directly although she knew exactly what he wanted.

"You're Esther Robertson." He didn't ask; he already knew. Esther's father's face was on the screen again.

"You on this flight?" He indicated the flight board. Esther nodded.

"Fuck if I am then," the man muttered and walked to the security agent who was standing by the entrance to the seating area. The agent looked at Esther and listened to the man rant. She could hear part of his words—terrorist, danger, murderer. Esther was none of these things, but that didn't matter. The agent was speaking now: "I'm sorry, sir" and "Nothing we can do, sir." The man stumbled off and out of the terminal. He'd tell the customer service desk before the flight boarded. Esther would have her purse searched again, the wand waved over her body before she got on the plane. The TSA officer would apologize. The flight attendants might even bring her a free drink if they were sympathetic; if they weren't, she wouldn't see so much as a cup of ice during the two hours to Denver. This had happened before. Now that the charity was recognizable, it usually ended with an apology and a free mini bottle of Bacardi on board. Before she'd started the fund for survivors and their families, Esther was politely asked to rebook the flight or wait on standby for the next trip.

Esther remembered an interview she'd seen with Dean Corll's sister. The Candy Man, the Pied Piper serial killer who'd murdered somewhere around twenty-eight young men in the 1970s. The sister said no one believed she didn't know. No one believed that she hadn't seen something, anything in him that would have clued her in on the idea that he was a murderer. Same interview happened years later with Samantha Krestin. Her husband, Stanley Krestin, had been burying bodies of prostitutes under the garage for twenty years before he was caught. Didn't she see the blood? Didn't she hear anything? Smell anything? Didn't Stanley ever act oddly? She had to have known, just like Dean Corll's sister; they had to have known.

Cooper Carlson had lost his big moment. He'd had Esther cornered. Her nonanswer would never have stood if the Dallas news hadn't been whispered in his ear. He would have circled back around, pointing out the evidence that she must have known, had to have known. Didn't she see the way the neighborhood treated him? At fifteen, didn't she see the Son of Abraham online? Didn't she recognize his face? His words? She had to have known. *Maybe I did*, whispered the tickling thought that lived at the back of her consciousness. *Maybe I always suspected.* Esther had known when she left Los Angeles that gray day in November that she would never see Sarai again. It was something Sarai had said. She'd leaned in and whispered in Esther's ear.

"You have to remember."

Sarai had been twelve, and her words had been wiser than any Esther had heard since. Maybe Sarai knew, and she let Esther leave without her. Maybe, maybe, maybe.

The flight was boarding. The businessman hadn't returned, and the flight attendants waved Esther on without any further hassle. She had a window seat and settled in for the two-and-a-half-hour flight to Denver. She fell asleep almost immediately, slipping into a dark and nonsensical dream. She was standing on the beach, but the waves rolled in and out as though drawn with black ink. They looked like the great rolling waves of a Hokusai painting. Meticulously drawn fishing boats fought the storm and dipped under the angry water, rolling back out again, dripping lines of ink. Esther watched as a spiny-tailed creature with talons for hands and sharpened hooks for teeth rose to the surface. Its unnatural eyes were that of a fish— pale, absorbing the blank space of the scene. It mouthed a word. Esther couldn't see far enough, couldn't understand.

She woke with a jolt, the man next to her staring curiously. Esther nodded and tried to ignore him. He still stared. *Another fan*, she thought without humor. It went a couple of ways: curiosity or horror. After LA, toward the end of her stay at Langley

Porter, she had attended a grief group. There were some survivors from LA and others whose losses had had nothing to do with her father. Some who had lost mothers, children, boyfriends to cancer or the flu; others whose fathers, sisters, aunts had been murdered. Grief, it seemed, knew no boundaries. Esther had met a woman there (hard to call her a friend, since they never spoke again after Langley). She had written a book about her sister's murder. It had sold thousands of copies. She said that everyone she was in line with at the coffee shop, everyone who took her temperature at the doctor's office, everyone who sat next to her on a plane asked her to recount the story over and over. "It's a fucking nightmare," she told the group one night. No rest, no quiet. "Would you have written the book if you'd known?" Esther had asked her after the session. The woman had shrugged. "I had no choice," she had replied sadly. "If I hadn't, it would have written itself." That was what the charity was for Esther. She could have changed her name, dyed her hair, moved far away. Instead, Esther endured the dead-eyed gaze of everyone who had ever seen her on television or in print news photos. Everyone who wanted her to recount her story. This man was just another.

Esther's phone told her they had about thirty more minutes of the flight. Esther's legs ached and her neck was stiff. Still the man in the aisle seat stared, his eyes wide and startled as though he had forgotten he was on a plane.

"We're not there," he said simply.

"No, we're not," Esther replied curtly and shifted her gaze out the tiny oval window.

"I know who you are," the man said, and Esther turned to look at him.

"Okay," she replied, steeling herself for whatever he was going to say next.

"I've seen your father," the man persisted.

"Everyone has seen him. He is on every news channel right now." Esther turned her head to look back out the window, hoping he would take the hint and leave her be.

"No. He speaks to me. He appears to me," the man said with an excitement in his voice that made Esther's skin crawl.

"No, he doesn't. Please stop," Esther said firmly. She was approached like this occasionally, by people who thought her father was their messiah, their Ceannaire. Among the letters she had received after Los Angeles had been those who exulted praise for the Son of Abraham and his daughter. Esther used to be afraid of them, but now she found them sad.

"You need to know something," the man whispered, and Esther turned to face him.

"If I let you tell me whatever you want to tell me, will you shut the fuck up and leave me be?" she asked directly.

"Yes, I will. I will shut the fuck up, but you need to know that we, your father's children, will never hurt you. Others threaten you, they blame you, but we would never harm the daughter of the Son of Abraham." The man looked around furtively even though no one was paying them any attention.

"Good to know. Alright, that it? You going to stop talking to me now?" Esther asked coldly.

"Yes. But remember, we would never hurt you. Your father would never allow it, Esther Robertson." The man smiled, and his eyes were strangely blank.

Esther turned as far away as she could manage from the man. If they had been any farther out on the flight, she would have demanded a new seat, but the "fasten seatbelts" signs were already lit. She had to endure this for only another twenty minutes. The man stayed true to his word and did not try to speak to her again. She was on the delirious end of tired, but she knew she would not sleep easily any time soon.

After Langley Porter, she had developed a variety of sleeping disorders. Her body had acclimated nicely to the institutional sterility, and once out, it could never rest without disturbance. The first ailment had been sleep screaming. Esther's neighbors stopped calling the cops when they found out, which always made her wonder what would happen if she really was being murdered. The sleepwalking had been next. Esther was busy in her sleep. One morning she woke to find she had swapped the food from the fridge with the plates in the cupboard. Warm, spoiled food sat on the shelves, and crisp, icy plates waited in the cooler.

Landing. The usual announcements. The man stayed silent and paid Esther no more attention apart from a polite nod as they disembarked.

The airport was a madhouse. As she had predicted, flights were being canceled and delayed. Anything going to, coming from, or stopping over anywhere near Dallas was out, sending everything else into a tailspin. Esther silently thanked herself for jumping on this flight when she could. If she had waited, she might never have left San Francisco. She hadn't informed the federal office that she was changing her flight, so the car they had promised to send would not be here. She grabbed her bag off the carousel and headed to the cab stand. Despite the man's assurance that none of her father's people would hurt her, she still found herself looking over her shoulder, as she always did. Threats on her life were a common occurance, even ten years after the bombings. She knew the interview with Cooper Carlson was likely to set off a whole new round of threats. Oddly, she had never assumed that they were from her father's people. The man's strange warning was a moot point in truth. No, the most virulent threats came from those who had lost someone—a wife or a daughter, a son, a mother or father. They came out of anger and grief. Threatening Esther was the only way they could strike back at a phantom who had disappeared after Los Angeles, resurfacing only a handful of times in over nine years.

Esther stared out the window of the cab. She was not going to go to the hotel that the federal office had arranged. Too many people would have access to where she was. She would stay as anonymous as possible and hopefully remain unseen.

13

COOPER

THE PHONE RANG FOUR TIMES AND THEN WENT TO voice mail. Cooper knew she had hit ignore, again. *Fucking Cecily*, he thought distractedly. The puddle jumper prop plane was cold, the seat sized for children, and the engine roared in his left ear. He wouldn't have been able to talk to her anyway in this piece of shit, but he didn't really need to talk. He needed two minutes. Two minutes to tell his daughter to pack a bag and get on a train out of DC, away from Georgetown, and head out to Boonsboro. Even that wouldn't be far enough if everything went to shit, but it was better. She could stay in the cabin. It had sat empty for months, but he'd paid the gas and kept the lights on, always thinking he was going to head out there for a weekend. It hadn't happened since last summer.

Frustrated, he dialed the Georgetown housing office. She'd kill him later, but if she wasn't going to answer her damn cell phone, then he'd have to have them send her a message. Abruptly he hung up. *A message that said what*? "Can you please tell my daughter I got a probably crazy email and she should go hide out in the country? Can you just put that on a sticky note and leave it on her door? Thanks!" Cooper started to dial again, hung up again. He couldn't say anything other than "Call me," which she would ignore, and had good reason to.

He ought to call Caroline. She wouldn't hang up immediately; she'd sit silently on the other end of the phone, let him say his piece, and then hang up. She was in Providence—not the most likely target, but still too much of a city for his taste.

"You get ahold of her?" a voice inquired hesitantly next to him. Cooper looked over at Bill. They'd been together all those years ago at the *LA Examiner*. Bill had been responsible for the first photos of the fire that destroyed Sinder Avenue back in 1996. When Cooper had moved over to the LA CBS office, he'd insisted they take Bill on as cameraman. All those early stories, before the bombing, it had been just the two of them, not even a producer. Bill was good people, mostly. He spent his free time gambling his son's ever dwindling college fund away, and drank enough to single-handedly keep Jim Beam in the black; but apart from that he was loyal, and one of the few people Cooper knew wouldn't gossip about his shitty home life.

"Nope," Cooper said resignedly. "She's not speaking to me 'ever again,' she said, and it looks like she meant it."

"She'll come around. Cecily's what... nineteen?" Bill asked, although he knew the answer perfectly well.

"Yep. I don't have time for her to come around. I need her out of that damn city." Cooper shook his head and checked his email.

Coop –

The email's been forwarded to the FCI facility in Denver, among others. Get there as soon as you can. We'll have a crew waiting in the satellite station in Lakewood. They're sending security.

CBS had begrudgingly arranged the plane to Denver directly after the broadcast in Fort Worth when they realized they couldn't stop him. There was no evidence the email that he received was connected to Alan Robertson—it could just as likely be some crackpot who fell off his meds—but the production team was intrigued enough that if there was a story, and Alan Robertson was involved, CBS wanted Cooper on it first.

Bill yawned. "That's some weird shit in Dallas. Those Geological Survery science types said there was no natural reason it should have or could have happened. I'm not ruling anything out. And Alan Robertson? Who the fuck knows, man. He was out a long damn time though, enough to hatch a whole new generation of crazies." Bill leaned over. "But tell me, what are you hoping to get out of this trip to Denver? You don't actually think he'll confess to anything, do you?"

Cooper sighed. It was a fair question. He wanted the first interview with Alan Robertson. He wanted that son of a bitch's cold-eyed stare. He wanted to be the one to get him to admit he had something, anything to do with Dallas. He wanted to know what was next. And he wanted his daughter to answer her damn phone and then get on a train to the cabin where they'd spent every summer when she was growing up. The cabin he'd bought with Caroline a year after they were married, when they couldn't afford it and hadn't cared. The cabin where all he could remember was happiness, where none of his fuckups had poisoned the well. But Cecily wasn't speaking to him ever again. He'd scoffed when she'd said it, and immediately regretted it when he saw the hurt in her eyes. She'd been true to her word; six long months had passed and nothing, not a word. But that wasn't what Bill was asking.

"There's not much reporting on a big hole. I know how that sounds, but there's no story there. Robertson, though...I think that message was real, and I think there will be more attacks leading up to his trial date. Someone is doing this with Robertson or in his name. Dallas is some kind of nightmare, and I'd end up reporting the same shit day after day. Denver is where the real story is."

Cooper sat back. Esther Robertson was also heading to Denver. His sources in San Francisco had told him she'd bumped up her flight right after the taping. *Figures*, he thought cruelly. She knew more than she let on. He remembered Cecily at fifteen. To a fault she knew the business of the house. Anything that even smelled like gossip, she was on it. No way Esther Robertson grew up in that shit, then willingly and silently left LA two days before the attack and didn't know what was going to happen. He'd had her too. He'd seen her defenses flickering, her story beginning to slide, and then that damn voice in his ear—end the interview, emergency, breaking news.

Esther Robertson who had raised millions for the survivors of the Los Angeles bombings. Esther Robertson who looked more child than woman. Esther Robertson who he knew wouldn't be surprised to learn exactly what was going to happen in Dallas. Maybe he'd have the chance to finish that interview as well in Denver. CBS had sent a skeleton crew with him and arranged this private plane, which looked more crop duster than charter jet. They'd pull the guts out of this story while the other vultures circled Dallas. He stared at his phone and resisted the temptation to dial. He'd try again when they landed. Staring out the window, Cooper let his eyes drift closed, and he slept for the first time in over twenty-four hours.

14

ESTHER

THE CAB DROPPED ESTHER AT MOTEL 6 IN LITTLETON, just a short distance from the federal detention center. The hotel that the federal office had arranged was considerably nicer, but she was spooked. *Stupid,* she told herself. Being paranoid was a family trait, but being stupid wasn't. Esther couldn't help but hear her father laugh at her in her head. Truth was, Esther never trusted anyone much, and right now even less so.

Early on, not too long after Esther left Langley, when she was living in a group home in South Sunset, a man followed her home from the bus stop. Esther was using a different name at that time; the CPS officials thought it best while she finished school. She had cut her hair and did everything she could to hide her face, which had been broadcast all over the news reports and documentary specials. The group home had only a few kids. They were all broken in one way or another. One girl peeled the paint off the walls and slipped it under her tongue. She ate dirt and wall plaster and caulk she'd pull out from in between the bathroom tiles. Another cut herself in elaborate patterns, bloody tattoos that scarred and warped with infection when left undetected. *I was probably the most normal of them all*, she thought with a snort of silent laughter. Her roommate swallowed a gallon of white vinegar the week she arrived; she had thought it was bleach. It hadn't done much except earn her a few days in the hospital. Esther thought mixing up the two was more indication of her being crazy than the actual act.

Esther attended a "special school for kids with special problems"—that was how it had been explained to her, as though she were a toddler. She took a school bus to the neat brick building and then again home in the afternoon. On one particular day, a white pickup had been parked outside the school. There was a label on the side with a plunger and a smiling roll of toilet paper. The staff hadn't noticed, but Esther had. The man in the driver's seat watched her as she waited in line to board the bus with all the other special kids. Esther sat in the back and watched him pull away as the bus did, watched him turn as they turned, stop as they stopped. As Esther exited, she had paused. The bus driver had looked at her curiously and asked if she was okay. In that moment, Esther realized that she didn't care if she was or not. The man in the pickup would either drive past or not, stop or not, kill her or not. Esther simply did not care what came of it all.

As Esther stepped off the bus, he stepped from the truck. She watched as a small black cylinder moved from his pocket and upward until it was pointed directly at her head. Esther had a faint memory of smiling; that's what anyone who was watching told her she had done. Esther didn't remember exactly. It was all like a dream that someone else had and she had borrowed. What Esther did remember was a high-pitched scream coming from the bus. She remembered the painful scrape of the sidewalk as the bus driver dove out and tackled her to the ground, barely in time to avoid her being shot in the head. Esther remembered yelling, voices, a numb fuzziness that surrounded her body entirely. Later they told her a man walking his dog had come up behind the man as he tried to shoot her and wrestled him to the ground. The bus driver was hit in the arm and forever lauded a hero. The man with the gun had a note in his pocket; he'd been intending to kill himself after he killed Esther Robertson, only living child of Alan Robertson the Butcher. He blamed Esther. He'd been hit in the LA blast. He'd watched the news, and he had been watching her. Esther's father was still missing then, but she wasn't. And for anyone paying attention, as he was, Esther was easy to find. Esther left the group home for another, and another after that, until she turned eighteen and moved into a basement studio in Chinatown. Esther took her name back; what did it matter anyhow?

There was a pay phone outside the 7-Eleven down the street from the Motel 6. She'd call the federal center from there. *Paranoid*, Esther told herself. *Weak*, whispered her internal voice as she splashed water on her face. Would they delay the trial now? Where would they send him? FCI Englewood was to be only temporary during the proceedings. It had held a variety of notorious criminals in its history, but it wasn't designed for long-term detention. It was a fortress that held a very limited number of guests, and then only while they were on trial.

Alan Robertson had been found in a Quonset hut in the plains outside Laramie, Wyoming. No telling how long he'd been there. The feds told Esther he'd claimed to have been living in a houseboat on Half Moon Bay prior to that. It was likely all lies. Esther could see her father walking across the border before the attacks. No one would have questioned him. From there, he could have gone anywhere. So why did he end up in a Quonset hut in the plains? Esther knew the answer to that too; he wanted to be caught, and now she knew why. This was a signal to those who still worked for him. And more would follow, she felt it.

The woman who answered the line at FCI Englewood put Esther immediately through to a line that rang once and then was answered by a man with a darkly smooth voice.

"Miss Robertson?" he said brusquely.

"Yes, I need to know if my visitation with Alan Robertson is still allowed." No point dancing around the topic.

"Miss Robertson, we've been trying to reach you. We offer our apologies for the airport confusion. We weren't alerted that you changed your flight until the last minute. I trust you found transporation?"

Esther paused. "I did."

"And the accomodations the agency arranged for you are acceptable?" he asked.

"I found my own hotel," Esther replied briskly.

"Are you alright?" he asked with a curious note to his voice.

Esther nodded, knowing full well how futile the gesture was.

"My name is Special Agent Carl Flagston. I've been in charge of much of the dealings with Alan Robertson's time here. It's perhaps best if you come in. Can we send a car to pick you up?" He paused, waiting.

"No," Esther said abruptly. "I'll get there myself." She hung up and slumped against the wall, staring out at the morning sky.

15

ESTHER

ESTHER STOOD AT THE ENTRY TO THE FEDERAL Correctional Institution, a building that had held some of the most notorious criminals in modern history. The holding cells in the lower floors were said to be more secure than any of the super-max prisons on the continent. She wondered if it was intentionally designed to look innocuous or if it was an accident that it could be mistaken for an insurance office or school administration building.

The front door opened, and a man in a gray sweater and over-large glasses that obscured his eyes opened the door and looked at her hesitantly.

"Miss Robertson?" he asked cautiously.

Esther nodded. "Are you Agent Flagston?"

The man shook his head. "I'm a clerk in his office. Let me take you to him." The man opened the door for her and nodded. With a deep breath, Esther entered into an equally unimpressive lobby. After showing her driver's license to the guard and allowing him to shine a flashlight around her shoulder bag, she followed the man with the overlarge glasses to the elevators. As the door shut, she turned to him.

"If you aren't who you say you are, I suppose you could kill me right now," she said flatly.

The man looked visibly shaken. "I assure you, I mean you no harm. I'm a clerk in the special crimes unit, which is a nice way of saying I'm a secretary. My name is Jeff. They sent me down to help you. They said you were arriving this afternoon."

Esther nodded. "Forgive me. It's been a weird day."

Jeff nodded. "Yes, yes, that's a way of putting it."

Esther nodded without responding. The elevator doors opened, and she stepped out into a bustle of activity. Women and men rushed back and forth with papers and file folders. Rumpled-looking agents sat at desks, leaning into their phones while nodding at whatever was being told to them from the other end. Jeff nodded at her, and she followed him through the activity to an office in the back of the room. The door was just slightly ajar. Jeff knocked softly once and then pushed it open, indicating to Esther to enter.

Special Agent Carl Flagston was well over six feet tall. Esther's first thought was he must have been asked exactly how tall every day for his entire adult life. His broad shoulders added to the imposing presence he carried as he crossed the room and stretched out a hand in greeting. His voice was deep, but not unkind. His expression was carefully controlled, and Esther could almost feel the waves of energy underneath his calm words.

"Miss Robertson, thank you for coming in. Have a seat. Jeff, can you get her a cup of something. Coffee?"

Esther nodded at Jeff and sat in the worn armchair that faced Agent Flagston's meticulously clean desk. He closed the door and then sat across from her, regarding her for a moment before speaking.

"It's a situation," he said simply. "I'm sure you can appreciate how dire it really is. I'm not sure how much you know. Where do you want me to start?"

Esther's head had begun to feel as though it were disconnected from her body, a response to the stress, she knew. Her doctors had officially termed it "depersonalization disorder," her body and mind's safety response to intense stress and anxiety. It overtook her like a wave at odd times, the feeling that her flesh, her eyes, her nose, her arms were all vibrating static. She felt miles away, as though she were observing herself from a distance. They'd tried to medicate her out of the disorder, and Esther had flatly refused. She felt safe in the static bubble while it lasted. And as she stared at Agent Flagston, who patiently waited for her response, she realized that this was the first time in weeks she hadn't felt as though she were being eaten alive by terror.

"Why was my father moved from Florence?" she asked quietly.

Agent Flagston regarded her for a moment and then leaned forward. "There was an attempt on his life. Even though he was in solitary and kept confined from the general population, word had gotten out that he was in the facility. His food was laced with cyanide. While that should have killed him outright, he was, by all accounts, unaffected by the poisoning. Regardless, he was moved here to our secure units as soon as possible. It was a move that was scheduled to happen anyhow. The attempt on his life simply hastened it."

"Wait," Esther interrupted. "You're saying my father ate a plate of cyanide and not only survived, but was unaffected? It didn't even make him sick?" Esther felt gooseflesh on the back of her neck.

"That's the report. I have no idea how. I can't even venture a guess." A look of concern and frustration crossed Agent Flagston's face. "I'm not sure how to address this with you. I do understand that despite everything, we are talking about your father and, from what I understand, your only living family member."

A cup of coffee had appeared before Esther at some point, and she looked down at it surprised. Agent Flagston caught her expression and gave her a small smile.

"Jeff is something of a coffee ninja."

Despite herself, Esther smiled back, the expression feeling stiff from disuse on her features.

"Agent Flagston," she began, "I do not harbor any loyalties to my father. The man I knew died ten years ago. Whoever is in that cell deep in your basement is a stranger. Please do not mince words."

The agent nodded and pulled a file folder from his desk and opened it to a series of black-and-white photographs. He reversed it and pushed it across the desk to Esther.

"Here are the surveillance photographs taken of your father before he was apprehended. We had almost caught him several times, but he managed to disappear at just the right moment, repeatedly."

The photos showed Alan Robertson, much as Esther remembered him, standing on the deck of a ramshackle houseboat. Notes at the bottom read "San Diego – August." Another showed him sitting behind filthy glass at a diner booth. He was staring right at the camera, a half smile on his face. He looked older in this picture, his eyes wild.

"He knew you were following him," Esther said softly.

"So it would seem," Agent Flagston agreed. "Mr. Robertson is under security precautions never before seen in this system. And even at that, we had an incident last evening where one of the outer entries to the holding area was found unlocked. It was discovered and obviously remedied immediately, but your father has a tendency to disappear."

Esther rifled through the photographs. Another showed him leaning against a Winnebago camper in what looked to be a rest stop. The notes read "Santa Fe – September." She flipped through to the bottom of the stack and gasped at the last image. A woman who looked more girl than grown stared out at her. Her eyes held just a hint of color; her hair was as pale as Esther's own. Her expression was unreadable, but the very image made every hair on Esther's arm stand at attention. The notes read "Ceit Roberston – DMV records 1995."

"Ceit Robertson," Esther read aloud.

"The other mystery attached to your father," Agent Flagston said. "You look identical to her, but I suppose you've been told that before."

Esther nodded. She had been told many times that she resembled her aunt but had never seen such a clear photograph of her, only had a few grainy Polaroids. And the news coverage after Los Angeles only mentioned Ceit Robertson's name; no one bothered to find her image.

"She disappeared before I was born," Esther said.

"Yes, she did. Not a trace. She disappeared following a major fire that destroyed the greater part of the cul-de-sac where she and your father grew up and where, by all records, she managed both the money and tenancy. The investigation from the time concluded that it was arson, and your father was the prime suspect. Two people died in that fire, including your great-grandmother, Shona Robertson. Your aunt disappeared and was presumed dead, although a body has never been found."

Esther closed the file and shoved it back across the desk. "What are you getting at? Do you think my long-lost aunt has reappeared and has been protecting my father all this time, tipping him off, trying to break him out of his cell?"

The agent looked confused and then shook his head. "No, I don't. I mean only that your father is far more connected and far more dangerous than anyone can possibly gauge. He makes Manson look like an amateur."

"You have a leak on the inside," Esther said pointedly.

Agent Flagston nodded. "Perhaps. But I'm not so sure. A large number of the photographs of your father—this one here at Half Moon Bay, another…here, marked Tombstone, Arizona—all of these were sent to us by an anonymous source outside of the agency. We never found out who. They were mailed from seemingly random places, impossible to trace, no fingerprints, nothing. It looks like your father knew he was being photographed. He's doing everything but smiling and waving. So we have to ask, is this someone he knows? Someone he traveled with? My point is, Alan Robertson seemed to want us to know he was out there. And even the shots caught by our surveillance, he seemed perfectly aware that he was being trailed, and disappeared every time. My guys are too good for him to find on his own."

"You don't know my father," Esther retorted.

"No one does…not even you," Agent Flagston responded.

"So why tell me all this?" Esther asked. "Will I still be able to see him, or is that off?"

"Not at all. We need you to see him," Agent Flagston said, leaning in. "I need you to go in there knowing everything possible. You're the last tie he has. All you need to do is talk to him. The footage will be analyzed by my team."

"I'm a spy then," Esther said. Her body felt numb.

The agent nodded. "If he is responsible for your aunt's death, if someone was harboring him for the last nine and a half years, if there is a leak in my office, all these things need to be brought to light and soon. You should know—and this has not been released to the public—but the Son of Abraham group has claimed responsibility for Dallas. Now, the official word on Dallas is natural disaster. There's no indication that this is a legitimate claim, and until the USGS and the emergency crews analyze the situation, there isn't any way to determine if Dallas was caused by an outside force such as explosives. But you can appreciate that we have to take this seriously. If your father had anything to do with Dallas, either directly or by association, we need to prepare ourselves for the possibility that there may be more attacks."

Esther closed her eyes and saw her father with his shaggy hair and light eyes smiling down at her. She heard his voice and felt the light roughness of his hand as it held hers. She could hear the beating of his heart as she lay her head to his chest, his hand stroking her hair. She heard her sister's screams in her imagination, saw her flesh burn. She saw her mother's body in her mind's eye, arms and legs blackened and splayed at unnatural angles. She opened her eyes.

"When do I see him?"

16

COOPER

"SO LET ME GET THIS STRAIGHT." COOPER BALANCED the phone on his shoulder while he flipped through the file. "Robertson was moved from Florence to the FCI facility a week early because of illness?"

There was a pause on the other end. Cooper didn't entirely trust his contact, but the guy hadn't lied yet. Cooper suspected he was a right fighter. He was anonymous now, but he'd come out after the story broke, accept all the thank-yous and accolades for his courage, but only after the story had been reported in such a way as to make him look more whistleblower and less rat. He claimed to be an employee at the maximum security facility in Florence. Cooper suspected he was a guard. He spoke in gossip that Cooper imagined he'd heard from inmates. It could be total bullshit or the most reliable information out there—no way to tell.

"Someone tried to poison him, but there wasn't any illness. You hear what I'm trying to say to you?" The contact's voice was scratchy; he was probably trying to disguise it. Cooper felt a migraine coming on.

"I thought he was in isolation at Florence. Wouldn't a guard had to have been the only one in contact with the food he was given?" Cooper asked. He already knew all this, but he didn't want his contact to know that. If the guy thought he was breaking a story to the media, he'd be more likely to spill. Cooper was listening for the details left out of the official investigation report. That piece of sterile shit said the poison had originated in the prison kitchen and the guard had transported it to Robertson unknowingly. But something didn't line up. Prisoners in isolation had contact only with the guards. The idea that a fellow inmate would have had access to the poison and the ability to lace Robertson's meal without being detected was fishy. Not to mention the fact that Robertson walked away from the whole thing without so much as a stomachache.

"Listen, it wasn't an inmate. It was the guard. But here's the thing—Robertson ate the whole damn plate. Then the guy on dish duty just touches that shit and spends the night in the infirmary barfing his guts up. That's something isn't it? You think that's something?" The contact paused, hopeful.

"Okay, maybe. But cyanide takes, what, ten seconds to kill you? And it takes only a spoonful. So help me understand what you're saying here." Cooper sat down. He was at the CBS Denver field office right outside of downtown, and it was getting too late for this bullshit if he wanted to try to talk to Alan Robertson before sundown. This contact had proven useful before, but Cooper couldn't help but think he was sniffing out a reward. The investigation at the Florence supermax had already shown that there were at least four guards who had lost people in Los Angeles. Any one of them would have had motivation to kill Robertson.

"Listen, man, it's fucking easy to get shit in here. You know that by now. They have rat poison and all sorts of shit that can kill a man. But this was harder than all that. This was one hundred percent pure, grade A cyanide." The contact's voice was excited.

"So Alan Robertson eats a plateful of poison that could have killed a dozen men and walks away." Cooper was half talking to himself. He was starting to see the picture the contact was trying to paint for him. "Okay, what else you got for me?" Cooper asked, trying to stave off the first hints of migraine that stretched at the corners of his eyes.

"Only this—they said all the time Robertson was in his cell he slept or sat perfectly still, like Buddha or some shit, never saying a word, just smiling and nodding." The contact paused.

Cooper tried to control his frustration. "And why is this significant?" he asked impatiently.

"There are three other guys in isolation right now. They shouldn't be able to communicate with each other, but they do all the damn time. Whole conversations through vents, all sorts of sneaky shit." The contact's voice was agitated as though he were telling a campfire story. Cooper breathed in, barely containing the urge to slam the phone down.

"Okay, so our guy sits silently in his cell and doesn't talk. Please tell me why I care," Cooper said in a voice far calmer than he felt.

"They had a security cam on him the whole time, and nothing. He just sat there like some kind of giant bird. But the other three in isolation? They said he whispered to them all night and day. He told them he was their Ceannaire, whatever the hell that is. He told them the devil was coming. He sang them a song, creepy little thing that sounded like something out of a fucked-up fairy tale. One guy tried drowning himself in the toilet after Robertson was taken away. Said he had to join his Ceannaire."

Cooper paused, the pounding in his temples abating a bit.

"That is interesting." He hung up with the contact and sat at the metal desk for a moment as the office bustled around him. Alan Robertson was still recruiting, in seemingly impossible circumstances nonetheless. A poisoning attempt that looked to be more orchestrated than the original report let on, and now this. Cooper stood abruptly. He needed to find Bill and get to Littleton.

17

ESTHER

"OKAY, PROTOCOL. I'M SURE THEY'VE BEEN THROUGH this with you already, but I'll go over it again. It is imperative that you follow the protocol. Any breach and the visitation will be ended immediately. You will be under video and audio supervision, and there will be guards present in the room."

Esther listened as Agent Flagston described how her father would be cuffed to the metal table, how there would be no physical contact, how every word and gesture would be recorded. She knew all this. Esther had no urge to touch her father. The last time his hands had touched her was when she'd left for San Francisco ten years ago. He had placed both hands on her shoulders at the Greyhound station and stared at her, as though he were memorizing every hair, every inch of her face. Esther had lied to Cooper Carlson, she realized. She had known in that moment that her father was going to destroy something, someone. She had seen the darkness in his eyes. It had passed through his pale irises like a shadow. She had left anyway. Not that she'd had much of a choice;

he had waited until the bus pulled from the station before he turned away. Esther had stared at him through the grimy Greyhound bus window as he grew smaller and smaller.

"Are we good?" Agent Flagston paused, sensing her mind wandering. "And remember, at the very least we are trying to read his actions, gestures, anything. At best, he might tell you something, open up, confess even. He hasn't seen you since the attacks. We're hoping it's enough to get ahead of whatever might be coming next."

Esther looked at the agent curiously. "What makes you think anything is coming next?"

A vein on Agent Flagston's left temple was slowly pulsing. "I've been doing this for twenty years. I did the preliminary interviews with Timothy McVeigh. I profiled Richard Ramirez and Dennis Rader. I sat alone in a room with each of them, the same way you will meet with Alan Robertson, and interviewed them for hours." He paused and seemed to be searching for words. "They didn't frighten me. I saw broken men. Monsters in a box. But I don't mind admitting, that's not what I see when I look at your father. He's not broken. He's been caught physically, but mentally, it's... different. It's almost as if it doesn't matter that he's in custody. Being in that cell is where he wants to be right now, where he needs to be. I, for one, take the Son of Abraham claim to Dallas very seriously. I have no doubt they were involved. How, I have no idea, but I *know* it. So when you ask me why I think there is a 'next,' I can tell you only that I am right. I feel it. I see it. I don't know his motivation, never have. But I do not think he will stop. And Alan Robertson will continue without ever lifting a finger on his own. The blood will never reach his hands. His followers will continue to kill and maim and murder forever."

Esther let the words sink in. "And what can I possibly do about it?"

Agent Flagston stared at her for a long moment. "I don't know. You're the last tie to his humanity that he has left. He chose to save you. I don't know what he will say to you. He might say nothing. He might talk about the weather. I straight-up don't know."

"What are you hoping for?" Esther asked quietly, her head buzzing.

"That he will see his daughter, the baby that was supposed to mean a new life for him, the chance to create his own family, away from the ugliness of where he came from. That's what I hope."

"I'm ready." Esther met Agent Flagston's eyes and nodded. "I'll try."

18

BENNY

BENNY WAS WALKING TOO FAST. HE CONSCIOUSLY slowed his pace and then sped up a bit. He tried to relax his face. His jaw was tight, and it made his smile look weird. He knew it looked weird; no one would ever tell him, but he knew.

"Afternoon!" A man he recognized from the base bellowed the greeting, the words overly cheerful. Benny nodded back, his weird, too-tight smile threatening to give him away. Benny had been in the custodial department at Hill Air Force Base in Clearfield, Utah, for four years now. He was considered a permanent, nonprobationary civilian employee, and on orders from the Ceannaire he had applied for the security clearance necessary to work in the records and research offices. He had gained his new security badge a year ago. Every evening at five o'clock, Benny dutifully reported to work. He clocked in exactly on time. His breaks never exceeded the allotted fifteen minutes. He took his dinner in the employee room, a bagged meal. He ate alone, reading a book, for exactly thirty minutes. Every single night. Benny would sweep the floors of the research floor and then mop. He ran the floor shiner on Wednesday evenings. He cleaned the restrooms and made the stainless-steel sinks shine.

Tonight, he was due to clean the concrete-floored research lab, a task that necessitated the security clearance Benny had meticulously worked for all these years. It was finally time. His skin tingled with excitement. Five years ago—before the Ceannaire had saved him—Benny had been a step away from the streets, sleeping on his sister's couch when she let him, a friend's when she didn't. He had dropped out of college, his engineering degree abandoned. The voices had kept telling him to do it. They said everyone was laughing at him when he couldn't hear. They told him his smile was weird and his manner awkward. They told him he wasn't smart enough and the only reason he'd been accepted to Colorado State was that his dad had gone there. Sometimes the voices argued amongst each other, and that was the only time Benny had had any peace before the Ceannaire. They told him that his food in the cafeteria was poisoned and described how the cook had spit in the potatoes back in the kitchen and wiped his finger on the meat. The voices said they were trying to help him, but Benny didn't believe that.

The night he met the Ceannaire, he'd been sitting outside his sister's apartment, pretending to smoke. He didn't, but the guise allowed him an excuse to sit by himself in the dark. He would light the cigarette and then watch as it burned down. When he'd heard the voice for the first time, Benny had tried to ignore it. It was just another of the crowd that ran circles in his head, stole his thoughts, blocked his intent. He'd ground the dead cigarette into the pavement, hating the stink it left on his fingers.

I see you, Benny. I see you. You're kind. You're smart. You are more than this. I see you.

Benny had shook his head and closed his eyes. It was a trick, another fucking trick. The voices did this; they'd say something nice and then start in on their shit. His mother never wanted him and resented him. His eyes were too narrow, his chin too pointed, his body too thin. No one would ever be attracted to him. No girl would ever sleep with him. She'd laugh. They'd all laugh.

I can take you away from this, Benny. I can make them stop. I can silence them all. Let me in. I can be your father and mother. I can be the soft place you land when you feel that all is lost. Let me in, Benny, let me see.

That night, Benny had lain on the stiff sofa, a thin blanket over him. As he had closed his eyes, he'd seen a face, graying hair and pale, kind eyes. A face with only the first hints of age beginning to show. He sat up, shaking. The man was in the room, sitting on his sister's Queen Anne wing chair with the faded yellow rose print. He was unextraordinary in every way. He wore a casual sort of tattered clothes that made him look as though he'd stumbled out of a yoga class. His face was calm, a subdued smile edged around the corner of his mouth. His hair was ill-kempt, but the unruly nature of it looked entirely intentional. He nodded at Benny, who stared and tried not to scream. The voices were silent, as though they too could not comprehend what it was they were seeing.

Hello, son. You can relax now. In fact, you feel your entire body relaxing, don't you? Why don't you take a deep breath? You can think a little more clearly now, can't you?

The man's lips never moved, but his soft voice filled the room. Benny felt his body doing exactly what the man suggested. His breath went in and out, and his muscles unclenched. For the first time in perhaps years, Benny felt perfectly at ease. He stared at the man, daring the vision to disappear.

I'm not a vision. I am real, Benny. I found you. I have been searching, and I found you. I have searched the edges of time, the dark spots where the broken and sad hide, and I found you. It's time to take back your life. The voices that fill your head will never bother you again, not so long as I am with you. I am your father, and you are my son. Doesn't it feel good to know you belong, Benny? To feel wanted, to feel loved?

And it did. Jesus, it felt good. Benny had let the feeling of perfect relaxation and guiltless release settle into his gut from that day forward. The Ceannaire came to him at night, told him of the Night Forest and how he would rule it one day. He told Benny that he was chosen, that he was special and smart, and that there was a place for him in the world beyond this. He had guided Benny off his sister's couch in Provo to Clearfield, where with his partial engineering degree and clean record, he had easily landed the maintenance job on Hill Air Force Base. He followed his Ceannaire's words, and for the first time, perhaps ever, Benny felt like he belonged, like he was loved.

His sister had hugged him and told him how proud she was. He had really gotten it together, she'd said. She helped him pick out furniture for his little base apartment and had given him a little houseplant for the window. Benny's supervisors gave him excellent evaluations and applauded his efforts. And when he closed his eyes in the early morning hours after the night shift at the base, the Ceannaire whispered in his ear. He told him about the veil between the waking world and the Night realm, how it would lift one day, and he, the Ceannaire, would rule the night with Benny by his side. *You'll be a king*, the Ceannaire whispered. Those who had been loyal, those who had fought to bring an end to the corruption and pollution of the waking world would be rewarded in the kingdom thereafter.

So Benny woke every day by three o'clock. He drank a cup of black coffee while sitting at the delicate round kitchen table his sister had picked out. He packed a meal in a brown lunch bag and left for the four thirty shuttle that would take him to the research lab on the north end of the base. But today was different. Today was the last day he would walk his way through what had become a comfortable, safe, engulfing routine. It almost seemed to him that even without the Ceannaire, the voices wouldn't bother him in this life, not here where everything made sense, where he was good at his job and secure in his life. *Maybe I don't need to be a king,* he thought sometimes. He would quickly banish the idea, ashamed that he had questioned the Ceannaire, sure he could read his thoughts.

Today he had packed a roast beef sandwich with extra pickles and horseradish. He had a baggie of chocolate cookies as well, a little extravagance that Benny never indulged in for simple meals at work. But tonight was different; it was the last night, and he would never again go back to the little base apartment. He had hesitated as the door clicked shut behind him. It was the first time he had ever had his own space, with his own things and sheets only he had slept in. It was small and unimpressive, but it was the grandest place he had ever lived. He would miss it greatly. The fridge was empty, the counters and floors spotlessly clean. The sheets on the bed had been changed, and his clothes had been neatly folded and placed in the appropriate drawers. Whoever came to clean up after him, Benny did not want them to think badly of him. He wanted them to see that he valued the little bit of normalcy that life had provided, even if it were only for a little bit.

So Benny slowed his pace, relaxed his jaw, and scanned his ID card for entry into the building. As he meticulously mopped every inch of the lab rooms, he let his mind wander. Once, when he was about eight years old, he'd become convinced the world was ending. This had been before the whole family had moved to Provo, back when they were in Colorado, in Cheyenne Mountain, the foot of NORAD. Benny couldn't remember how he'd found out about the underground base that was designed to hold all the political and military essential personnel in the event of a nuclear disaster. He had found out that there were bunkers with beds and food, enough to outlast nuclear winter. He'd dreamt about living in the eternal darkness of the nuclear bunker, the smell of concrete and dust, the damp sterility. He'd woken in a panic, the sound of the fighter planes that carried the A-bomb ringing in his ears. He had run to his mother's room, shaken her awake, cried and screamed.

She'd slapped him hard across the face. She had slapped him and then rolled back over and gone to sleep. His sister had pulled him off the floor, sobbing and hurt, and taken him back to his bed. "Hush," she'd whispered, "hush. Tell me your nightmare, tell me about it. Don't bother momma. Tell me instead." She'd always listened to his nightmares and tucked him back into bed. Benny would miss her. Maybe the Ceannaire would let her rule in the world to come alongside him. Maybe.

As he sprayed the metal toilet bowls with blue-colored cleaner and scrubbed along the rim with a wire brush, Benny tried to recall the scent of his father's cologne. He'd been so young, he hardly remembered it, except when someone walked by with the same sweet spicy pull, and he'd spin around, his mind flooded with nearly lost memories. His father had passed away, that was what his mother told him. Passed on, passed away, moved on—it's what everyone said. Now Benny knew where he'd gone. The Ceannaire had promised him that his father would walk this world again, young and healthy, his mind free from the ugliness and distraction that had haunted him. Benny had been five years old when he'd found his father in the garage with the car running. He hadn't understood why his mother started screaming, why his sister pulled him away, why everyone refused to talk about how and replaced all his whys with passed ons, passed aways, moved ons.

Benny leaned against the metal counter and stared at his reflection in the mirror. He didn't remember what his father looked like anymore. He didn't know if he resembled him or not. His sister wouldn't say, and his mother had destroyed all the photographs in the weeks that had followed the loss. Benny wondered if his father had heard the voices too. Before the Ceannaire had chased them away, the voices had told Benny to drive off the side of the road, to jump from the balcony, to swallow the bottle of bleach under the sink. They'd been relentless and creative in their desire to destroy him. Once they told him to stuff a jar of cotton balls in his throat, let the cotton asphyxiate him, let himself slowly drown in the dry ocean. Benny wondered if the voices had told his father to close the doors and turn on the engine. He wondered if they'd stayed with him until the very end or, like the betrayers they were, if they'd abandoned him and left him alone and too weak to save himself.

"Soon," Benny whispered the word so faintly that his lips did not even move. Soon his father would be free from the Night Forest. Soon the veil would lift and the souls of the departed would join the living. Soon the Ceannaire would lock his pale eyes on Benny and, with a small nod, would grant him eternal freedom from all the ugliness of this world. *Soon.*

Benny ate his sandwich and the entire bag of cookies. The other night workers came and went, not paying attention to him, not realizing the entire world would change that night. The only one who ever spoke to him was a man named Luke, who had a wife and baby girl at home. Sometimes he showed Benny photos, not on his phone either, but folded and the edges scarred with use. The Ceannaire had been very clear that Benny was not to tell anyone what was to come that night—not a soul, not a breath. But Benny couldn't get the image of the round-cheeked baby girl out of his mind, her dark chocolate-brown cheeks, her curly hair sitting up in erratic spurts. Luke had always been kind to him. He greeted him at the top of every shift and nodded a goodbye before leaving. As Benny threw his trash into the can, he took a deep breath. Not a warning, but a push—that was what he would give Luke. Just a push.

He found Luke in the equipment room, getting the floor polisher ready for the east wing reception area. The man smiled at Benny. His hair was graying around the temples the same way as the Ceannaire's. He'd been doing this job for twenty years, he'd told Benny, and he liked to keep an eye on the new hires, make sure they all fit in just right.

"Whaddya know, kid?" Luke had a voice that could fill the room. Benny would miss him. He was the closest to a friend he had made in years.

"I… I…" Benny stuttered, unsure of what to say. His heart was pounding. What if the Ceannaire heard? What if he was in his head right now and knew what he intended to do? What if the rewards he had promised were held as punishment? What if the voices returned? What if, what if, what if…

"You okay? You look like something's eatin' at you." Luke pushed the polishing brush he was affixing to the side of the unit and took a step toward Benny, who instinctively stepped back. "Whoa, calm down, son. What's going on?" Luke's voice sounded genuinely concerned.

"I…I just had to tell you…had to ask, I can't say, I…you should go," Benny blurted.

Luke looked confused and then deliberately wiped his face of the emotion, reaching out a hand to Benny. "Why don't we go back to the break room, let me pour you some coffee, and let's just take a break. Whaddya say? This doesn't need to get done right now. We have all night. Let's just take a break and talk a little. How does that sound?"

Benny nodded. It sounded so nice, with the weight of the secret he was carrying seeming suddenly unbearable. In his pocket was a cloth bag that had been passed to him by another of the Ceannaire's followers. It had been left in his base mailbox, but not sent through the mail. No, it had been hand delivered by another family member, another who had been promised passage to eternity when the veil was dropped. The cloth bag had been given to that family member by yet another, and another before that. The chain wrapped around the globe. The idea that the Ceannaire whispered in each and every one of their ears every night made Benny want to crawl out of his skin. He wasn't special, he wasn't chosen; he was convenient, he was easy.

Luke took another step forward, and Benny collapsed into the man's arms, great heaving sobs racking his body. Luke gently rubbed his back and whispered, "There you go, let it out. This world gets heavy sometimes. Just let that out." Benny sobbed until he felt his entire body was rung dry. Then Luke held him at arms distance, his kind eyes searching Benny's. "Now, how about that coffee?" Benny shook his head. It was too late—too late to save anyone, too late for himself.

"You should go," he said in a shaking and weak voice. "You should leave." At that, he turned and ran back down the hallway to the research labs in the far west wing.

The Ceannaire had instructed Benny every night, walking him through the ritual he would need to perform. Benny was to open the door, and through that door his Ceannaire would arrive. The Ceannaire had whispered in Benny's ear every night, describing the ceremony, telling him exactly what he needed to do. Benny knew every step. But his hands were shaking and his lungs were on fire. Through the door, the Ceannaire would arrive, and with him a vengeance. He would take Benny by the hand and lead him to his rightful seat in the Night Forest. He would never feel alone again.

Benny slammed the door to the research lab behind him and removed the cloth bag from his pocket, carefully laying the contents out on the concrete floor: a razor-sharp athame, a simple piece of black chalk, a small bag of salt, a jar of oil that stank of dead things. The bag had been passed from one family member to another, all the way from the Ceannaire himself. Only through these tools could the Ceannaire enter this space, and only then could he bring the power of the Night Forest, as he had done in Dallas when he ripped the earth apart and sank the wicked city into the ground.

Benny tried to calm his shaking hands as he anointed himself with the foul-smelling oil. It burned his nose and skin, but he smeared it on his temples and forehead all the same. He murmured the words he had been taught to memorize.

"Éist liom trasna."

Benny felt his body begin to vibrate, and the Ceannaire's voice whispered in his ear.

Now the circle, Benny, now the circle.

Benny reached inside the bag of salt and began rubbing it all over his skin. It would keep him safe, the Ceannaire had said. It would purify him for the sacrifice to come. Benny then took the black chalk and drew a circle on the concrete around him. In the hallway, he could hear voices. Luke, talking to someone else. Benny felt a stab of panic. Of course Luke would know where he went. He had worried him, and now Luke was trying to get the supervisor to open the door. Benny realized that he had only minutes before he was interrupted, and once that happened, the chance to bring his Ceannaire through the door, his chance for eternity, would be gone forever.

Benny, hurry, Benny.

Benny took the athame in his hand as he heard the code for the secure research lab door begin to sing on the other side of the concrete wall. He held it against his wrist, a thin line of blood already rising to the surface. Benny jumped back. Even the razor-thin line burned and sent a spasm of pain rolling up his arm.

Open the door, Benny, let me in.

Benny swallowed his breath and drew the blade across his wrist, thick blood spraying the parameters of the circle. It stopped as it hit the chalk line, just as the Ceannaire had said it would. Benny smiled. He needed to fill the circle. He needed to build the door. He needed to be brave and do as his Ceannaire had taught him.

Fill the door, Benny, let me in.

His ragged wrist dropped, his arm shaking from the shock. As the lab door swung open, Benny raised the athame to his throat and plunged it into his neck. The circle filled with blood as he fell to the ground. He faintly heard Luke's voice shouting and the clap of feet on the concrete floor as the figures ran toward him, but it was too late—the door was open.

Benny looked up, his vision dimming. He saw the walls beginning to shake and crack. His Ceannaire stood over him, a hand outstretched, barely touching Benny's forehead. Then Alan Robertson, the Son of Abraham, raised his fingers to the ceiling and closed his eyes. The room rocked back and forth. Luke and the other man were thrown to the ground, where they lay still. Benny felt a pang of regret. Luke had been a good man, a good friend.

Thank you, Benny. You are no longer needed.

"But, Ceannaire, I am going with you..." Benny sputtered through the thick blood choking his airway.

The Ceannaire shook his head.

No, friend, but you will see the Night Forest soon enough. And when this world and the next collide, we will meet again.

The pain of the betrayal was more than that of the searing bite at his neck and wrist. Benny writhed in his misery as the building collapsed around him, the wind roaring with an unearthly intensity and a rain that scorched his flesh pelting him. Every drop made his skin burn. He felt his throat closing, and the light faded. The monstrous howl of the wind overtook him, and the blackness became entire.

Benny lay on his side, his knees against his chest. His last thoughts were of Luke's little girl with her bright eyes, how she would never see her father again. There would likely not even be enough pieces to bury. And he thought how this was a thing he had done, a thing he had made happen. He had murdered Luke, and the other men who walked the halls that night and lay asleep in the base dormitories. He had opened hellgate, and he would now be lost to the darkness he had been promised passage from.

Benny heard a faint song winding its way through his head as he lay dying, a song that the Ceannaire had sung to him, a song the Ceannaire had said held power in the hands of those that knew how to wield it.

> *I sing of the fae and the wood and the vine,*
> *And the night that lasts forever.*
> *The ghosts of your loves and the ghosts that are mine,*
> *Will linger there forever.*

The sun had just started to peak in the sky as the sprawling base was devoured by the winds and acid rain that dissolved metal and glass. If anyone screamed, it was lost in the grinding horror that echoed and rang closer, closer, ever closer to the bit of floor where Benny let the darkness overtake him.

The dead never sleep and the night never breaks,
You're alone until forever.
With teeth that can bite and the claws that will tear,
Your soul it will not weather.

19

COOPER

COOPER WAS JOLTED OUT OF A DREAMLESS SLEEP BY the mad buzzing of his phone. His face froze and his heart forgot to beat as he read the text from the Denver field producer. Within minutes he was out of bed, teeth brushed, water splashed haphazardly on his face, and clothes thrown on. He managed to pour a cup of coffee into a metal travel mug before he headed out the hotel door. His skin felt numb, like it was buzzing with an invisible energy. At the airport, Bill would probably already be waiting. They would fly to Salt Lake and then head out on a crew bus to Clearfield, Utah, where a research lab and the greater part of Hill Air Force Base had just been obliterated, taking with it hundreds if not thousands of lives.

CBS had a car waiting out front, and Cooper nodded a hello to the driver as he threw his bag into the trunk and settled in. He wasn't far from the airport. The sun wasn't even fully up, the sky a pinkish gray. The last twelve hours had been a nightmare of its own sort, and now this. Cooper felt a chill in his gut that he had never felt before, not even after Los Angeles or Dallas. This was different; it had a dreamlike quality that made him continually wonder if he were still asleep, if this moment was real or a thing he had imagined. *It won't stop*, he realized. *It won't.* After this attack, another and another after that. There was no stopping it, because there was no one person to stop. Even dead, Alan Robertson would still hold a grip over those who were putting this into action.

Yesterday afternoon, following the conversation with his Florence contact, Cooper had driven to the Englewood prison. Bill had smoked a cigarette while Cooper had organized his plan of attack. The producers had arranged a meeting with the lead agent, a Flagston? Flaglen? This guy had been heading the investigation since Robertson had been brought in, but he'd been a junior investigator all the way back to the cult days in Venice Beach. Cooper knew this could be a benefit or a drawback; either the guy was dedicated to bringing Robertson in or he had fallen for the hype. The second option meant that Robertson was more celebrity than prisoner, which made for a dangerous distinction.

Cooper had wondered how he'd never heard the agent's name before. One of his first assignments had been the coverage of Sinder Avenue and helping to archive and label all the grainy photos the field photographers brought in of Ceit Robertson and the others in the years that led up to the fire.

Alan Robertson had been just a kid then, a lanky teenager with the same unsettling eyes that his sister and daughter had. He'd skulked around doing typical teenager things. At the time, he appeared to be the most normal of the lot. Cooper remembered one particular photo of a girl—Esther Robertson's mother, in fact—sneaking out of Alan Robertson's bedroom window. The photo showed one arm helping her to the ground, and her face tilted upward, a small smile on her lips. Cooper had thought the whole operation was bullshit then, all this attention for nothing. Up until the fire, Alan Robertson and the rest of that damn cul-de-sac had been nothing but a street full of eccentrics. Ceit Robertson was barely more than a girl herself, several years younger than her neice was now.

As the sun threatened to start setting, Cooper had pulled up to the Federal Correctional Institution in the borrowed CBS news van and sat a moment, watching the front of the building. It was innocuous, the prison spread out behind it like a labyrinth. Underneath, Cooper knew there was a maze of steel-enforced tunnels that housed a holding system said to be more secure than the military's NORAD bunker.

He and Bill had been checking in at the front desk when Esther Robertson had gone streaming past them out the door, a harassed-looking man in a button-up shirt running after her. He was too young to be the Agent Flagston or Flaglen or whatever his name was. Cooper had watched as the man caught up to Esther Robertson on the steps outside, where she had abruptly stopped, doubled over, and was vomiting all over the concrete.

"Isn't that…?" Bill had asked, his tone incredulous.

Cooper had just nodded. He'd known Esther Robertson had beat him here and that she had a scheduled visit with Alan Robertson that day. He surmised from the scene on the steps that it hadn't gone well. A woman had hustled out from an invisible office and headed outside to assist. The security guard who had been checking Bill's camera bag had paused, taking in the scene, and then shook his head.

"Any idea what's going on?" Cooper had asked.

The man had just shot him a look that said that even if he did, he wouldn't be telling Cooper. At that point, an elevator opened, and a man with graying temples and expensive shoes had stepped out, headed for the front doors. As he drew closer, Cooper had called out, "Agent Flagslenn? I'm Cooper Carlson, from CBS."

The man had stopped, still watching Esther out front, who had stopped vomiting but was now leaning against a handrail, a blank expression in her eyes. He'd turned and looked Cooper up and down, a dark surveillance that Cooper had felt clear to his bones.

"It's Special Agent Flagston. You are the one who received the communication from the Son of Abraham group." The man had regarded Cooper curiously and then cleared his throat. "It was sent on to my office. I do want to speak with you. However, we are in the middle of a bit of a situation, so I'll need to ask for your patience. I'll have someone take you upstairs." His voice was definitive, inviting no debate. Still, though, Cooper had worked with this type before. He knew he and Bill would wait upstairs on a stiff sofa all night before anyone remembered they were there.

"Actually, Special Agent Flagston, my appointment was arranged by CBS central office, and I rather expected to be going downstairs, not up." Cooper had stepped forward as the security guard regarded him warily. Agent Flagston had cast him a long look and then again returned his gaze to the front steps.

"If you think I'm impressed by the CBS central office, you'll have to try harder. We've had a situation erupt here, and your appointment is canceled. I will grant you a few minutes upstairs, but you will need to wait. Yes?" It wasn't a question.

At that, he had exited out the door and to the girl, who had looked like she was going to shake into a million pieces in the winter wind. In the distance, Cooper had heard the wail of ambulance sirens.

The car stopped, and Cooper was snapped back into the present moment and looked out at the small plane, soon to be headed for Clearfield, Utah; the scene of new horror was waiting for him.

• • •

Cooper opened the door, swinging his bag over his shoulder. As expected, Bill was already there, standing at the entry to the private plane, inside which would be the production crew. They walked up the steps and took their seats without speaking. Cooper nodded a hello to the rest of the plane's occupants, none of whom he recognized. They were Denver crew, and already well ensconced in the preplanning of the production. The air held a static charge.

As the engines roared to life and they took to the air, Cooper turned to Bill, who was paler than usual. His hands were shaking just slightly.

"You okay, pal?" Cooper asked gently.

Bill shook his head. "Not so sure. After yesterday, I had a bad feeling, and I hate being right."

"Yeah, I had that same feeling," Cooper said softly.

"I worked at Hill back in the day, right out of high school," Bill said.

"I didn't know that," Cooper said, honestly surprised.

"It wasn't for long. I was in the mess hall. Glorified busboy really, but they were damn nice. The officers out there tried every which thing to convince me to enlist. I used to joke around with them. All the crew members out there were damn nice. I spent only a summer, then I left for school, but they were good people." Bill took a swig from his travel cup, which Cooper suspected held more than coffee.

"They tell you what happened?" Cooper asked.

Bill nodded. "Tornado. Since when is there a tornado in Utah?"

"I have no idea. But not just a tornado—CBS central said there was some kind of acid rain or corrosive liquid. They said it was as though the place had been melted," Cooper replied.

"Jesus," Bill muttered.

"Cooper?" A producer, with her hair tied back in a messy bun and a strained look on her face, leaned over his seat. "I'm sorry to interrupt, but we need to clarify some of the details of the report you sent to the office last night."

"Of course." Cooper stood and crossed to the cluttered work area, where he could see printed copies of the email he had sent when he'd finally made it back to the hotel.

"Okay. What do you need to know?" he asked as the team stared at him with overcaffeinated anticipation.

"We know your meeting with Flagston was sidelined. The daughter met with Robertson at a quarter after four, and we know that visit lasted approximately twenty minutes before the incident, which you were not present for—is that correct?"

Cooper nodded. "I just saw the aftermath. I wouldn't have been present for Esther Robertson's visit with him anyway. There are rules, and all sorts of other reasons she wouldn't have welcomed me there. But no, Bill and I arrived after it happened."

"To the best of your knowledge, what occurred? You gave a recounting here in the report but we just need to make sure we're getting it right. It all sounds a bit..."

"Horrible? Fantastical? Pick a word, I surmise it was all those things. Look, I didn't see it. You need to pin down Agent Flagston or Esther Robertson for firsthand. I only played back what they told me."

With a deep breath Cooper recounted his arrival at the prison, seeing Esther Robertson get ill on the front steps, and subsequently he and Bill sitting on a stiff sofa in a waiting room on an upper floor of the administration office, watching while people raced by, one degree away from panic, and listening to the hushed conversations being had all around. It was the youngish man who had immediately followed Esther Robertson who had eventually come to their rescue. Jeff was his name. He was an assistant, which Cooper knew was just a glorified intern. Jeff had been cleared to give them the basics and send them on their way. And that's precisely what he had done, so Cooper's report was vague to say the least.

"What agent-in-training Jeff told us was exactly what I wrote. About fifteen to twenty minutes into the meeting between Esther Robertson and Alan Robertson, there was a malfunctioning of the lock system, and the doors in the secure holding room were unlocked simultaneously. Jeff told us there was no indication that Alan Robertson moved to escape, but a guard who had been with the facility for some time—well-trusted, all that jazz—evidently had some sort of breakdown and caused injury to himself in the room right in front of Esther and Alan Robertson. Other guards rushed the scene and locked Alan Robertson back up. And we saw Esther's exit as we were entering."

"'Caused injury to himself'? What do you think it means? Why was Esther Robertson's reaction so strong?"

Cooper paused, considering his next words. If false, he was spreading nothing more than sensationalistic gossip; if true, they marked a phenom beyond their comprehension. "Jeff followed his orders and gave us the bare bones, but Bill managed to do some eavesdropping of his own."

"And?" The multiple sets of eyes watching were twitching in anticipation.

"And… by 'caused injury to himself,' the guard evidently clawed out his eyes and shredded his tongue with his bare hands. Alan Robertson smiled the entire time."

20

ESTHER

HE SMELLED OF ASH, OF DIRT AND THINGS THAT ARE beginning to turn to rot. Esther had been momentarily paralyzed by the foul odor and the faint memory it carried with it, a hint of her childhood she had tried to forget. Sarai had wrinkled her nose when they smelled it and whispered that daddy was angry. And Esther had known to take her sister outside, stay quiet, stay out of sight. The smell came and went, and their father would once again carry the normal odors of soap and laundry. Esther hadn't smelled his angry scent since that day at the bus station when he had sent her away, and she had almost forgotten it existed.

He sat across from her—his wrists in cuffs that were chained to the metal table, his feet in irons—and regarded her with his uncannily pale eyes that matched her own, but not entirely. He smiled as though they were meeting at a coffee house and she was in town on a break from college. He smiled as though there was some sort of normalcy to be found, and Esther almost smiled back, wanting it to be so.

"Hello," he said simply, his voice as rich as she remembered, like a slow, hot summer breeze.

Esther nodded, her throat closed.

"I thought I was looking at my sister, you've grown so. You favor her. I suppose everyone tells you that." His voice was wistful, soft.

"Who's left to tell?" Esther replied, her voice cracking sightly as she forced the words out.

"You'll see her soon, daughter," Alan Robertson replied. "You all will." He looked around the cave-like room and offered a conciliatory smile to the guards who lined the space. They ignored him. An older guard named Sid, who had led Esther to the underground room, cast her a worried look. He had told her not to touch her father in any way, not to take his hand, not to have any contact whatsoever. Sid had told her that at any time she could end the meeting. "Just give me a look," he had said. He had worried in a way that made Esther think he had a daughter of his own at home somewhere. She gave him a small nod, trying to tell him it was okay, that she was still alright.

"Where is she?" Esther asked.

Alan Robertson laughed, a thin, musical sound that seemed to bounce around the room. "Here and there, here and there. Right on the other side. You'll see soon. You all will. Soon. She's always waiting. Left us so long ago, too good for this world. But she'll be the one cast out this time, and you and I will walk the Night Forest together, daughter."

"You're insane," Esther whispered.

"Maybe," her father replied, staring at her curiously. "They sent you in here with a mission, didn't they? Sneaky, sneaky, sneaky. They should know that you cannot keep anything from me. None of you can," he barked over his shoulder to the guards who stood by the iron bars.

"Why did you save me?" Esther asked, the quaver in her voice gone, her words steady.

Alan Robertson cocked his head, regarding her with amusement. "That's not the mission. Special Agent Flagston will be disappointed, little one." He sat back, the motion making his wrist irons clank against the metal table, sending a chill up Esther's spine. "It's not the question, but it's a much more interesting one, isn't it? Why you, you, you?"

"I begged you to send Sarai with me. I begged," Esther said evenly. "Why did you kill her? And mother? Any of them? Why did you save me?"

"Because." Alan Robertson shot forward, causing Sid and the rest of the guards to step closer, eyeing him nervously. "Because you came from the cul-de-sac, daughter. You were conceived there. The energy of that place is inside you. You are the last of the Society, the very last, and I'm sentimental. You have her blood in you, dear Esther. I knew it the day you were born. I could *see* it. She denied me, but she will know you. You will be my voice and my ears, and you will sit at my right hand in the world to come, revered and honored. Do you know what I am, dear daughter? Do you really know? I am Gef the Talking Mongoose, the Dalby Spook, a hungry ghost. I was *left behind*. You have the blood of the demon in you. I saw it on the day you were born. You've always had one foot in this world and one in the next. I was never quite so lucky, imprisoned as I am this side of the veil. But you...you walk the line. You can talk to the divine, my girl, and so you shall. You will get me across the veil. I saved you because even then I knew she would deny me passage. And so she did. But you will convince her to *let me in*."

Esther stared at the man across from her. His pale eyes no longer held the shadow she had seen as the bus pulled away from

Los Angeles all those years ago. Now she knew it was because he had released that darkness into the world. He spoke like a madman, but she knew he was not. His mind was clear. His truths sounded like riddles, but it slowed her heart to hear them spoken aloud. The ash and dirt scent of him intensified, and he met her gaze, unblinking.

"Ask me what they sent you here to find out, daughter. Ask." He spoke so softly, Esther barely caught the words.

"Who else? How many more attacks? How do we stop it?" she whispered.

Alan Robertson laughed, a mocking, shrill cry that resonated off the cold walls of the cell.

"As many as it takes to draw her out, daughter. You cannot stop it. I have too many in my service. They see me in their dreams. I bring them comfort, I love them. I feed on the souls of those who wander this world lost and alone. They are my family. They will never stop, and they are everywhere." Alan Robertson leaned forward, his expression imploring. "You have nothing of your mother in you. A shame—she was a beauty. You should have seen her when we were young. She was still in high school when we were matched. You came into being one night as we lay together, as my world was ending. My sister, your aunt, was destroying my home, destroying my legacy. You favor her, you do. I was the true leader of the Society. It should have passed to me, and it would have if not for the demons that my sister called to her side. She stole what was rightfully mine, just as Mór Ainsley had stolen from her father. They are the darkness, and they hid in the shadows. I am the sun. I love my family. I am bringing us all to the light. I am freeing us all, don't you see?"

"You're a murderer," Esther breathed, her skin clammy and ears ringing.

"You're mistaken if you think that death is the end. What I bring is eternity, true eternity. The souls that flood the Night Forest live forever, and soon I will be their Ceannaire." Alan Robertson's eyes had a fevered look. Blue veins pulsed behind the thin veil of his pale skin.

"How do we stop it?" Esther repeated softly, her voice steady and unwavering.

"Stop?" Her father laughed loudly, the sound alien and otherworldly. "Stop? There's no stopping. There's no cell that can hold me, no limit to what I can do, no death that can touch my eternal heart." He paused, looking around the room at the visibly unsettled guards. "Watch," he whispered.

An alarm siren wailed through the space, making Esther jump in fear. The iron gates, which had been firmly locked in place, buzzed with electricity and rolled back simultaneously. Alan Robertson held his hands up as far as the chains allowed, and Esther swallowed a scream as the shackles fell away, hitting the table with a terrible clamor. The guards rushed Alan Robertson and wrenched his arms around his back, sending him face-first into the table. Behind him, the others were swiftly shutting the open gates. The sound of renewed connection to the lock hissed through the room. Esther looked to the side where Sid had returned as her father was recuffed and the locks restored. She was done. She couldn't breathe. She would never be safe; he would always be inside her head. His followers could be anyone, and they were always watching. She had never been safe, and never would be.

Sid was swaying back and forth, his skin waxy. The others had noticed, and an officer was talking into a radio while another steadied the older guard. Still more guards pulled Alan Robertson from the table and toward the gates.

"This interview is over," declared the officer as he spoke into the comm box. "We're taking him back to lockup. Double the security protocol."

As the lock released for Alan Robertson to be pulled through the exit and back to his cell, he turned his head to stare directly at Sid, a wickedly empty grin on his face.

"Wait," Alan Robertson whispered, turning his gaze to wink at Esther. "Just wait."

Sid began to convulse and fell to the concrete floor, his spine arching and falling, his head attached to a serpent's neck, writhing uncontrollably. Bloody froth spewed from his lips, and his eyes rolled back into his head, showing only the red veins popping from the white sclera. The guards were in a panic, some trying to protect Sid, others trying to hold Alan Robertson steady as he twisted around to watch, an amusedly fascinated grin on his lips.

Sid reached both hands to his face and, to Esther's horror, dug his fingers into his eye sockets. Blood sprayed the walls as the guards tried to pry his hands down to his sides. Esther didn't scream. She was frozen solid, her spine an unmovable thing, her breath ice. She had seen this before, in her nightmares, in the shadows that passed through her father's eyes. The stink of ash and dirt filled the room and intermingled with the metallic tremor of blood. A guard vomited, and the sour stink of it joined the cacophony of scents. Sid broke free from the guards' grasp. The slick blood coated everything, making Sid's broad face unrecognizable. The fingers that had stroked his daughter's hair at night and had held Esther's arm gently as he guided her to this room latched onto his tongue, and he shredded the flesh in chunks. Meaty cords of blood and matter lined the walls and floor.

Alan Robertson laughed and twisted his head back one final time as he was dragged from the room, locking his eyes on Esther. "See you soon, daughter."

*

Ashiks@qmail.com via Kqur.ber
to: Cooper_Carlson

You're on your way to Utah by now I expect. We brought hell rain down onto the earth and scorched the land. The Son of Abraham will rise, and the world will kneel. Godspeed, Cooper Carlson. Hope you get the scoop.

21

COOPER

THE SALT LAKE CBS AFFILIATE TEAM MET THEM AT THE airport and shuttled them into a makeshift greenroom. Cooper had long since stopped trying to remember the names of the young production assistants and field producers. He nodded a hello before his face was assaulted with a makeup brush and a wardrobe intern was thrusting button-up shirts into his hands.

"Is this really what we're worried about?" he muttered. Bill nodded at his chest, and Cooper looked down to see a long, dark line of coffee stain that ran from his neck to his belly. Cooper grimaced and shook his head. He had turned into an old man who drooled on himself and didn't see it happening.

"Fine," he said in a conciliatory tone and took a blue-striped button-up from the wardrobe girl.

"Cooper? We're in the van in ten, live in forty," a voice called from around the corner.

"Fine," Cooper called back. He was staring at the briefings he had been handed, his vision starting to swim. "Bill, can this be right?" He looked up at his cameraman, who was also poring over the paperwork that had been thrust into their hands by one of the field producers.

Bill shook his head. "Jesus," he said quietly.

Ten minutes later, they were all streaking down the empty highway toward what had been Hill Air Force Base. The roads had all been closed, and the stillness of what had once been a busy commute made the landscape apocalyptic. As they drew closer, ambulances, fire trucks, emergency vehicles, and police cars lined the side of the road. Already, tents could be seen in the distance, a makeshift base camp taking form.

"Why aren't they transporting anyone?" a production assistant wondered aloud.

"There's no one left to move," Cooper stated grimly.

*

Cooper
CBS Breaking News Report
*

We are reporting live from Hill Air Force Base in Clearfield, Utah. In the early hours of the morning, an EF6 tornado destroyed the greater area of Hill Air Force Base. Winds from this storm were greater than 250 miles per hour, and there was no warning. In addition to this unprecedented cyclone, rain containing high levels of sulfuric acid flooded the desert, causing castrophic damage. Of the men and women on the base at the time of the disaster, there were no survivors. The tornado combined with the sulfuric rain was so destructive, there is little left. What was concrete and steel is now dust. The bodies of the victims were incinerated, the structures vaporized. It is unlike anything we have seen on American soil. In the wake of Dallas, in the not too faraway shadow of Los Angeles, this is the most recent tragedy to stain our land.

There are many things we do not know. We do not know why two disasters of this magnitude have struck in less than two days' time. We do not know how they were not detected in either Dallas or Utah. This is difficult to say, and it makes as little sense to me as it will to you, but these incidents are not natural. They are not freak acts of nature. They are stemming from the same evil machinations that were responsible for Los Angeles ten years ago. I do not know how, I do not know why, but I know this is true.

I want to speak directly to the Son of Abraham and his followers. Alan Robertson, your people have claimed responsibility for Dallas and now Utah, just as you did in Los Angeles ten years ago. Alan Robertson, you sit in a cell awaiting judgment. Your people are angry, and they are killing in your name. I implore you to make them stop.

I do not know what will happen tomorrow. But this tragedy happened today because there is a greater evil lurking in the shadows. Wherever you are, whatever you do, pay attention. We have said "if you see something, say something" for years, and now I will say it again. People came together to do this terrible thing. People can stop it.

This is Cooper Carlson reporting.

Good night and Godspeed.

22

COOPER

BILL PULLED THE CAMERA AWAY FROM HIS GAZE AND stared at Cooper for a moment. "Holy shit. I'm going to stop these live feeds. You're cracking."

"Look at this," Cooper growled, shoving his cell phone with the email from the mysterious address toward him. Bill read it quickly, a vein ticking in his right temple.

"Jesus, Coop, and you thought the best time to share this was on live TV?" Bill stared at him, his eyes a shade below panic.

"Who do I share it with then? The feds? You read that report from the Esther Robertson interview. Whatever we're dealing with here is way beyond law enforcement." Cooper shoved past him, annoyed. His hands were shaking and his head buzzing with a static that only grew in intensity.

"I'm serious, Coop!" Bill yelled after him.

Cooper ignored him. He heard the shuffle of the crew behind him. He heard his name being called, but he charged forward. He had to get out of here. According to the network, he was supposed to have given a perfunctory report—straight reporting, don't spread panic, all that bullshit. He was scheduled to drive out to the blast site with the feds in an hour and record shots and a few pieces to be sent to the bigger markets. But Cooper was done. He hadn't stuck to the script. He hadn't tried to calm people down, and he knew that everyone was flailing, trying to clean up his mess. Cooper didn't give a shit right now. He was headed back to the parking lot and was going to take the first car he found with keys in it back to Provo, and from there he was going to get a flight back to Denver. He had to talk to that fucker one way or another. Something was throbbing in the base of his spine—not just a need, but a warning. If he didn't reach Alan Robertson and soon, this would happen again and again and again.

He could hear Bill's voice in his head. *What are you going to do? How can you stop anything?* Cooper knew it was crazy, but the pulsing sensation was climbing the ladder of his spine, one vertebra at a time. He had no choice; he had to go. A red Dodge with faded paint and a sun-cracked dashboard was sitting unlocked with keys in the ignition. It was likely the property of one of the teenage-looking production assistants. Maybe the network would buy her a decent car if it came out that the great Cooper Carlson had stolen hers.

He squealed out of the lot and floored the gas, flying past the emergency vehicles sitting impotently by the side of the empty highway. As Salt Lake grew closer, Cooper felt the oscillating need in his bones settle in like a compass needle. When he blinked, he could see Alan Robertson's cold eyes, feel the radiation that seemed to emanate from his very skin. Cooper shook off the chills that suddenly overtook his shoulders and neck and continued on his course.

23

ESTHER

ESTHER FELT A WAVE OF RELIEF AS HER FEET LANDED in the dew-damp grass of the field. It was night, and the neatly trimmed grass oval was lined by a wall of tall oaks that created a seemingly impenetrable border. She could smell the fresh rain and the sweet night air. Esther took a tentative step and then another and another. With a cry of joy echoed across the expanse, she ran as fast as she could, fully in control of her body. She stopped running and spun in circles, feeling the heady dizziness overtake her until she fell back, the ground as soft as a pillow, but real and visceral. This was a dream, but it was one of her making. She was in charge here. She could feel and hear and smell the air around her. Nothing entered this space unless she permitted it.

Esther wasn't always able to slip into a lucid dream. Sometimes the most she could hope for was a vague awareness that her actions were not her own and the faces and sights that passed her by were the stuff of sleep. But how sweet it was when she broke through the veil and found herself in this place. Sometimes it was this field. Sometimes she walked the streets of a city that she did not recognize. Here it was always night. The field resembled a bit of a memory she had from her childhood, a soccer field where she remembered laughing and playing with other children, a place from before the terrible, a place utterly disconnected from the tension and sadness that had surrounded her all her life.

She twirled a blade of grass in her fingers and stared at the night sky, whose stars were nothing she recognized from her waking life. Maybe it was the sleeping pill she had taken after she'd returned to her hotel room. The news, the destruction in Utah, the guard in that dark room at the prison, the blood streaming from his face—it had been too much to carry. Esther shook. That wasn't welcome in this place. The dark thoughts she sought to chase away would not survive the purity of the air in her dream. Esther sat up, eyeing the line of trees that edged the field. She had never crossed its border. But tonight she could not take her eyes off the pitch darkness that lay beyond the twisting layer of branches and bark.

Esther rose to her feet. She didn't know how much time she had left here. She could wake at any moment, and god knew when she'd make it back to this state. With a heightened sense of urgency, she walked steadily toward the line of trees that seemed to distance themselves with her every step.

"No," she stopped and said the word aloud. "I want to see."

It was her dream, and she commanded the space to stop distorting the distance to the tree line. She felt a slight tremor beneath her feet, and suddenly the impossibly complex maze of oaks was directly in front of her. A voice whispered in her ear, a man who spoke with a practiced crispness.

"If you are sure, banphrionsa."

Esther did not bother turning her head. The voice, like everything here, was part of her dream—an undigested bit of beef, as

Charles Dickens would have said. She smiled at the thought. It was all in her head, and utterly infinite. With a deep breath of the fantastical air, she stepped into the darkness of the forest.

ESTHER

THERE WAS MOVEMENT ALL AROUND HER. HIDDEN IN the darkness, shapes slipped here and there, none taller than her knees. She could hear the faint rustle of a winged creature above her. She felt herself tugged forward from the center of her chest, as though an invisible cord had hooked itself into her very ribs. She walked slowly forward, mindful not to step on any of the swiftly invisible creatures that she felt darting back and forth. The air had changed in this place. It was still impossibly crisp, but it held an undertone—not rot exactly, but the smell of things that grow other things. The smell of rebirth, of the turning of the soil. Before her a small clearing revealed itself, a warm glow shining directly down, illuminating the dark forest floor. A tug at her chest pulled Esther into the circle, where she immediately felt a wave of pervasive calm. Her rabidly nervous mind, the storm that constantly raged in her gut, all these things were drowned in the light that seemed to wash through her skin and deep into the marrow of her bones. It was unlike anything she had ever felt. Even in the waking dreams she treasured, she had never felt this level of peace.

Esther sank to her knees, feeling her mind disconnect from her body. *I must be waking up.* The thought mumured at the edge of her mind.

"You'll wake when you wish to wake, not before."

Esther's eyes snapped open to see her mirror image, a young woman with light hair and skin so pale it was translucent. Her eyes were of no particular color, so pale they seemed to house light that emanated from the outside in. Esther stared at the creature. In the universe that existed in its eyes, Esther could see great waves rising and crashing, storm clouds forming and clearing, flower petals circling in the wind.

"Who are you?" Esther asked quietly. The sound seemed to float from her mouth, as though even speech wasn't assigned to the laws of gravity here.

The creature smiled slightly. "I haven't taken this form in so long, so very long, I hardly know how to answer that. This is my realm. You have come here before, but you stayed in the meadow. You were content to roll in the grass and look at my stars. We're glad you have joined us. You are so very welcome here."

Esther gave a small nod. This creature was familiar, and not just because it wore her face. It felt as though she had known this person, thing, monster, all her life. She suddenly was overwhelmingly aware that the figure who sat across from her in the golden light of an imagined place knew every single thing about Esther; in this place there were no secrets, no shame, no darkness.

"It's my fault." Esther felt words float from her mind across space.

"You must be very important for that to be true." The creature's lips never moved, but the lilting sound of its voice wrapped around Esther's head and neck. "No, child, you cannot take fault for the chaos of the universe. You cannot claim responsibility for human drama. It exists whether you exist or not. It has always been such. It's a problem of incompatibility, you see. Mankind is a bit of a rash on the waking world. It scratches and spreads. The world responds back by shuffling and sighing. And in the midst of this dance, unhappiness and chaos leak into your lives. In the world to come, you will find that the problem of incompatibility is quelled. The Night Forest is a balm to the soul."

Esther felt as though she were floating. "Why live in the world at all?"

The figure gave another calm smile. "It's the passage. There was another world you clawed and scratched your way through before this, and another before that, even rougher and full of sharp points. The world you reside in now is by far the best you've ever known. And the next will be greater still." The creature paused, her infinite eyes cyclones sweeping across a vast plain. "Do you know me now?"

Esther looked at the thin shoulders, the curve of the creature's jaw. She had seen this image her entire life, been haunted by it. "You are Ceit Robertson."

"Once I was. I am the Bandia Marbh, Lord of the Night Forest. I reign over the fae and the wood and the vine. You are of my blood, when it still ran in my veins, and you are welcome here. We have awaited you." The creature held out a single hand, the fingers long and unnaturally slender. Esther stared at the open palm and then gently placed her own atop it.

"Show me." She felt the words sail from her mind and cut through the golden light. The world began to spin, and Esther felt the forest and the oaks, the night, the meadow with its perfect grass and air all spin farther and farther away. She fought the waking sensations that pulled at her fingers and toes.

Esther woke with the stiff hotel sheets twisted around her limbs, as though she had been bound by a force outside herself. The fog cleared from her mind entirely as she bolted up to rhythmic pounding at her room door.

25

COOPER

"ALL FLIGHTS HAVE BEEN GROUNDED. THERE'S NOTH-ing we can do." The Yasper Airlines ticket agent glanced nervously over Cooper's shoulder to the ensuing chaos that was building behind him. All flights canceled, all currently in the air ordered to land at the earliest opportunity, and then...what then? Cooper stared at the young man in front of him, barely out of his twenties. He wasn't old enough to remember anything like this. Cooper himself had never seen anything of this magnitude.

"What about private? I'll pay," Cooper insisted.

"Sir, please, there's nothing to be done," the young man repeated.

Cooper turned around and stared behind him. No use taking out his frustration on this kid. All this was out of his hands, out of all their hands. Who in here was working for Robertson? Cooper stared at the bustling forms of men and women, toddlers being drug along by the hand, nervous-looking children following their parents through the crowds. *Who is communicating with that fucker right now?* Cooper felt the back of his neck buzzing. His skin was covered in a thin layer of cold sweat. Without looking back, he charged out the door back to the Dodge he had left in the lot. He'd drive. It was a little over seven hours to Denver, less if he floored it.

The car wasn't bad for what it was. Solid, like a tiny little tank. *Appropriate,* Cooper thought as he pulled out of the lot, the attendants not even bothering to stop anyone for payment. He didn't know why he knew he was headed into war, but he was sure of it. Cooper pulled onto I-15 south and hit the gas. The roads were apocalyptically empty, and for a moment, Cooper wondered if he were caught in some kind of fucked-up dream. Maybe this had all been a dream and he was in bed, the night before that goddamn interview with Esther Robertson, before Dallas, before Hill Air Force Base, before whatever came next. Hell, maybe he was back in bed at that shitty hotel in Lancaster where he'd been when Los Angeles had been leveled. Maybe none of it had happened.

Caroline had been pissed. He was going to miss Cecily's basketball game. She was starting that year. And if the opposing team hadn't been burned to death in the blast that melted their bus as it had the misfortune to be on the I-10 freeway headed east to Pasadena, Cecily would have shone. As it was, Cecily and her mother took shelter in the gym that should have housed the high school championship game. The next morning, Caroline, Cecily, the dog, and a few boxes of the most dearly held possesions were stuffed into the SUV, and they drove across the country to Caroline's parents' house in Georgetown, where they stayed.

Cooper was supposed to be covering a fracking protest in Lancaster but instead found himself thrust into a war zone— twisted metal, blackened concrete, bloodstains, and broken glass. He reported day and night on the single worst terrorist attack the world had ever seen. He became the face of tragedy, the voice that never stuttered, wavered, or broke. He told the stories of the lost and of the survivors. And within the month he was teleported from a slightly recognizable local news personality to what the *New York Times* called "the most trusted journalistic voice in the Western world."

For months after the bombing, he visited hospitals, Bill following behind documenting the entire affair. It was Cooper who tracked Esther Robertson after it became known she had left town two days before the bombing. He was the one who arrived at the glorified garden shed with Bill and a skeleton production team, ready to get answers from the only known living relative of Alan Robertson, the only one who might know where he was—if he had even survived.

He'd found a child, lips and skin blue from the San Francisco winter, huddled in blankets by a portable heater. He had looked at her face and seen a ghost. The man who lived in the main house, Hector Ramirez, had left long before they had arrived. He'd stacked bottled water and a box of granola bars in the doorway of the shed for Esther Robertson. She had claimed not to know him, only knew that her father had told her he would take her in. She was shaken by the news of Los Angeles, in shock, the doctors later said when the production crew took her to the hospital. Cooper didn't see her again until the interview. She'd been hidden away in the foster care system, her identity blocked, any information she might hold, lost.

The bombings had made him famous; finding Esther Robertson had made him a legend.

Cooper had never lost the image of her face as she cautiously opened the door of the shed—the haunted look in Esther Robertson's eyes, her skin so pale you could see the blue and red blood pulsing on the other side. Bill had dropped the camera. The producers had immediately called the local hospital and told them they were bringing her in. Cooper had just stared. She wasn't innocent. She knew exactly what this was. She could have stopped it. He'd never said that aloud to anyone. It would have been career suicide to blame the child of a madman for her father's crimes. But Cooper knew what he knew, and child as she was, she was no innocent.

Cooper eased onto US 6. Now all he knew was that he had to reach Alan Robertson before the sun rose on another day. He felt an invisible cord pulling him along the empty expanse of highway. He could hear a pulsing in his ears, the rythmn of his own heart, but it felt a hint out of step, just enough to send his blood racing through his veins in a panic. His phone buzzed incessantly in his pocket. It would die soon enough, and with it, all the messages and texts that it carried. He knew Bill was among them, not to mention a great number of CBS producers and organizers. Their star reporter had delivered an apocalyptic live report, revealed classified information, stolen a car, and then disappeared. None of this mattered if he didn't reach Alan Robertson in time.

He flew past a billboard, long forgotten on the side of the highway, "Son of Abraham" spray-painted across it. Cooper slammed on the brakes, and the Dodge skidded to a stop. The ugly letters stared down at him from their metal perch. *Someone is watching me.* Cooper shook his head at how irratonal the thought sounded. Still, he felt eyes on him. He felt a hook driven deep into his flesh, and he heard the faint edges of whispers in his ears. With a deep breath and a sudden realization of how thirsty and tired he really was, he straightened the car back out on the highway and headed toward his goal.

26

ESTHER

"ESTHER? ARE YOU IN THERE? ESTHER?" THE VOICE on other side of the Motel 6 door was tightly controlled panic. The cheap wood rattled. If he kept knocking at that pace, Esther knew the entire door would blow down, like the little pigs'. Irrationally, she giggled. The dream, or visit, or whatever it was still clung to her limbs. Slowly, she attached a face to the voice—Agent Flagston. But how had he found her? Esther answered her own question almost immediately. Of course, she had been followed. She'd been too rattled when she left the prison to pay much attention.

"One moment," she called out and rose from her bed, pulling a sweater over her head. The air held a hint of ice, and the room's noisy heater had tapped out. She crossed to the door and peeked out the window, the scent from the smoke-stained curtains filling her nostrils. Agent Flagston was standing with his hands nervously resting on his hips. Two other agents she didn't recognize were behind him.

It could be a trap, she thought. Her father could have sent them, eaten their minds, destroyed them from the inside out. But she didn't think it was. He was too nervous. If her father was behind this, they would be calm, smiling. She remembered how blank Sid's eyes had been before...With a swift motion before she could change her mind, Esther unlatched the door and pulled it open.

"There's been another incident, and your father's followers have claimed responsibility. I have no concept of how they could be responsible, but I just...I feel like I don't know what's possible right now," Agent Flagston said urgently. It was clear that he hadn't slept; his face held deep lines she hadn't seen before.

"Where?" Esther asked softly, her hands growing slowly numb.

"Utah. A military base was wiped out by what looks to be a tornado. We can brief you in the car, but we need to get you out of here as soon as possible."

"Why?" Esther asked, her head swimming.

Agent Flagston took a deep and somewhat impatient breath. "We've received threats against you. And they named this hotel, so there is good reason to believe that you are being watched and the threats are credible. You should know, Cooper Carlson gave a rather alarming live report early this morning and then disappeared, according to the folks at the CBS office."

"You think Cooper Carlson is threatening me?" Esther asked, trying to make sense of all the thoughts swimming in her head.

"No, we don't. But he named Alan Robertson and the Son of Abraham group specifically, which might be driving the threats against you. We are not ruling out that the threats are from members of the Son of Abraham group themselves. It could be backlash from your television interview as well. There's no way to know until we investigate further, but we need you safe first." Agent Flagston glanced at his watch and then back to Esther.

Esther nodded. "It's not my father's people. I can't tell you how I know that, but it's not them. But I'll come with you."

"Get ready, and take your things. We are going to house you

in a medical lockup facility not too far from here. I know how that sounds, but there is an isolation ward at the facility that we've used for inmates who had death threats that we deemed credible. It's the safest place for now until we can regroup. We'll work to get you far away from here as soon as we can secure your immediate safety."

Esther gently closed the door, leaving the men in the cold air on the other side. She pulled on her clothes and then brushed her teeth, staring at her face in the mirror. She wasn't the same as the vision she had seen in her dreams. Her face was plain, where Ceit Robertson's had held a sort of unknowable beauty. Her eyes were pale, but there was no light behind them, as there was in Ceit's. She was an imitation, a watered-down version of the majesty and the horror that she was spawned from. There was nothing of her mother anywhere in her being—her poor, sad mother, whose only real fault had been not seeing that the young man she ran away with died in that fire on Sinder Avenue all those years ago. Meg Robertson had left that place with the demon that had took his place, and now the world was burning.

The agents walked her to a blatantly nondescript SUV with darkly tinted windows. As the van pulled out of the parking lot and toward her isolation ward hiding spot, Esther felt the pull of the Night Forest and knew where she would find her answers.

27

COOPER

THE SUN HAD SETTLED INTO THE MORNING SKY BY THE time Cooper pulled into Denver's city limits. The Dodge was limping along on fumes when he pulled into a gas station. Helicopters circled overhead. The other customers standing in the crisp Colorado air looked up disinterested, but Cooper felt the hackles rise at the back of his neck. The black-and-white copter circled in ever-tightening loops, looking for something—a person, a car, movement far below it. Cooper felt inside his pocket and breathed a sigh of relief that his wallet was still there. He hadn't bothered to check before he tore out of what had been Hill Air Force Base; he hadn't stopped for anything. He poured himself a cup of too-strong coffee from the pot at the back of the store. It smelled of burned liquid and long nights. He dropped cash on the counter and, without waiting for change, started to walk toward the door, fixated on the helicopter and the faint sound of sirens in the distance.

"We've been expecting you," a voice from behind him said clearly and deliberately. Cooper spun around and stared at the clerk, no more than a teenager. He had acne irritation across both cheeks and stubble that was trying to be a beard. His eyes were milky, as though a fog lay over them. For a moment, Cooper thought he must be blind, but the irrationality of it made him shake his head. *He couldn't be blind and at the counter by himself, could he?*

"Who? What? Sorry, are you talking to me?" Cooper stuttered.

The kid smiled, revealing yellowed and chipped teeth.

"The Son of Abraham is coming home. He's getting ready to open the gates and let us into his kingdom. Soon we shall all be rewarded." The kid recited the lines as though from a script, no emotion, no inflection.

Cooper felt his body grow cold. Outside the helicopter sounded as though it were directly overhead. The din of the sirens echoed in his head. "Who are you?" he managed to ask, his hand threatening to crush the Styrofoam coffee cup he was holding.

"A voice, a face, an ear. Do you have anything you want to be heard?" the kid intoned, and Cooper knew whoever he had been was long gone.

"Who will hear me?" Cooper asked, forcing the words from his throat.

"I will, of course," the kid replied with a sardonic smile on his thin lips. "I. Will."

"I know what you are," Cooper said in a voice barely above a whisper. "Where's next? Let me warn them. Let me stop you."

The kid laughed, the incongruous cackle alien to his lanky body. Overhead the helicopter sounded as though it were hanging in mid-flight. Boxes of cereal began to rattle their way off the shelves. The magazine rack swayed back and forth, threatening to tumble. A police siren screamed in Cooper's ear. The kid leaned forward as a bin of candy bars toppled to the ground, spraying the floor. Behind Cooper a freezer case door swung open, the contents flying out on their own accord, hurling themselves into the glass front window. All the other customers—the men and women fueling their cars, the old man sipping coffee on the bench outside—they were all gone. The landscape was deserted but for Cooper, this kid, and the descending cacophony. The kid motioned to Cooper to come forward. The coffee cup finally burst in his hand; he barely noticed the scalding hot liquid as it sprayed his arms and torso.

"Come here, quickly. You don't have much time." The kid nodded outside. "They'll be upon you any minute. Don't you know? Wolves to the kill."

Cooper was thrown forward as though hands had shoved him from behind. "But, me…I can't…"

The kid leaned in. His breath was sour and sulfuric. "It's a funny twist about man. Sacrifice is so noble, until it is you on the altar. Then you will sell your own mother to make sure some other soul is the one who pays the price, picks up the tab for your sins."

"Is that what this is about?" Cooper could hear boots on the concrete outside and the excited shouts of officers running. The helicopter roared. The fluorescent lights swayed in the commotion, the long plastic coverings crashing to the ground, knocking over everything in their wake. "Are these murders sacrifices?"

The kid leaned farther in still, his lips grazing Cooper's ear. "No, love. They are a means to get the attention of the one who has been sitting in my house for so long. They are a flare in the darkness, a scream into the void. We need you, especially now. We're about to give you the story of a lifetime. My associates will fill you in on what we expect from you, which is nothing short of the best. We thank you."

Cooper felt paper-dry lips on his cheek, and then he was pulled violently backward, his arms twisted behind his body. Voices in his ear shouted, so loudly that the words were incomprehensible. He was lifted and slammed to the ground, his chest taking the brunt of the impact. He looked up from the filthy floor to see the kid, his eyes clear now, talking excitedly to a black uniformed officer. The kid caught Cooper's eye over the officer's shoulder and winked, then went back to his story.

As Cooper was pushed toward the open door of the squad car, an officer read him the rights he had heard only in movies.

"What am I being arrested for?" Cooper asked quietly.

The officer leaned in until Cooper could feel his breath against the back of his ear, and then a faint tickle, the touch of a snake's forked tongue against his flesh. Cooper jumped and fell forward.

"Relax..." the officer whispered, his voice a soft hiss. He hauled Cooper back to his feet by the cuffs, the metal digging into his skin. Cooper started to object, but he bit his lip. *Best to stay silent.*

"We're taking you where you want to go," the creature whispered in his ear as he shoved him into the back seat of the police cruiser. As the squad car pulled out, a caravan of police cars followed.

Cooper closed his eyes. Whatever reality had been in place before the sun rose was obsolete, replaced with this new world of Alan Robertson's creation. Cooper felt his throat closing, and he struggled to breath in through his nose. What would the day bring?

28

COOPER

COOPER SAT IN THE COLD METAL CHAIR OF THE INTER-rogation room. His wrists ached from where the metal handcuffs had cut into his skin. His hands were free now, and he rubbed the swollen and sore skin absently. He had been in this tiny, airless room for what felt like hours, though he had no way to tell how much time had passed—no clock, no window. The temperature had been crisp when he'd arrived but had steadily risen. Now he could feel beads of sweat trickling down his back. It was a tactic, he knew that much. Keep him here as long as legally possible, make him uncomfortable, make him desperate. But the confession they hoped to extract would be disappointing. No one had actually stated what he was suspected of doing. Cooper ran each of the disasters through his head. To draw a connection to him was madness; but wasn't that the word for all of this?

He looked up as the metal door creaked open and two officers entered like characters from a bad TV drama. One was older, his stubble a couple of days old, his shirt worn and in need of a change.

The other was a young woman, fashionably dressed, perfectly poised. Cooper stifled a guffaw. They looked like they could have been drawn in a comic book. He stared back at them, trying to keep his face impassive.

"Well, the great Cooper Carlson," the man said in a voice that matched his stained shirt and rumpled appearance. "I'm Detective Bowen, and this is Officer Metzger."

Officer Metzger gave him an amused smile.

Cooper met Detective Bowen's gaze and said, "I want to talk to my attorney."

The detective nodded. "I don't think you do, not really. You haven't heard what we're offering."

"Am I being charged with a crime?" Cooper asked.

"What crime should we charge you with?" Detective Bowen said flatly.

"Well, if I'm not being charged, you can't hold me, can you?" Cooper said in a tone that sounded more confident than he felt.

"Where do you think you are?" Officer Metzger asked. She leaned in, clearly enjoying Cooper's discomfort, and he automatically felt the flesh on the back of his neck begin to crawl.

"I assume I'm in the federal lockup? Maybe the Denver Metro Police Station," Cooper replied, realizing he had no idea. The trip here was suddenly foggy. He remembered that last moment in the back of the squad car and then, this room. He shook his head.

"Can't quite remember, can you?" Officer Metzger said, her lips curling into a crooked smirk. "You looked out the window, didn't you? Can't you remember anything?"

Cooper shook his head, realizing that the entire trip from the gas station to wherever he was existed only in the fog.

"Journalists." Detective Bowen grinned, showing the same yellowed and stained teeth that the kid in the convenience store had displayed. "You'd think your lot would be more observant."

"Who are you?" Cooper whispered, afraid of the answer.

Officer Metzger leaned forward, and Cooper caught the scent of sulfur on her breath. "We're the ones who were sent to interrogate you. To see if you are ready." She tapped her finger on the tabletop, and Cooper looked down with fascination as he noticed her fingers were extraordinarily long and thin—too long in fact. They seemed to stretch into points, the nail beds nonexistent. He blinked, and her hand was perfectly normal again, clear nail polish catching the light from the overhead lamp.

"You're..." Cooper stuttered.

"Aware that you know things," Detective Bowen said, finishing his thought. "So let's talk about small stuff. You met Esther Robertson ten years ago in San Francisco. You were the one who found her, actually. Do you think that's something of a coincidence?"

"A coincidence?" Cooper sputtered, his body feeling increasingly numb. "A coincidence of what? What does it coincide with?"

"First on the scene in LA all those years ago. First to find Esther Robertson. On live air when Dallas was hit. Your team was given exclusive rights to the coverage at Hill. You seem to be attracted to this tragedy like a moth to the flame, obsessed really. You seemed in an awful hurry to make it back to Denver." Officer Metzger sat back, her lulling voice a little hypnotic.

"Where am I?" Cooper asked. "How did I get here? Why can't I remember?"

Detective Bowen slammed his hand down on the table, nearly knocking it over, and making Cooper jump back in his seat, his heart pounding.

"Concentrate!" he barked. "You're somewhere you've never been before, and let's leave it at that."

Cooper's hands were shaking, his skin clammy. "You're not police, are you?"

Officer Metzger laughed, sharing a look with the thing posing as the detective. "Journalists," she said. "They never miss a thing, do they?"

29

ESTHER

THE ROOM WAS MORE PRISON THAN HOSPITAL, BUT IT would take an act of God to break into it. *Trouble is,* Esther thought wryly, *those seem to be occurring more and more often, and God has nothing to do with it.* She had a small en suite bathroom, and a security officer had brought her a metal pot of coffee and a breakfast tray from the hospital cafeteria. Esther regarded it warily. It was impossible to say who her father's followers were. They could be anyone. They could be the cooks in the kitchen, the guards outside the door.

Still, Esther doubted it was her father or his followers who were behind the threats. She was no stranger to this. Esther had received death threats all her life, and never once had her father's people been behind them. It was hard to say why she knew this, except that they wouldn't do anything without his say-so, and if he wanted her dead, he had had his chance ten years ago. No, Alan Robertson did not wish to harm her. But that left everyone else. And the numbers of people who had lost their wives, husbands, children, parents, and friends to her father's actions were growing exponentially.

A tornado nearly three miles in diameter—the largest in recorded history—and sulfuric rain that dissolved steel on contact. *How is he doing this?* Los Angeles was the result of man. Hundreds of followers had worked their way up in jobs and security clearances over the course of years in order to be in the position to assemble and detonate a series of bombs. It was a human effort, a suicide mission, an evil act perpetrated by blind followers of a dangerous man. But this was something entirely different. It was impossible, or should be. What happened to Sid in the prison, the way the locks just fell from her father's wrists, it was all impossible. Esther thought about her dream or vision, or whatever it was. The idea of clawing her way through world after world, that there had been more suffering, more pain, more more more in the last world. She closed her eyes and lay back on the stiff hospital bed.

A sound at the door made her sit up, and Agent Flagston entered. He had straightened his tie, but his eyes still belied his exhaustion.

"Esther? We have some information. Are you up for it?"

Esther nodded, and Agent Flagston pulled a metal chair to the side of the bed, laying a file folder next to her.

"Okay, so our investigators in Dallas discovered this security camera footage." He pulled out grainy black-and-white images, stills from a video. Esther squinted to see a figure sitting in what appeared to be a circle. Something dark streaked the figure's wrists and chest. The face was indiscernible, but Esther could see an open mouth. A scream? The next frame showed a second figure standing in the circle, a man in loose clothing. His face was grainy, but Esther felt her spine turn to ice and her hands start to shake.

"How..." she whispered.

"We have no earthly idea," Agent Flagston said. "At the time this footage was taken, Alan Robertson was in lockup at the FCI facility. He had multiple guards and video surveillance. Our video and eyewitness accounts have him in his cell, sitting on his bunk with his eyes closed, sleeping or meditating. The figure in this photo is identical to him, wearing the clothes Alan Robertson was arrested in. The only logical assumption is this is a look-alike who is impersonating your father. However, we have no idea what is happening here, or how it is connected. We were hoping you had some insight."

Esther shook her head. "Is that blood?" she asked, pointing to the sitting figure's arms and chest.

Agent Flagston nodded. "We think so. This was ground zero for the sinkhole. This footage was sent electronically moments before the camera was destroyed. Do you have any idea what is happening here?"

Esther shook her head. "Did this happen in Utah as well?"

"We don't have any footage of it if it did. There's no security footage of anything like this." He indicated the photographs. "But we did get an upload from the base of the hallway outside one of the research labs, here."

Esther looked at the still shots. She saw what appeared to be a custodian entering a door. The next frame showed two somewhat larger men at the same door, and the frame after that showed them beating fists on the surface before the final frame caught them entering.

"No cameras in this room?" Esther asked quietly.

"No. It was a secure research lab, so no security cameras. And no evidence this is connected. The first man to enter is"— Agent Flagston shuffled through the paperwork—"Benjamin Hoefer. Custodian, model civilian employee. He was assigned to clean this lab, so no alarms, nothing. The other men entering are Luke Cristins, also a custodian, and a custodial supervisor, a Dan Reynolds. Neither have business being in this area, so we can assume they were going in after Hoefer. But why? There's no indication." Agent Flagston stared at Esther for a long moment. "Do you have any idea how this could be happening?"

Esther shook her head. "I've never understood my father. I don't know anything. I never have."

30

COOPER

"WE ENJOYED YOUR BROADCAST FROM HILL AIR FORCE Base," Officer Metzger said, her gray eyes locked on his. "You're doing a very good job. We're here to help you. The Ceannaire has requested an audience with you."

Cooper nodded his head. "Alan Robertson? Yes, I want to talk to him, but how?"

Detective Bowen sat back and regarded Cooper stoically. "What the Ceannaire wants, he gets. We were sent to intercept you, prepare you. We'll go to the FCI facility next. In fact, in a few moments you might find you were there all along. Weird how time works, isn't it?"

"Prepare?" Cooper stuttered. "Prepare for what?"

"Father is capable of a great many things, and he has a great many more to share with the world very soon—hours in fact. But he needs a messenger, a voice to the world. Just like you did in Hill, you need to make sure our word is heard by all. You are, after all, the most trusted voice in journalism." Detective Bowen said this last bit with sardonic mockery.

"Where is he striking next? What is going to happen? How is he making this occur?" Cooper spat out the questions, his mind racing.

"I don't know what he sees in you, I really don't," Officer Metzger said as she glanced at the detective. "It's all been arranged. You listen, he talks. You will remember what he says, and you will spread the word. That is all that is required of you."

Cooper stared in horror as the same thin, snakelike tongue he had felt on the back of his neck in front of the gas station slipped from between her teeth, flicked around her lips, and then disappeared.

"What are you?" Cooper whispered.

"You wouldn't understand it if we told you. Let's just say we are made of the same stuff as our father. We were cast out just as he was. We walk the earth the same as he does," Detective Bowen said. "Right now, we are Detective Bowen and Officer Metzger of the Denver Police Department. We met you at the police head-quarters when you got into town a little bit ago. We briefed you on Alan Robertson's request. We told you how he promised a confession to the feds if they granted your visit, and the feds being the feds are frothing at the mouth to know what the hell is happening. We drove you to the FCI facility, and you're sitting in a waiting room right now. It's very nice. You could almost pretend you were in a hotel conference room. In a few moments, Special Agent Flagston will take you to a little metal room downstairs, where you will be briefed on the security protocol, and then Alan Robertson will be led into the room. There will be guards on order to intervene if he so much as lifts a finger. But don't worry—he will not. He wants to talk to you. Father needs you."

Cooper felt an intense wave of vertigo, and the room seemed to tilt and then straighten back out. He closed his eyes, the blackness spinning. When he opened them, he was alone in a room that, indeed, looked like a hotel conference room. Functional, generic furniture and a glass water pitcher on a side table. Cooper blinked several times and tried to stand, but the dizziness forced him back down. He cursed under his breath. Cooper had made his living reporting facts, not fairy tales, not stories, and not magical bullshit that was probably some sort of delusional meltdown. What had he said at Hill? What had made him drive all this way, and what the hell had just happened with the police? Cooper reached into his pocket and pulled out his cell phone. It was dead, and Cooper groaned with the realization that it had been over twenty-four hours since he had charged it. He looked around the room and saw a desk phone on a round conference table. Keeping a firm grip on the arms of the chair, Cooper gingerly rose to his feet, making sure to let the blackout wave of vertigo pass before he walked slowly across the room to the phone. He glanced at his wrists, but there was no sign of the rough marks left by the handcuffs, not even a line of redness. Cooper felt a chill run up his spine. He had been asked to take psych evaluations repeatedly since the Los Angeles bombings but had always refused; now he was wondering if that had been wise.

Cooper picked up the phone and was surprised to hear an operator's voice.

"Hello, can I help you?"

Cooper paused. "Um, yes. I...I...need to make a call."

"I can connect you to whatever office you are trying to reach, Mr. Carlson," the voice intoned.

"Yeah, I need an outside line," Cooper said, trying to keep his voice from shaking.

"Certainly," the voice responded. "All you need to do is hang up with me and dial 9 and your number, if you need to call internationally—"

"Wait," Cooper cut her off. "Where am I?" He cringed at how desperate he sounded.

There was a pregnant pause on the other end of the line. "You are at the FCI Federal Lockup Facility." Another pause. "Are you feeling alright, Mr. Carlson?"

Cooper sat back down in a stiff-backed chair. "Yeah, no, it doesn't really matter. I'll just take that outside line."

Cooper quickly dialed Bill's cell phone. He had no idea how long he had before whatever the hell was going to happen happened. Bill answered on the first ring.

"Dude, about time. I tried the hotel, but they said you never checked in. The production office is going nuts."

Cooper rubbed his temple with his free hand. "I...I don't understand what happened in the last twenty-four hours. I need you to tell me like I'm a five-year-old. Just humor me. Walk me through everything that has happened since I was on air at Hill."

"Buddy, seriously. You okay? You sound shaky." Bill's voice had switched from annoyed to concerned, but there was no hint that anything was out of the ordinary.

"I...I don't know. Just do it, please. Tell me everything that has happened since Hill."

Bill sighed. "Alright, Coop. You made that nutso broadcast, and then you stole or borrowed—not sure what you'd call it—one of the PA's cars. We were about to send out the troops to get you, but then the call came from Denver that Alan Robertson was willing to do a bones-for-bars kind of deal and he'd confess to any involvement in Dallas and Hill if he talked to you. We all figured maybe you had gotten a call and just taken off. That's all I know, buddy. Denver office left a message for you with a hotel reservation, and times and whatnot, but we never heard back, until now. You're due in there in what...fifteen minutes? You okay? You sound rattled. You're never rattled."

Cooper felt a throbbing headache coming on. "Rattled is a good word for it. I get it. I know what I'm supposed to do. No crew, right? Just me and him, no recordings, nothing."

"Those were the terms," Bill replied. "Look, no one would fault you for backing out. There's no way this guy is causing freak natural disasters. The scientists and everyone in Dallas didn't find anything like explosives. How does one man rip a hole in the earth from a prison cell in Denver? How does he make it rain sulfuric acid?"

Cooper stood up as the door opened, revealing Agent Flagston. "That's what I'm about to find out."

ESTHER

ESTHER LAY BACK ON THE STIFF COT-LIKE MATTRESS. Agent Flagston had left some time ago. Her father had offered a deal, a confession to be given exclusively to Cooper Carlson in exchange for... ? Agent Flagston didn't know, and Esther couldn't figure out what Alan Robertson's angle was. There was no hope of clemency, even if he was able to explain how he was involved in recent events. She had a sick feeling it was all a game, a chance to use Cooper Carlson to send up a dog whistle, a message to those who were waiting for him, waiting for the next opportunity to destroy. She hoped the great Cooper Carlson would see through it but was not sure he would. It was an opportunity that no journalist would pass up.

She remembered his face from ten years ago, at that shed in San Francisco. Hector had taken off days before and locked the main house. Esther had tried for hours to get in, break a window, anything, but it was all barred and sealed tight. So she had huddled in the shed, listening to the tiny radio Hector had left her. It was difficult to describe what she felt as she listened to the broadcasts. Esther heard Cooper Carlson's voice, heard his interviews with the survivors, the FBI, the analysts. She heard his live reports as he walked through the destruction and visited hospitals.

Esther had known her mother and sister were dead. No one had to tell her that they hadn't made it out of Los Angeles. Likewise, no one had to tell her that her father, the Son of Abraham, would not be found until he was ready to be. Esther hadn't cried in that first month; her tears seemed an insult. She listened, and listened, and felt her body atrophy from disuse. She felt her limbs grow numb and watched with fascination as her fingertips became increasingly blue. Hector hadn't left much food, and her stomach clenched stoically at the sight of it, but when the hunger pains overcame her, she forced herself to eat. It didn't make sense that she should do anything that brought her comfort, eased her pain. All Esther could see was her sister's face. All she could feel was her mother's hand on her cheek. She must have slept, but for that month, Esther didn't remember dreaming. She faded in and out of consciousness, drifting from one dark place to another.

When she'd opened the door of the shed and the light of the camera shone in her eyes, she had thought maybe she'd finally died. Then she saw Cooper Carlson's face and knew that this was yet another fresh hell. Esther had a vague memory of people rushing around, trying to talk to her, the wail of sirens in the background, concerned faces concealing panic. But the one clear memory from that day in December when the winter rain was freezing on the San Francisco sidewalk was Cooper Carlson's eyes. They held no pity. He looked right through her. And while he never said a word, he knew her guilt. Cooper Carlson had always known what she was.

All the time she spent at the hospital, all the time in group homes, all the days and nights since that terrible year, Esther had made it a point to read the names of the victims to herself. She would go alphabetically on the list printed in the newspapers and silently repeat the names of as many as she could before the print began to swim before her eyes. Now she had new lists. Dallas, Utah, and where next? As irrational as she knew it was, she felt the blood of the freshly dead on her hands. She could have stopped him ten years ago. She could have refused to get on that bus, gone to the police instead, demanded they listen. She could have, could have, could have.

Esther closed her eyes. She wasn't tired, but she needed to make her way back to the meadow of her waking dreams. She needed to see the Lord of the Night Forest, the Guardian of the Dead—her aunt.

32

COOPER

THE ROOM WAS UTILITARIAN AND CLAUSTROPHOBIC. No windows, no natural light. A metal table on a metal floor, metal chairs, surrounded by steel bars. The air was cool, cave-like, and it smelled of things kept deep underground. Cooper had been briefed by a weary Agent Flagston and then again by the FBI security officer who walked him to this dungeon. There were agents lining the room. After what had occurred when Alan Robertson had talked to his daughter, they weren't taking any chances. Cooper had nothing prepared, no questions ready to ask, no trap waiting to be set. It was perhaps the first time in his career that he felt like an imposter, an actor playing the role of a journalist, and he expected to be exposed at any moment.

The idea that he might be in the middle of a nervous breakdown permeated his thoughts. Cooper wondered if knowing that he was cracking was a good sign or if it was yet more evidence that he'd had a very real psychiatric episode. He ran the timeline over and over in his head. The hallucinations, the loss of time, the voices, the paranoia—it had all started on the way to Utah, if he was being honest. He remembered a very real feeling of wanting to crawl out of his own skin while sitting on the plane headed to Clearfield. It had probably been building for a while, ever since that interview with Esther Robertson. Cooper nodded his head; of course, that was when it started. He had botched that interview, and he never botched interviews. He had prepared for that taping meticulously. He had done his research and knew every angle. There was no way Esther Robertson was going to be able to leave that studio without the truth coming out. But she had, and he had looked weak. He had been bested by a twenty-five-year-old child, so slight a strong gust of wind would overtake her. If he thought about it, it had always been Esther Robertson who had stood in his way. All those years ago, finding her in that shed in San Francisco, that had shifted the entire story. Perhaps this breakdown had been brewing for ten years. Perhaps a blood clot was inching its way through his brain, waiting to burst. Perhaps Cooper Carlson was washed up. Perhaps he had always been a fraud.

"Ready?" the guard behind the steel bars asked.

Agent Flagston was in a control room behind Cooper. The only surface that wasn't cold steel—a one-way dark glass panel—hid Flagston and others who would be standing by in case things went sour.

Cooper nodded. "Let's do this," he said in a voice he hoped sounded confident.

He heard the slow shuffle of footsteps, and then Alan Robertson appeared on the other side of the bars flanked by officers. He smiled, his teeth irrationally white and perfect. His face was haggard, but his eyes, *Jesus.* They were the same colorless pale that Esther Robertson's were, and her aunt's before that. It was as though no one in this family had a soul. They were flesh and bone framing a void.

The gates buzzed open, and Alan Robertson was walked to the metal chair opposite Cooper. He was seated, his wrists cuffed to the links in the table so he could only lift them less than an inch from the surface. His ankles were shackled to links on the ground. He was immobilized, but Cooper doubted very much that would matter if Alan Robertson meant him harm.

"Well, the great Cooper Carlson, the most trusted voice in journalism in the Western world. Thank you for meeting with me." Robertson's voice was smooth, practiced.

Cooper nodded. "Why did you want to talk to me?"

Robertson stared at him unblinking for a moment. "You know the answer to that. I believe my associates filled you in. Yes?"

Cooper shifted uncomfortably. "I don't know what you're referring to. I received a call while in Utah that you wanted to confess, and I know we're all very interested in what you have to say. So what do you have to say?"

"You're not having a psychotic break or nervous episode or whatever. You aren't. You are the most rational man in the room, Cooper Carlson. My associates explained to you in very clear terms what we need from you. Are we in agreement?" Robertson leaned back, and Cooper was distractedly amazed at how he appeared to be perfectly at ease in spite of the conditions.

"You want me to tell the world, report what it is you tell me here," Cooper replied, a chill building at the base of his spine. The idea that what he had experienced hadn't been a delusion was unacceptable. He pushed the thought back before it overtook him entirely.

"Yes. I'm trying to get the attention of a particular party, you see. And while my efforts have most certainly woken her up, I need an antenna, so to speak. I need you to ring the alarm." He smiled again.

Cooper found himself resisting the urge to smile back. Robertson had a pull about him that made you want him to like you. Cooper had a moment of clarity about how Robertson had convinced so many people to do such terrible things.

"I'm not going to help you commit terrorism. I won't send up a dog whistle to your people. I won't glorify you," Cooper said, feeling his hands start to shake.

"You don't need to. I glorify myself. My people, my children, already know their roles," Robertson said softly.

"You killed your children, all but one," Cooper replied, feeling the fog start to clear from his head.

"Yes, about that one," Robertson said. "She's been a sort of thorn in your side, hasn't she? Always the puzzle you couldn't figure out. Did she know? Did she help me? You saw her all those years ago in San Francisco. You knew then, didn't you, Cooper Carlson? You knew she was no child. She was much more than that. She was the continuation of a curse that was set in motion many, many years ago. That one has demon blood in her veins. You saw it even if no one else did."

"Why did you save her?" Cooper asked.

"I need her," Robertson said. His gaze flicked around the room, and then his pale eyes locked once again on Cooper. "She has the old blood in her veins. She is the conduit. When my dear sister, the Lord of the Night Forest, returns to see my work, I need Esther. She is my voice, and the voice of the Bandia Marbh."

Cooper shook his head. "Make some sense."

"Do you know the story of the Gef? No? I thought not. They also called it the Talking Mongoose. An earthbound spirit, bound to the flesh for eternity. Isle of Man, 1930s—you should look it up. It's a gas of a story. But there are things they don't write about. Gef was cursed, you see. He was cast into the Sluagh, the restless dead, for his crimes, his atrocities. His physical form faded over time, but what a long time he had to wander this earth. What a long time he was given to feel pain and hunger and loneliness, and to know that he would never, ever be redeemed. To know that no matter what he did, he would never see beyond the veil, he would never enter the next world. Gef was immortal, and that was his punishment. But Gef did not have a daughter. My daughter, my Esther, you see, will be my voice and the means by which I will speak with the Night Forest. She is how I will end this torture."

"I'm not interested in fairy tales," Cooper replied coldly. "You said you wanted to confess. Tell me what's next. You didn't ask me here to discuss your daughter. No matter what happened ten years ago, she had nothing to do with Dallas or Utah. You said you would talk, so talk."

"That's the Cooper Carlson I know!" Robertson nodded with approval, and Cooper again felt a surge of misplaced pride that he had pleased him. "I will tell you what I promised, and you need to listen. I'll even tell you what's next." Roberston leaned in, his face changing. The lines disappeared, and his eyes glowed with a light that had no source. "Agent Flagston will share some information with you after this is over. Pay attention to what you see. I can do only so much from this cell. I need my children to invite me into the circle, and then I have a precious few minutes to call the winds and rain, to tear the earth asunder. But the window closes, and I find myself entirely in the present. Do you hear me, Cooper Carlson?"

Cooper shook his head. His body was buzzing, and he felt disconnected from his spine, as though he were floating a few inches from the chair. "Quit talking in riddles. What do you mean a circle?"

Robertson lowered his voice, forcing Cooper to lean forward. He noticed, out of the corner of his eye, the agent closest to him take a protective step forward.

"You will see. Special Agent Flagston will show you. My children draw a circle, they fill it with their blood, and I ride their pain into their reality for a few precious moments. My sister wasn't the only one born with gifts, you see, Cooper Carlson. My sister was the Matrarc, the Bandia Marbh, the Lord of the Night Forest, but she wasn't the only one who knew a little magick. My children invite me in, and I bring hell upon earth for as long as my window lasts."

"You're insane," Cooper said softly, his hands shaking. "You expect me to believe this? What did you do, Robertson? Explosives? What? If you caused Dallas, if you caused Utah, how? I know how you destroyed Los Angeles—the whole world knows—but you're saying you're God."

"No. Not God. Rather the opposite. Los Angeles was clumsy. I was bound to the limitations of humanity then. I hadn't found my feet, so to speak. But if there is any silver lining to my current . . . what to call it? Situation? It would be that I am no longer bound by such pedestrian chains." Robertson gave Cooper a crooked grin.

"How? How did you cause a sinkhole? A tornado? Acid rain?" Cooper spoke softly but urgently. He knew his time was coming to a close; Robertson would clam up soon.

"You're asking the wrong questions. I already told you how. You want to know *why*. Ask yourself the question no one else seems to be putting to words. *Why* Dallas? *Why* Hill Air Force Base? What did those places have that other places did not? That's how you'll find out what's next. Of course, you will have to work fast. It's going to happen soon . . . very soon in fact. And after that . . . well, that's when the show really gets started." Robertson had an amused smirk on his face. He sat back; he was enjoying this.

Cooper felt a wave of anger and the disconnected feeling snapped, and he was thrust back into his body sitting in the cold metal chair in this dark place. "You haven't told me anything. This was a waste of my time."

"Only if you waste it," Robertson said, an edge to his voice. "I'm telling you how to find the next location. Make the connections, do your research. Nothing happens in a vacuum. Everything is deliberate. Everything I do leads to the end."

"Which is?" Cooper asked, feeling for the first time like his old self. "What's your endgame? Why?"

"This is the way the world ends—whimper, not a bang and all that. I was never much of one for school, but I remember that. Well, I intend to end it with a bang. And when it does, you'll see my sister again, the great and wonderful Ceit Robertson. She will open the veil, and the Night Forest will lay open to us all. And when she does, I will take my throne the same way it was taken from its original Ceannaire, back in the old times. I will take back what was stolen from me. My dear little daughter is talking to Ceit as we speak. She doesn't understand what she is hearing though." Robertson spoke as if in a trance, his eyes half-lidded. Cooper stared as the nonsense words tumbled from his mouth.

"This isn't real. You're not giving me anything real. What was it? Bombs? Talk to me about Dallas. How did you trigger a sinkhole? Or is it just more bullshit you're trying to take credit for? I bet you had nothing to do with this at all. You're not God or the devil. Your sister wasn't either, was she Robertson? Where is she? Where'd you dump her body? Did you kill her before or after you burned down the cul-de-sac? You killed your own grandmother, why not your sister? Hell, you murdered over fifteen thousand innocent people, including your own kids, your wife. You don't have powers, Robertson. You aren't the Son of Abraham. That's a line you've been selling. I know you. I saw you when you were a skinny, confused teenager living in your sister's house. You're damaged goods. What did they do to you all those years ago when you got snatched off the street? What did they break? No, I think the last time you were a person was when you were a kid, all those years ago when your great-grandmother died. That was the last time you were whole, wasn't it? You've been looking for a way to be special all this time. Well, you're not special—you're a fucking monster."

Robertson was silent, his pale eyes staring into Cooper's, his face expressionless. He raised the index finger on his right hand and flicked it to the right. The metal chair next to Cooper fell over with a clatter that echoed around the space. Despite himself, Cooper jumped. The agents lining the room shifted uneasily.

"You think this can hold me?" Robertson glanced down at the chains that wrapped around his wrists. "I am nowhere I do not choose to be. You need to heed my words, Cooper Carlson. There will be another incident, and it will be soon. You cannot stop it, but if you want to try, you need to stop waiting for your turn to talk and instead listen." Robertson looked to the agent at the entry. "I'm done here."

"So am I." Cooper stood and was met by an agent on either side who escorted him out of the cell-like room. As they passed through the secure doors and began ascending to the upper levels of the building, one of the agents cleared his throat.

"For what it's worth, he said more to you than he has to anyone. We expected him to sit out the trial next week, not say a word. You got more out of him than anyone yet." The agent gave Cooper a conciliatory nod.

"What did he mean that Flagston had information to show me?" Cooper asked the man.

"Can't speak to that, but Special Agent Flagston does want you in his office, if you're up for it," the man replied.

"Yeah, I am. What did he mean about his daughter? He said she was talking to Ceit Robertson...which doesn't make any sense. Is she in a safe place?" Cooper asked as they stepped from the elevator and headed to Flagston's empty office.

"Flagston will fill you in. Wait here. I'll get you coffee." The agents nodded and walked like well-trained soldiers down the hall. Cooper sank into the office chair and rubbed his temples. His nervous breakdown was beginning to feel a little too real. Robertson's words hadn't made any sense, but yet they had. As crazy as they sounded, Cooper had the sick feeling they were true. But how? He took a sip of coffee from the mug that had appeared before him. He would do as the Son of Abraham commanded. He would look for the patterns, and he would stop this thing.

ESTHER

ESTHER LAY ON HER BACK IN THE MEADOW, THE grass soft and damp under her bare arms. The air smelled of fresh rain and soil that's beginning to sprout seedlings. She forced herself to sit up. She wanted to stay in this place forever, away from the world, but she knew she had to go into the forest and find the creature that had once been her aunt. Esther stood, feeling the warm breeze wrap around her body, and she shivered with the delicious feeling of comfort it gave. She turned to the woods and began walking. Esther did not know how Ceit would help her, but she was aware this was the only place she would find any truth.

The woods were thick. The overhanging branches, laden with their ancient greenery, blocked the light of the stars. Esther stumbled, and she suddenly felt a small hand take hers. It had the same texture as smooth tree bark, it's fingers no larger than a child's. Her impulse was to be afraid, but she had no fear of this creature. Gently it pulled her along until light began to shine through the canopy once again. Esther saw she was in a small clearing similar to the one she had found before. The owner of the tiny hand stood before her, barely reaching her knees. Its skin a dark maple, it was more branch than creature. Overlarge eyes of liquid amber stared at her, curious. It pulled its tiny hand away and let out a sound that could have been a giggle. Before Esther could speak, it darted into the woods.

"Hello, love. Please sit." The silky voice floated on the breeze, seemingly everywhere at once.

Esther sat, and as she did, a figure appeared before her. The pale hair, the light eyes, the slight frame in a long white tunic. The Bandia Marbh nodded. "You found us again."

"Something helped me … it was … " Esther stuttered.

"One of my children. You'd call it a wood elf if you saw it in your world, which you're not likely to. My great-grandmother could see them in the forest outside Cork where the Society came from. Did your father or mother ever tell you the stories?" Ceit asked gently.

Esther thought carefully. "My mother used to talk about the cul-de-sac, but she didn't know where it had come from. She hated it there."

"For good reason," Ceit said, a small smile on her unearthly face. "One day I will tell you how the Society came from Cork and about the deal my great-grandmother made for her passage. It's the reason my brother haunts your world, although I do not blame Amon. No one is responsible for the path Alan chose."

"Amon?" Esther asked.

"My demon," Ceit said simply and smiled at Esther's wide eyes. "You need to change your perception of demons. There was a saying I used to know from your world … 'nothing is good or bad, but thinking makes it so.'"

"Hamlet," Esther whispered.

Ceit nodded. "You need to know what comes next, and I need to show you what could happen if my brother is not stopped. I'm afraid it will not make much sense, but you have to believe and trust that what I am about to show you exists."

Esther nodded. "I've seen too much in my world to think you false."

Ceit smiled. "Good. Now open your eyes, and see."

A pool of water opened in the space between them. It was clear and perfect. Tiny ripples echoed across the surface. Esther had an inexplicable urge to dive headfirst into it, to feel the perfect chill on her skin.

"Go ahead." Ceit nodded. "You will see but not be seen. You are seeing what has already been and what could be, but it is not reality. Go ahead." She nodded again to the water.

Esther tumbled forward, feeling the rush of water cover her head and shoulders, sucking her all the way down. Her eyes were open. The water was infinitely deep and crystal clear. Esther realized she was holding her breath and opened her mouth. Water did not enter her lungs; instead, crisp, clean air filled her nose. She smiled at the weightlessness of it, the feeling of perfect calm. Suddenly, all around her, images began to form. They startled her, but she heard Ceit's voice in her head. "You will see but not be seen." She saw her father, his ragged hair long and unkempt, his eyes wild. He stood in a circle of blood, his arms raised. He muttered words she could not hear, and the ground began to shake. Esther saw the bottom drop from the room, concrete, metal, wood, and glass dissolving into the earth. Her father floated in place for a moment more and then dissipated as though he were no more substantial than smoke.

The image changed. She saw a young man with sad eyes. She saw the name tag on his coveralls: Benny. Then she watched as he drew the knife up his wrists and plunged the blade into his skin. She felt his pain, his regret, his despair. Esther reached for him, but she was a voyeur in this reality. This had already happened; this boy's pain was already passed. He was dead, along with so many others. Again, her father appeared. This time the image was grainy, unfocused. The concrete walls began to crumble, and Esther could feel the pull of the wind. As the roof crumbled, the sky held a greenish tint. Even in the silence of her viewing, Esther knew the terrible scream that emanated from the sky. She felt it in her bones. She saw rain pelting down, everything it touched hissing in protest. The scene began to fade, the images becoming darker and darker.

Another, a cabin lined with metallic monitors and computers. Esther knew this was not the same as the others. This image was barely visible, only outlines with faint colors. Long tables, unfathomable equipment lining the space. A framed picture of water spraying into the air. Esther had a moment of clarity; it was Old Faithful, the geyser in Yellowstone Park. She strained to see what was happening. An older woman, her face lined with age and exposure to the elements stood still in the center of the room, her eyes closed, her body radiating sadness. She raised a knife to her throat, and Esther screamed silently as the woman drew it across her flesh. The image crumbled before her. It faded into the clear, perfect water, and Esther found herself shaking convulsively.

Another image began to form. Esther tried to swim up. She had had enough. She had seen how her father was making these atrocities happen, how he had used those who had sworn allegiance to him. *No more*, she begged Ceit. *No more, I understand.* But her efforts were futile. Esther stayed anchored in place, her arms and legs flailing uselessly. Around her she felt oppressive heat. She felt her skin burn and her lungs fill with smoke and ash. She saw bright sprays of fire in the sky. Esther gagged and tried to scream. The image faded, and the sky overhead appeared, dark gray clouds filling the space. Her nose and throat burned. Esther looked around her and saw a wasteland—no life, no vegetation, ash piles covering the burned soil. Felled trees lay dead and rotting; a few survivors stayed upright, their trunks blackened, their limbs stripped of life. Esther turned in circles, but the view remained the same. The world was dead. Her father had scorched the earth and salted the ground. Nothing would grow. There was no redemption.

Suddenly she felt herself being pulled upward, the feeling of movement washing the ash from her lungs. She was flung into the Night Forest once again. Esther lay gasping on the shore of the ever-shrinking pool. She was dry, as though she had never been submerged. Struggling for breath and her mind spinning, she sat up. Ceit sat motionless, her pale eyes watching Esther.

"You saw," she said simply.

"What did it mean? What did my father do?" Esther gasped.

"You know the answers. The real question is whether it can be stopped," Ceit said.

Esther felt a sob stuck in her throat. "Can it?"

Ceit gave her a small, sad smile. "If not, your world will end. But remember what I said, love. You have been through many worlds already. When you leave your reality, you move to the next, and the next after that. When you die, you enter my Night Forest. Some are here for an eternity, some for a moment. But they pass through and move to the next world, and on and on. There is no death, only a new way of living. So if this is not stopped, if your world ends before its time, you will be with me, until."

"But, why show me then?" Esther whispered. "Why should I try to stop it?"

"It's in your nature to want to survive," Ceit said. "You weren't built to accept the inevitable. You want more time in your world, and you should have it. You are young. There are so many wonders yet for you to see. So go back, and use what you have seen. Try."

"My father..." Esther murmured.

"Yes. Once upon a time, he was a little boy who had terrible and dark things happen to him. They broke him. I could not welcome him into my kingdom. I barred his entry. You also had terrible and dark things happen to you, but you are not broken. You chose not to allow the pain to destroy you. Remember that. Now it's time to wake up. We are here always." Ceit smiled, and in a brilliant flash of light, disappeared.

Esther opened her eyes and stared at the ceiling of the hospital room. She knew where the next attack was going to be, and there wasn't much time. She pulled her cell phone from her bag and dialed Agent Flagston.

34

COOPER

COOPER STARED AT THE PRINTED STILLS OF THE surveillance footage. The circles, and Alan Robertson's face, his arms reaching upward. He put them aside and examined the hallway footage from Hill Air Force Base. As he did, he heard the unwelcome voice of Alan Robertson in his head. He needed to see the connections. He needed to understand why these places had been chosen.

"We don't really know what to make of this footage, to be frank," Agent Flagston said, and he took a long drink of his coffee. "There is no perceptible way that Robertson was out of his cell. We have footage of him in the cell at the time this happened. So maybe it's a look-alike, someone working on his behalf—"

"It's him," Cooper interrupted. "I don't know how, but it's him. I'm not for anything that can't be proven, but this is … this is something else. Tell me, what were they researching in this lab at Hill?"

Flagston pulled another file from the pile and shuffled through a messy stack of papers. "Largely classified, but we know that the

USGS basically built this lab. All the equipment came from a grant that originated from that office."

"What does the United States Geological Survey have to do with this?" Cooper asked. He looked up at Flagston, trying to read the man, but failing. "Why are you talking about any of this with me?" Cooper asked suddenly. "Seriously, you have an entire agency devoted to investigation."

"Yes, we do. And Robertson won't talk to any of them. He wanted to talk to you. And you have been deeply ingrained in this case since Los Angeles. Before that even, right? I have you back in your *LA Examiner* days on Society surveillance. You were following Alan Robertson and analyzing the movements of the Society back even before the fire. You probably know more about them than any single person out there, except Esther Robertson maybe. And you are the only one she would talk to on the tenth anniversary. You had the exclusive. Our guys are stumped. They deal with clues, facts, logic. This is none of that. So I'm asking for help. Robertson said there is going to be another attack. I don't know how he's making this happen, and I don't really care. I care about stopping it."

"Fair enough," Cooper replied softly, shuffling back to examine the photos from Dallas. "What is this building? You said it was the epicenter of the sinkhole. What was the building used for?"

"An outfit called Connexion International." Flagston pulled a paper from the pile and handed it to Cooper. "Satellites used to track global weather patterns and environmental impact on the atmosphere."

"It doesn't make any sense," Cooper said, feeling the migraine that had finally gone dormant start to rise back up. "How am I supposed to know what is next?"

Flagston jumped as his cell phone rang. The conversation was brief, but Cooper had a feeling who was on the other end. Flagston ended the call and stood, stretching his neck from side to side.

"It's Esther. I need to go talk to her, and I would like you to come."

Cooper stood, loose ends of information swirling in his sleep-deprived mind. "Yeah, okay. Does she know I'm coming?"

"She asked for you," Flagston said as he ushered Cooper out the door.

35

ESTHER

THE FIELDS OF ASH AND DEATH ROLLED BEFORE Esther's eyes as she sat in the hospital cell waiting for Agent Flagston and Cooper Carlson. She knew he had met with her father, and as repugnant as she found him, he knew more about her family than she ever would. The lab with the framed photo of the geyser—it had to be Yellowstone. And the destruction she had seen could only be the result of an eruption. But surely there were limits to what her father could do. There were detection systems in place; it was monitored. Esther lay back on the stiff mattress, staring at the ceiling. She felt clammy, and her hands held a slight tremor. She realized suddenly that she hadn't really eaten in nearly twenty-four hours. Her entire body had been tied in knots. The idea of food still seemed terrible, but her stomach cramped and growled. On the small table, the untouched breakfast tray had been replaced with lunch. Esther pulled herself to her feet and lifted the lid.

She was finishing the cafeteria standard tuna fish sandwich when Agent Flagston and Cooper Carlson walked in the door.

"Good," Flagston said, offering her a smile. "They said you weren't eating. That helps no one."

"Thank you for coming." Esther nodded to the two men. Cooper looked worse than she felt. He was pale, and his eyes had taken on a hollowed-out appearance. "You look as though you aren't eating either."

Cooper extended his hand, and Esther shook it. He had no strength left in the grip. This was a man who had seen something that had shifted everything he thought to be true. For the first time, Esther felt a measure of pity for him. He had always been so sure he was right, so confident that he had the angle, the truth. There was no truth in this, only riddles and the requirement that you stop believing that anything was impossible.

Both men sat, and the three of them stared at each other for a moment.

"The next attack is going to happen in Yellowstone National Park. I don't know exactly where, a lab of some sort, lots of equipment. I saw the person who opens the circle for my father, but I don't have a very specific description, and I don't know where they are, only that they are in the park." Esther felt their eyes on her as she spoke and knew how mad she sounded.

Flagston tapped the table distractedly, thinking. "How do you know this, Esther? Did you receive information? No one except our guys should know you're here."

Esther shook her head. "I did receive information, but not in a way that you would believe."

"I would," Cooper said softly and looked up, meeting Esther's eyes. "I believe you. Alan Robertson said you would be talking to his sister, that she would show you things."

Esther nodded silently. Flagston rifled through his bag and pulled out a map. On it were marked Dallas and Hill Air Force

Base. He spread it out on the table. "Okay, let's talk impossible. It's the best intel we have right now. Any clue at all where you were?"

"No," Esther said. "But it has to do with the volcano. I know that much."

"Hold on," Flagston said and pulled out a small laptop. He rapidly typed, waited a short moment, and then spun the screen around so Esther and Cooper could see.

"The Yellowstone Volcano Observatory has offices that span five states—Wyoming, Colorado, Utah, New Mexico, and Arizona. There are multiple labs in Wyoming, but the biggest is right up here on the border, in the Yellowstone Caldera." Flagston pointed to a little triangle on the northern corner of Wyoming.

"You said Utah. Where?" Esther asked. She was beginning to see the pattern that Ceit was trying to show her.

"Salt Lake City, the University of Utah lab. Jesus, that must have been the target at Hill." Flagston swung the laptop back around and typed some more, quickly reading. "Yes, yes, yes. The Clearfield lab on base was being upgraded. That must have been what was going on at Hill—they were moving the lab from the University onto the base."

"Okay, so he knocks out two YVO labs, why? To impact early detection? It doesn't explain Dallas." As Cooper rubbed his temples, Esther could see a little vein beginning to pulse where he massaged.

"None of that matters if we don't stop the next attack," Esther said. "I saw a woman, forties or fifties. She was wearing what looked like a park or government uniform. Can you get people to the Caldera lab now? See if this woman exists, close the lab, guard the door?"

Flagston nodded. "On it." He stood and pulled out his cell phone, exiting the room into the hall.

Cooper stared at Esther. She felt deeply uncomfortable. His eyes held a disdain that she was not unaccustomed to, but she had invited this into her space, which felt unbearable.

"Why did you ask for me?" Cooper asked, his confident reporter voice entirely gone. He sounded unsure, lost.

"You know my father better than anyone. Agent Flagston knows that too. You know him better than I do. I saw my aunt," Esther said calmly.

Cooper nodded. "Alan Robertson said you would. He also said you wouldn't know what to do with what she showed you."

"Turns out my father doesn't know me very well either," Esther replied, a crooked smile on her lips. "I'm made of sterner stuff than he gives me credit for."

"I imagine that's true," Cooper said, returning the smile.

"So what's next? They lock us both in here while we wait for the FBI to find this lab and maybe, *maybe* stop something that none of the agents will believe is possible?" Esther asked, staring at the door where she could hear Flagston's muffled voice.

"No, I think not," Cooper said. "In fact, you might be the only one who can stop it."

"They're not likely to let me out. There were death threats called in after your show," Esther said, feeling a seed of excitement in her belly.

"They can't hold you," Cooper replied, standing and circling the room.

"We can make it in ten hours driving, unless you have a plane," Esther said, feeling her spine grow straighter.

Flagston reentered the room. "We're coming with you to Wyoming," Cooper said in a tone that didn't invite debate.

"I was hoping you'd say that," Flagston replied. "We leave in an hour."

36

COOPER

THE DENVER CBS AFFILIATE HAD LOADED COOPER UP with a body camera and an audio recorder. Bill wouldn't make it in time to leave with Flagston's crew, and Cooper had turned down the offer of a field team. He didn't know what they were walking into, but he didn't want to give it any more media attention than it needed. Alan Robertson wanted a circus, but Cooper was determined not to give him that satisfaction. He would not be the flare that Robertson wanted to send into the world.

He'd had time to make one hasty call before Flagston had ushered him onto the prop plane that would take them to the YVO office in the Yellowstone Caldera. He felt a wave of relief as he heard Cecily's voice on the other end.

"Dad?" She sounded young, like she was nine years old again and scared of the dark.

"Cecily, thank god you answered." Cooper paused, he hadn't expected her to answer and now found himself tongue-tied. "I need to say some things."

"Dad, I...it doesn't matter. What's happening, Dad? I saw you on TV. What does it mean?"

"I don't know, kiddo, I don't know. Look, I have only a few minutes. I'm following the story, and my ride will leave me behind. I need you to get to the Boonsboro house. Can you do that? The cabin?" Cooper felt beads of sweat rolling down his neck despite the chill in the air.

"Why? What's going to happen? What does any of this have to do with Alan Robertson?" Cecily sounded on the edge of panic.

Cooper lowered the tone of his voice, remembering how he'd talk Cecily out of a panic attack when she was a child and later when she was a teenager—smooth, calm tones, repeating facts, reminding her to breathe. "Listen, listen, you don't need to be worried about a thing. He's not after you...he is not after you. I want you to go to the cabin. Call your mom, tell her to go too. Have her meet you there. You're safer away from cities, okay? Take a breath, can you do that?" He heard the faint noise of traffic in the background. *She must be in the car*, he thought distractedly. *She must still be in Georgetown.* "Honey, just go to the cabin. The lights work. You can pretend it's a vacation—but go."

"Okay...look, I'm sorry," Cecily said in a voice that sounded more little girl than grown.

"I am too. Let's not worry about that," Cooper said.

"Wait a minute, I had a dream." Cecily was talking fast, and Flagston was waving at him to get on the plane. Cooper held up a hand, silently begging for a minute.

"I had a dream, I did. It smelled like sulfur. There was a lake of blue and gold and red. I knew you were going to die there, I knew it. You fell in. Your skin...Daddy, your skin melted. I tried to pull you out, but you were dead. Dad..." her voice broke.

"Cecily, I'll be okay. I will. Get to the cabin. Call your mother, make her join you, okay? I'll get to you as soon as I can, but don't think on that dream. I'm okay. I love you." Cooper headed for the plane as the engines started up. The roar drowned out Cecily's last words, but he knew what they had been.

Cooper took his seat on the plane. Flagston shot him a glare and gestured to the front. He had already had to delay while the CBS affiliate ran equipment out to the airport, and now Cooper knew he was steaming about the lost minutes. Esther leaned against the window, her knees drawn up to her chest, eyes closed. She looked so young, so fragile. The opposite of Cecily. He smiled to himself remembering Cecily's constant scrapes and bruises, the sheer number of times they'd had to take her in for stitches from being tackled, knocked out, kicked in some sport or another. She was muscular, solid, not like this wisp of a girl that seemingly held the fate of the world in her hands. Cooper watched her. His distrust of her was irrational, he knew that, especially after meeting Alan Robertson face-to-face. It was clear the girl had never had a real father. She was all alone in the world, always had been.

The plane reached altitude and leveled out. He thought over what Alan Robertson had said in Denver. All that talk about wandering spirits and ghosts. What did it mean? But the truly perplexing part of the whole thing was that despite the insanity of the words that had left his mouth, Alan Robertson had a magnetic quality about him. It was overwhelming. No wonder Esther Robertson had such a tragic air about her. She had only ever been an offering to the altar for the Son of Abraham.

Cooper closed his eyes, he let himself relax into a light sleep for the rest of the short flight. God or the devil awaited them in Wyoming; he wasn't sure which one he was hoping for.

37

REBECCA

REBECCA SAT AT HER DESK AND STARED AT THE framed photographs that lined the space. She reached out and straightened the one of Toby, age five, in the front lawn playing with the garden hose. The water was spraying up into his face, and his mouth was open in laughter, eyes squeezed shut. Next to it, Toby, age seven or eight, sleeping on the couch, the faint glow of the television illuminating the scene. In his arms was a kitten, her tiny head on his chest. The kitten had disappeared shortly after this picture had been taken. Rebecca suspected the coyotes that roamed the woods surrounding the house, but she'd told Toby that someone must have stolen her. The idea that his cat was simply living a life far away was better than the reality that she was dead. Toby, age twelve, posing with a soccer ball on a green field, his jersey smeared with grass stains and his smile wide. Fourteen, first day of high school. His hair under a baseball cap, the smile forced. He had been embarrassed, and she had insisted. He stood in front of the carved stone sign: Calvin Carver High School.

He was shot a month later and died right before Christmas, ten days before his fifteenth birthday. There was a photo of him on the ventilator, but that was locked deep in the closet. Rebecca sometimes took it out and stared at it, time slipping away as she remembered the deep rhythmic whirring of the hospital equipment. A fighter, that was what the nurses had called him. For the first month, kids from the high school stood outside the hospital, some putting flowers and teddy bears on a makeshift altar with Toby's photo on it. The audience had tapered off by December. Only a few stray roses had remained. People forgot.

The incident, too, was forgotten by December. Toby's death had revived it for a few days. A montage of photographs appeared on the front page of the *Tulsa World*, and a few news broadcasters mentioned his name—Tobias Parker—in earnest voices. She even received a letter from the White House; Rebecca never opened it. She expected it was a form letter much like the parents of the other victims had received. *A terrible tragedy, loss of a bright light, we will not forget*...Blah-blah—that's all it was to Rebecca. Empty words. Nothing could bring her boy back to her.

Toby's death made five killed, seven injured on that day in October. The boy who brought the gun and opened fire was arrested that same day. Rebecca had spent too many hours staring at the photos of that kid. His eyes were dark pits, his face pale and lifeless. Did Toby know him? She would never find out.

It was on Christmas Eve that she first met the Ceannaire. She'd been sitting on the bathroom floor, holding a full pill bottle of Xanax. She was working up the courage to swallow it all and chase it with a bottle of vodka. She'd been working through every memory she had of Toby, and every time she had failed him. He hadn't wanted to go to school that day. He had said he felt sick, and she had snapped at him, sure he was faking. She'd picked up his backpack and set it by the door, pointed to the knob and told him to go. He had sulked out, not even a goodbye. She had been frustrated, annoyed, and for a minute allowed herself to think of what her life would be like when he was grown and gone, when she had her time and life back. Maybe she had killed him, wishing her dark thoughts into existence.

The Ceannaire had appeared as a figure sitting next to her. Rebecca had been so startled, she had dropped the Xanax, the tiny white pills scattering over the floor. The Ceannaire had calmed her. He had told her she had a purpose, and he had promised to take away her pain. Even though Rebecca had been sure she was losing her mind, she had talked back to him, telling him about Toby, about the killer who was due to be released from the juvenile correction facility in a few short years. Just a few years in exchange for the lives he had extinguished.

Father had appeared to her every night after that. He would be sitting across from her, wearing a sort of tunic, his hair long, his eyes containing galaxies. He listened to her grief. He promised her that she would see Toby again, that he was just across the veil, and he, the Son of Abraham, could guide them together. And then, one night, as Rebecca sat before the fireplace, the Ceannaire appeared with a smile on his face. He had a gift for her, he had said. He had done something for her, and she would be pleased. He instructed her to turn on the news, and when she did, she saw the image of the shooter. The sad-looking boy with the bottomless eyes was all over the screen. He'd been found dead in his cell at the juvenile lockup. Suicide they said. He had made a rope from his bedsheets. There were reports of the boy talking to an unknown person the entire night leading up to his death. Guards had checked and no one was there, but two distinct voices had been heard by his neighbors and guards alike. One was the boy's; the other, a man's voice.

The Ceannaire had nodded at Rebecca as she turned the television off, overwhelmed by the images. *He won't have the life your son should have had. He will never be free.* Rebecca had cried the entire night—for her Toby, for the other victims, for the boy's mother who had lost a son in this too. But the next morning, she felt a weight lift from her heart, and slowly she entered the world again. The Ceannaire guided her. He needed her; she was vital. Rebecca had a geology degree, and on the Ceannaire's instruction applied at the Yellowstone Caldera with the Yellowstone Volcano Observatory. She took the national park licensing tests and another semester's worth of classes to make her eligible for the United States Geological Survey posting. She sold the house in Tulsa, giving Toby's clothes and soccer cleats to charity. She would see him again soon, so she no longer needed the remembrances. Once settled in, she became a model employee. She lived on-site, and worked every holiday so the other scientists and engineers could be with their families. She was efficient and smart, and within a short time, became indispensable, unquestioningly reliable.

Every night, Rebecca would see the face of her Ceannaire before her, instructing her on her role in the world to come. Her son would be waiting for her. They would be reunited, all the pain of his passing erased. The other children, too, would be welcomed into the world that the Son of Abraham would create. He had shown her a great, sun-filled meadow where the souls of those he had collected in Los Angeles all those years ago danced and sang. He had rescued them from this wicked world, and he would not rest until he rescued all his children. Rebecca was indispensable, important. She would open the gates in preparation for the final awakening. With the elimination of the Clearfield and Yellowstone Caldera YVO offices, Father would be free for his ascendance.

...

The satellites that tracked the volcanic pressure had been off-line since Dallas. Rebecca closed her eyes and whispered a prayer for the chosen ones that Father had tasked with opening the doors in preparation for this day. She would join them in his inner circle soon. It was almost time. He would bathe the evil from the world of man and reunite the dead with those who mourned them.

The phone rang, breaking her reverie. Rebecca was alone in the office. She had sent everyone home; she needed privacy for what she was about to do.

"Beck? It's Phil here at the university. You okay up there?" It was the Bozeman field office. Much of the business of the YVO lab was managed through the university.

Rebecca took a deep breath, pulling herself back into reality. "Sure, Phil. Quiet day around here. What's up?"

"Phone's been ringing off the hook. You have visitors on the way. FBI, if you can believe it." Phil chuckled.

Rebecca felt a length of ice form along her spine. She forced a light tone. "Well, what do they want? Bear up a federal tree?"

Phil chuckled again. "No idea. They wanted to know who was up there today, and I told them you were there every day. Hell, I can't remember the last time you weren't at your post—"

"Phil, they asked about me?" Rebecca cut him off, confused. How would the FBI know about her? One of the other family members must have leaked information.

"Well, not in so many words. They asked who was working the station, and I told 'em. Don't tell me you're running a crime ring up there, Beck, without asking me to join." Phil laughed at his own joke.

Rebecca felt her heart racing. As calmly as possible, she said, "Not without you, Phil. No worries, buddy. Look, when are they all supposed to be here?"

Phil hesitated. She heard the shuffling of papers. "Huh, let's see. Less than an hour to land here, and then they'll be driving out, I expect—unless they have choppers. You probably have at least two hours, maybe. Why?"

"I'd hate for the FBI to find me in a dirty house. Just want to make a good impression." Rebecca forced a laugh.

"Well, call me later. This is the most excitement we've had in years!" Phil hung up, and Rebecca stared at the photos on her desk. She needed Father. He needed to tell her what this meant. She wasn't supposed to open the gate until sundown, but with the FBI all over the place that would be impossible. She closed her eyes and prayed with all her soul. *Ceannaire, I need you. Ceannaire, tell me what I must do.*

38

ESTHER

THE AIRFIELD IN BOZEMAN WAS NOTHING MORE THAN a short strip of concrete in the woods accompanying a few metal-sided structures. The prop plane made a rocky landing, and Esther had to swallow the vomit that rose in her throat. Cooper was acting oddly polite. She wondered if he was buttering her up for some sort of final interview sneak attack. She hated that she needed him here, but her father's side of the story could not be the only one to be told. A helicopter was waiting on a landing pad when they stepped off the plane.

"Courtesy of the bureau. It's about two hours to drive. This is faster." Agent Flagston ushered them off the plane and across the otherwise empty airfield. "We're losing time," he shouted over the din as Esther climbed up into the helicopter. Her heart was beating fast. She'd flown plenty before, but never like this. The noise was deafening. The pilot turned his head and pointed at the headphones that were hanging on the arm of the tiny seat. Esther put them over her ears and immediately felt calmer. Beside her, Cooper did the same. They were joined by Flagston and another agent, a woman with rough black hair and kind eyes. Agent Lander was local and worked in the state office near the university. She knew the station and the woman who lived on-site—who might be the woman Esther had seen in her vision.

The chopper lifted into the air, and Esther gripped the armrest. The helicopter felt like it had no business balancing. It wavered and leveled out, then shot forward toward the Wyoming forest. Flagston leaned in, shouting over the noise.

"The Bozeman office likely told her we were coming. Rebecca Parker is her name. Is this who you saw?" Agent Lander tapped on her cell phone, revealing a USGS employee site showing a woman in her late forties, early fifties maybe, unremarkable in every way— limp hair, undistinguished features, slightly doughy but not overweight. She was utterly unmemorable. *No wonder my father chose her*, Esther thought. This woman would be overlooked and underestimated. Rebecca Parker's eyes though, that was what caught Esther's gaze. They were sad black pits that held no hope.

"I think so. Like I said, it wasn't very clear," Esther shouted back.

"She's been there for years." Agent Lander leaned in to be heard. "Very dedicated, but also . . ."

"Also what?" Esther asked.

"I don't know. Intense. She had a son. He died in a school shooting some years ago, back in Oklahoma. I don't blame her for being off. I can't imagine how you'd ever be normal again." Lander shook her head.

Esther looked out the tiny window. Another broken and lost soul. No wonder her father had adopted her. She would have been at the lowest point a person could be. What did Alan Robertson promise her? Her son brought back to life? Eternity without pain? Whatever it was, the Son of Abraham had orchestrated this. Esther hoped they weren't too late to stop it.

REBECCA

REBECCA SANK TO HER KNEES ON THE WOODEN floor. She was supposed to wait until sundown. If she opened the circle now, would it be wasted? Would the Ceannaire be displeased? If she waited, would those who were coming here interrupt? Would they take her away and destroy her chance at eternity? What was the right answer?

Quiet, my child, quiet. You've done no wrong. You are in no danger.

"Father...what do I do?" Rebecca whispered. The Ceannaire's face appeared before hers, his hazy form sitting cross-legged inches from her.

Let me in, child. Let me in.

For a moment the Ceannaire's eyes went entirely blank. A wave of fear washed over Rebecca. She had the hunting knife in her desk, the black salt and chalk. She had held the blade to her wrist many times before, trying to work up the courage to draw it across her skin, trying to imagine the pain. She was overcome with a sudden crashing doubt.

"Father, I'm scared," she said softly.

Your son is waiting for you.

Suddenly, the Ceannaire's face began to change. The features morphed and melted, becoming indistinguishable. They began to reset, reshaping and reforming until Toby sat across from her, his hazel eyes bright, a peaceful smile on his perfect lips. Rebecca felt tears on her cheeks. Toby reached up one hand as though to wipe them away, but his touch was invisible against her skin. The fissure that had separated her heart and soul was healed. She felt a sense of calm she had not felt since that terrible day all those years ago.

"Hi, Mom," he whispered softly.

"Baby," she murmured, a sob choking her throat.

"We'll be together soon, Mom. You just need to let him in," Toby whispered. But the voice was wrong; it had a raspy, polluted quality, an inhuman hum to the words.

"This isn't real," Rebecca said, anger rising in her gut. "This isn't real. You aren't my son."

He smiled, and the grin widened and then melted as the features began to shift and move once again. The faceless creature sat before her dressed in the last thing Toby had worn. It was a mockery, an insult. Why would the Ceannaire do this to her? He had promised she would be reunited with Toby, that he would take away her pain. But she felt more pain in this moment than she had in any of the days she had sat by Toby's bedside, tubes and wires protruding from his arms and chest. Maybe it had been a lie. Maybe this pain was eternal and Toby was long lost to her.

The figure shifted again and changed back into the Ceannaire, but his face was agitated, his eyes intense.

You are losing time, child. You need to let me in.

"Father, why would you show me that? That wasn't my son...If I could only see him." She felt, for the first time since the night he had appeared to her, a measure of fear. What if this had been false? What if she had believed a lie?

They will be upon you any moment. You have to let me in.

Rebecca heard the roar of the helicopter as it descended onto the landing pad in the field out behind the observatory. She rose to her feet, her legs shaking so much she was surprised they held her weight. She needed to make a decision. Not knowing if the Ceannaire was false or if her son was nothing more than a memory, she pulled the hunting knife and small jar of supplies from her desk. The roar of the helicopter blades stilled, and she heard voices through the trees. They were walking to her now; she had only moments. Clumsily, she drew the outline of the circle, just the way the Ceannaire had taught her. She murmured the words he had made her memorize.

"Éist liom trasna."

They made no sense to her, just sounds, an ancient language that spoke only to those beyond the veil. Rebecca took the foul-smelling oil and frantically rubbed it on her exposed skin, then followed with the thick grains of salt, covering her neck and wrists. She could hear her heart as it frantically beat against the confines of her chest. This would purify her and hold the energy within the circle. Her blood would create the door through which the Ceannaire would enter. A sharp knock at the office door nearly made her drop the salt. Rebecca gasped for air. Her lungs felt as though they were folding in on themselves.

"Rebecca? It's Mia Lander. Can we come in?"

Rebecca heard the familiar voice. She resisted the urge to run to the door, beg for help, tell whomever stood on the other side to take her away, far away from this lie she had created for herself. Instead, she methodically lined the circle with the black chalk and, once it had been sealed, took the hunting knife from its sheath.

40

ESTHER

THE WOMAN BEFORE HER WAS THE FLESHED-OUT version of the rough sketch from her vision. Rebecca Parker stood in the center of the room, in what Esther knew to be a circle drawn from chalk and salt, sealed with ancient words and curses. Rebecca stood with a black-bladed knife in her right hand. Esther could see she was shaking. The two agents stepped carefully into the room. Esther and Cooper hung back. She saw Cooper quietly press the record button on his body camera. *Traitor.* Anger flashed through her. *All that bullshit about not glorifying my father, not here for the story.*

"Beck, you okay?" Lander said in a gentle tone. "What are you doing with that knife?"

"Hi, Mia," Rebecca said in a small voice. She was defeated. Esther saw it in every muscle in her body. Her father had taken this woman's grief and used it to control her all these years, and now he would ride the wave of her depair into this world to cause more destruction.

"Rebecca, I'm Carl Flagston. I came here to see you from Denver. Can we talk?" Agent Flagston edged slightly closer, his hands at his side. "Can you put that knife down?"

Rebecca shook her head. "It's too late," she said so softly, Esther had to lean in to hear.

"Rebecca?" Esther said loudly and clearly. The two agents shot her looks intended to keep her quiet, but Esther knew there was very little they would be able to do to stop this woman. "Rebecca, I'm Esther Robertson. My father is Alan Robertson."

At that, Rebecca broke from her haze and looked up with a mixture of fear and fascination.

"The Ceannaire?" she said questioningly.

"Yes," Esther said soothingly. "Your Ceannaire is my father."

"He promised me that he would reunite me with my Toby. He killed the one responsible for his death. He guided me... he loves me." Rebecca looked down at the knife. "I'm so afraid of letting him down."

Esther stepped past the two agents. As she did, Flagston hissed at her to stop. She blocked him out and kept going until she was at the edge of the circle.

"I know he did. My father makes many promises. You know who I am?"

Rebecca nodded.

"Rebecca, listen to me. He lies." Esther reached out a hand. "Give me the knife. We can keep you safe."

Rebecca shook her head violently. "He promised me my son. He promised me that I would hold special counsel in the world to come."

"He cannot do either of those things. My father holds no sway in the next world. That belongs to the Bandia Marbh, and he cannot speak to her. He knows some magic that seems like miracles, but he uses it for destruction, for death. He has killed so many. He cares very little for your pain." Esther slowly sat. Rebecca sank to her knees and cradled the knife to her chest. The woman began sobbing, emitting deep, racking noises that sounded as though she were dying.

"He's right here. He says you are a demon and that you are false. He says he loves me." Rebecca looked past Esther to a vision only she could see. Esther felt the tiny hairs on the back of her neck rise.

"Maybe I am a demon—I have the blood of my aunt, the ruler of the Night Forest, in my veins—but I am no liar. I do not want anything from you, except for you to stop listening to empty threats, for you to put the knife down and come with us. We will help you."

Rebecca looked at Esther, her grief palpable. "That day, the day it happened, I sat at the school gate. Everyone was waiting for their kids. They came running out in groups, and then one by one, and then there were just a few of us left, and the police and the ambulances, and the cameras...oh god, the cameras...I think I knew then he was gone, you know? I think I knew. Even when they told me he was alive, that he was being taken to the hospital, I knew he was gone. I felt him leave, I think I did." She looked imploringly at Esther, her eyes now dry. "I would give anything in this world to see him one last time, anything at all."

"I understand that," Esther said softly and held out her hand. "My father killed my sister and my mother. I still see them when I sleep. I know what it is like to want to erase what has happened. I know what grief is."

Rebecca tentatively took one hand off the knife and reached out to lay it flat against Esther's. "I would give anything," she repeated with an icy resolve in her voice, and Esther knew she had lost her.

Rebecca pulled her hand back and stood to her full height.

Esther fell backward. She screamed, but it was lost in the cacophony that overtook the room. The two agents rushed the circle, and Cooper yelled something Esther couldn't understand. She felt him pull her back. The roar of a gunshot echoed through the room, and Esther saw Rebecca fall to the ground, still in the circle. Blood seeped through a wound in her thigh. As though in slow motion, the woman raised the hunting knife and brought it straight into her neck. Thick black blood sprayed into the air, which took on a charge that sent shock waves across the floor. Agent Lander tried to pull Rebecca from the circle but was stopped by an invisible barrier. It threw her backward and into a metal table.

"It's too late," Flagston shouted, motioning Esther and Cooper out the door.

Esther watched in fascination as a hazy image of her father rose from the blood that pooled within the confines of the circle of chalk and salt. He wore the last thing she had seen him in as a child, loose cotton pants and a tunic. His hair was long and unkempt, his eyes were vacuous orbs. He locked his gaze on Esther and smiled.

Hello, daughter. His lips never moved, but the sound swirled in space.

Esther wordlessly shook her head. She had renounced him long ago. This was not her father; this was as close to the devil as existed in the waking world.

You should run. Alan Robertson's voice swept through the four figures in the room like a gust of wind, and it was then that Esther smelled the smoke and, with a great hacking cough, realized that soot was already raining in through the open windows.

Run! the voice screamed, and Esther scrambled to her feet, taking one look back at the thing that had been her father. Flagston was pulling Lander from the floor. Her forehead was bleeding. Cooper pushed Esther out the open door.

"For fuck's sake! Run!" Cooper yelled as he took off for the helicopter that was already hovering in the air. A wall of fire washed toward them from the far hill. The sound was deafening. Esther forced her legs to move. They had only moments before it would be upon them. Flagston and Lander stumbled out after her, but Esther was already in motion.

Cooper reached the helicopter first, as the fire licked at the YVO cabin. He held out his hand, pulling Esther forward and roughly throwing her into the helicopter. He then paused to reach out for the struggling agents. Flagston pulled Lander along. *She seems disoriented*, Esther thought distractedly. Lander fell backward, her head gushing blood. Flagston reached back for her as the fire raced up the hill to the helicopter.

"I have to take off!" the pilot barked.

Cooper jumped up into the chopper. Esther reached out to pull him in. They looked at each other. Flagston was pulling a now unconscious Lander along, feet from the helicopter.

"Now!" The pilot sounded frantic. The heat was overwhelming. Esther felt the smoke and soot burning her lungs. She gasped for breath, but Flagston's terrified face shook her from her frozen state. She jumped across Cooper and leaned out as far as she could go.

"C'mon!" she screamed. Flagston reached out for her hand. The fire was surrounding them. The entire forest was ablaze. In a moment that seemed to stretch forever, Flagston hauled Lander close enough that Esther could grab one hand and Cooper the other. Flagston clambered on board as they hauled her dead weight into the helicopter. They soared straight up, Esther falling back and nearly out the open hatch. Below them, the forest was already decimated. An electrical sizzling emanated from the YVO cabin just as the helicopter spun out of the fire zone. Esther saw a spray of fire and debris rise into the air, the air pressure from the explosion knocking the helicopter forward. For a terrifying moment, they swung madly about trying to regain balance.

"Jesus, Lander?" Flagston was checking the agent for a pulse.

"She's alright, just unconscious," Esther said, gently lifting his shaking hand away and then wrapping Lander's head in a bandage she'd pulled from the first aid kit.

"We were too late," Esther said softly.

"What happens next?" Cooper asked, his voice small and distant.

Esther looked back at the raging fire, which was sending apocalyptic plumes of smoke into the sky.

"I wish I knew."

COOPER

THE FOREST FIRE WAS RAPIDLY SPREADING AND HAD already destroyed hundreds of acres by the time Cooper, Esther, and Flagston found themselves back in Bozeman. An ambulance met them at the airport, the siren's screams becoming fainter by the second as they transported Lander to the university hospital. Cooper had managed one call to his producer. She had argued with him, telling him he was hysterical and not making any sense. Cooper hoped she at least heard his warning before he hung up.

"Broadcast the footage. Tell everyone who will listen to evacuate, to get as far from Yellowstone as possible. Tell them to run."

He had sent the footage of the unbelievable sight in the YVO cabin. Cooper hadn't reviewed it; he had just uploaded it in the Bozeman office and hit send. It might show nothing, or it might prompt people to get the hell out.

"Where would they go?" Esther had asked, standing in the corner of the Bozeman office with an accusing look on her pale face. Cooper didn't have an answer. He understood what was likely to happen next. There was no safe place. Thousands of miles surrounding not just Yellowstone but the whole of Wyoming would be destroyed straight out, and then what happens? The world chokes to death on the ash and soot?

"You said you weren't going to glorify him," Esther had said quietly, her voice tinged with anger.

"I'm not. I need people to believe this is real. I need people to get out now," Cooper had answered, knowing it sounded like a weak defense.

Esther had walked away to wait with the others as the plane was refueled so they could take off again. But where? Denver wasn't far enough away.

Cooper sat once again in the small prop plane, the sky clogged with thick, black smoke from what had been reported as the worst forest fire in history. They had failed, and he was faced with the fact that everything he had ever thought possible was wrong. He had seen Robertson rise from that woman's blood. He had seen the bastard. But that was impossible; Alan Robertson was locked in a cell in Denver. Magic didn't exist, neither did evil or God or the devil. Cooper had made his life reporting facts, not the impossible, and he was not about to start believing in fairy tales.

But that didn't change what he had seen.

"Cooper?" Esther leaned forward. He could see dark circles under her eyes.

"Yeah?" he replied, looking up from his reverie.

"When we land in Denver, where will you go?" Esther asked softly.

"I'm heading out to the East Coast, and I want to see you on a plane to San Francisco." He felt a paternal tug of fear for the girl. She had been so fearless back in the cabin. He'd had to fight the urge to rush forward and pull her away from that crazy bat.

"I have to stay in Denver. I have to try to talk to my father," Esther responded and then tilted her gaze up at him. "I guess this means you finally believe that I had nothing to do with Los Angeles?"

Cooper sighed and rubbed his temples. "Look, I don't know what I believe anymore, but I've seen enough over the last few days to know that you are not responsible for anything your father has done." He paused. "Do you know what he means when he says you will speak for him?"

Esther leaned back, took a sip of water, and looked up at the sky. "Yes. I do."

Cooper waited, watching her mentally sort out the words. Finally she spoke, her voice barely audible.

"He thinks he can use me to talk to his sister—Ceit Robertson. But Ceit hasn't existed for years. She died that night that Sinder Avenue burned."

"I always knew he killed her," Cooper said, feeling a small spark of vindication. "I always—"

"Not in the way you think," Esther cut him off. "Alan Robertson had very little to do with it. He couldn't have harmed her if he'd tried. You do remember what happened to my grandfather, don't you? And she was only a child then."

Cooper nodded. Boyd Healy Robertson was a vegetable in an Inglewood nursing home when Los Angeles had been bombed. He hadn't survived. From all accounts, he had been in a comatose state every since his attempt on Ceit Robertson's life all those years ago. Cooper shivered. Daughters weren't safe from their own fathers in this family, not by far.

"Yeah, I know the story," Cooper said gently.

"Ceit Robertson abandoned her mortal form that night on Sinder Avenue. She is the ruler of the Night Forest, the next world, the Bandia Marbh, goddess of the dead." Esther gave him a sardonic smile. "Sorry you asked, aren't you?"

Cooper shook his head. "I like fairy tales. I just don't want to live in one. Pretending this is true, why does he think you will speak for him?"

Esther gave him that same humorless grin. *Jesus, she must be exhausted*, Cooper thought.

"My father told you that nonsense story about the Gef, the earthbound spirit? He believes that she cast him out of the next world. She will not speak to him, and so he believes he needs me to be his voice." Esther closed her eyes and stretched her arms out in front of her.

Cooper was confused. That weird folktale made no sense then or now.

"So why you? You make it sound like that's not true. Is it?" Cooper queried, feeling increasingly delirious. All this talk of fantasy and superstition made him feel disconnected from the reality they were facing.

"In my father's wormy little brain, you see, he thinks I can communicate with Ceit Robertson because he believes I have the same demon blood. I carry the same curse—if you want to call it that—that followed all the women in my family back to my great-great-grandmother Ainsley in Ireland. I don't know all the stories. He only hinted at them, and my mother was never privy to it all. Is it true? Who knows. It doesn't really matter, does it? Alan Robertson thinks it is, and you've seen that he can obviously do things normal human men shouldn't be able to do," Esther said.

Cooper tried to wrap his head around what the girl was saying. "He's insane."

"No doubt," Esther responded. "But that doesn't make him wrong. I might carry the curse in me. I might be more closely connected to the Bandia Marbh than him. He might be right—he may need me to be his voice. However, I have no intention of bartering a deal on his behalf."

"So why all this?" Cooper waved his hands. "Why kill tens of thousands of people? Why destroy? Why is he doing this?"

"You've followed him for years, before I was born. You followed him back in the nineties, when he was living on Sinder Avenue. He asked to talk to you personally. Why do *you* think he is doing this?" Esther's voice contained a challenge.

Cooper sat up. "Okay, I get you. I'm the 'most trusted voice in journalism,' star investigative reporter. I must have a theory, right? I must know something." Cooper paused, faced with the biggest insecurity of his entire existence, the single thing that kept him convinced someone would find out he wasn't really a reporter, that he didn't know what he was doing, that he was just impersonating an actual journalist. "Truth is, and I've never said this out loud to anyone before..."

"I'm honored," Esther said, raising her water glass.

"Truth is, I have no fucking idea." Cooper's voice cracked sightly. Esther stared at him. A dark laugh born of exhaustion and complete emotional depletion overtook both of them. Flagston stirred from his sleep and glanced at them, confused, before he closed his eyes again.

"Alright, Cooper Carlson, 'most trusted voice in journalism in the Western world,' I'll give you the scoop of a lifetime. You ready?" Esther said, her light eyes seemed to be glowing in the dark of the plane.

"Go for it," Cooper said as he sat back.

"He told you he was trying to get someone's attention, didn't he?" Esther asked.

"Yeah, but that made no sense," Cooper responded.

"It doesn't, if you're talking a living, mortal person. He's trying to get Ceit Robertson's attention. He thinks if he disrupts this world enough and she is forced to open the veil so wide as to allow in the not just tens of thousands, but millions that will die if he succeeds—then he can take the throne. He needs me to get him in, barter his passage. Once there, he thinks himself strong enough to usurp the goddess of the Night Forest." Esther grinned.

"Ah, fuck me. That headline will be a real bitch." Cooper sighed, then paused. "You're serious, aren't you? Your father said as much when I interviewed him too. Alright, going on the theory that any of this actually exists and we aren't just dealing with a garden-variety madman, can he do that?"

Esther shrugged. "My father has some of the skills that his sister possessed when she was on this earth, but none of the true magic. He doesn't understand where it comes from. He has been angry for most of his life, and he blames everyone but himself. It doesn't really matter if you believe. You have seen what he is capable of, and you know what he will do next." Esther looked out the window. "We're almost to Denver. I'm staying, are you?"

Cooper took a deep breath. "What makes you think you can talk to Ceit Robertson?"

Esther smiled again. "I already have."

42

ESTHER

COOPER'S FOOTAGE FROM WYOMING WAS EVERY-where by the time they landed. They were met by a CBS team, and there were a dozen other news crews outside the landing strip. Cooper put his arm around Esther protectively as they rushed past the cameras and into the town car sent by CBS. Esther had flinched but then allowed him this paternal moment. He was worried about his own daughter. Ever since her last lucid dream, and the visions shown to her by Ceit Robertson, Esther felt different. She could see the shape of other people's thoughts—not quite a literal translation of them, but more the intent. She had purposefully eschewed any notions of telepathy or psychic sensitivity before; she had enough in her life that isolated her. But now it was unstoppable. She could see Cooper's carefully masked panic wrapping itself around him like a string of dark smoke. He ushered her into the car as cameras flashed and questions were shouted.

Flagston waved as they headed out. He was met by a host of other agents, and would meet them at the detention center. The reporters, seeing that they had lost Esther and Cooper, took off in his direction. He artfully ducked into another black town car before they could swoop entirely.

Esther was anxious to get to her father. She had to try to reach him. *Maybe it isn't too late to stop this*, she thought.

Cooper looked as though he were deep in a puzzle. His confusion emanated off of him in waves.

Esther regarded him carefully for a moment, but as the car pulled out onto I-70, she ventured a question. "You're wondering about something?"

"Since everything else impossible has turned out to be true, I suppose I'm questioning my memory," Cooper said, his voice detached. Esther just nodded, hoping he would continue.

"I don't remember leaving Utah. I mean, I remember leaving, and I remember driving to Denver, but not the way everyone said it happened." Cooper paused. "I . . . I was, I don't know, kidnapped? Arrested? Taken by two people who said they were officers—FBI and a detective. They told me he wanted an audience. They called him their 'father.' Time . . . it moved. I was in one place, and then I was at the FCI. Their fingers were . . . I don't know how to describe it . . . they were *off*. I guess I thought it was all a dream. I mean, what else could it have been?" Cooper looked at her, and for the first time, Esther saw genuine fear in his eyes.

"Are you sure they were people?" Esther asked, trying to keep her voice level.

"No. I'm not actually. If that was real, and not some sort of fucked-up dream, I'm not at all sure they were people. But what does that make Alan Robertson then?" Cooper asked, his voice distant.

"I don't know. But you know the history of Sinder Avenue. You were part of the surveillance on the Society all those years ago.

You know there are stranger things in heaven and earth than can possibly be explained by the FBI." Esther watched the man for a moment. "I have a question of my own."

"I hope I have an answer for it," Cooper said, giving her a small smile.

"Flagston told me the first time we met that my father was poisoned when he was in the Florence supermax prison. He said it was cyanide."

"Yeah, he was. I have a contact down there, and he can usually be believed. He said Alan Robertson ate an entire plate of cyanide-laced food and walked away without a single consequence. My contact said the guard was in on it. Could've been anyone really. He was rather unpopular, as you can imagine. They had him in isolation, so it could have been the guard who brought the food, the kitchen crew, anyone." Cooper stretched and yawned.

"He didn't die," Esther said flatly. "He should have been dead in minutes. Even if he had a single bite, he'd have been hospitalized." Esther framed her question carefully. "So why didn't he die?"

"A true mystery of science and nature," Cooper answered. His voice held light sarcasm. "I can only say that, according to my guy, there was enough poison in that food to kill a dozen men, and Alan Robertson walked away from it. Only reason anyone even found out about it was the poor sap in the kitchen who washed his plate got sickened and taken to the infirmary, then someone ratted it out. Whoever did it expected Robertson dead, you see. When he didn't die, they spread the word he was some sort of devil or something. They actually moved him to Englewood early because the inmates were threatening to riot. Turns out quite a few of them lost people in Los Angeles. There was too big a price on his head."

"He didn't die," she repeated, her mind circling. "What does Alan Robertson want more than anything?"

"He wants power, control," Cooper answered, leaning forward.

"Why you?" Esther was thinking out loud. "You're a reporter, not a president or a king. You don't control anything but—"

"The media," Cooper finished. "Holy shit, I think I just saw how we can stop this. Or delay it at least." Cooper took out his cell and began madly texting someone.

Esther realized immediately what Cooper's plan was—a feature story with cameras, broadcast live. A chance for her father to tell his story, a chance for recognition. She shivered. The idea of giving him a stage made vomit rise in her throat. He would use it to rally his followers, and god knew what else. But Cooper was right, they could dangle logistics, planning, preparation of a telecast in front of him and maybe, just maybe, delay what might already be inevitable. Maybe they could evacuate as much of the area as possible, figure out a way to stop him. Esther shivered again. She knew the only way to stop him. As long as he drew breath, no one was safe.

COOPER

BY THE TIME THE TOWN CAR PULLED UP TO THE FCI facility, Cooper felt feverish with renewed intent. He had frantically explained the plot to the Denver CBS office and also CBS central in a combined conference call. He had also managed to text Flagston that he needed an audience with Robertson as soon as possible. Esther had watched him quietly the entire time. She retained her pensive silence until they were through security and in the elevator heading to Flagston's office.

"What aren't you saying?" Cooper asked while madly checking his phone. CBS would need to start sending equipment as soon as possible, and he needed Bill, who should have gotten in from Utah by now. He also needed his archive research, which meant the San Francisco office would need to send the file in the next hour. There was a lot to plan in a short time, and Esther's passive-aggressive stare was grating.

"You are missing the point," she said.

"The point?" Cooper responded distractedly. The Denver producer had just messaged that a full crew, including Bill, was on the way, and she was talking to the network about an emergency time slot in the prime hour.

"You can delay this, maybe. But you can't stop it until he's dead." Esther's voice was cold.

Cooper looked up from his phone. The elevator opened, but neither of them moved.

"You're suggesting that I . . ." Cooper began.

"Kill him," Esther said bluntly. "He will love the idea of this interview. As soon as you can get close enough to him, kill him. End it."

The elevator door started to close as curious faces walked past looking in. Cooper let it close and then hit the stop button. "I'm not a killer, Esther. That's your father."

"But you'd watch him kill the world," Esther stated, no question in her voice.

Cooper felt his whole body grow tense. She was right, he knew it, but if he killed Alan Robertson, if he even could, what did that make him? A hero? A monster? If he didn't, what would Alan Robertson become?

"How would I even do it? You're talking about a guy who ate an entire plate of cyanide and walked away from it." Cooper looked at her. "What could I possiby do? Launch across the table and take him on with my bare hands? Even if every agent in this building didn't stop me, I couldn't, I just couldn't."

"Get a knife, or a gun, or a rock or a stick. Jesus, he will kill all of us, interview or not." Esther's voice held an edge he had never heard before. It sent gooseflesh across his skin.

"I can't, Esther. Even if there was a way to get a weapon in there—which there isn't, I might point out. Even if there was a way to get every single agent in this building to look the other way. Even if I thought I could do anything before Alan Robertson made me eat my own tongue or shoot myself with my own gun, I couldn't. I just cannot do it." Cooper hit the Door Open button and strode out toward Flagston's office, where he could see that the agent had returned. He turned around to see Esther still standing where he had left her, and he knew that even if he was not capable of killing Alan Robertson, his daughter most certainly was.

44

ESTHER

THE TRANSITION TO THE MEADOW WAS NEARLY effortless this time. Esther had feigned a headache and asked for a place to lie down. Once she had locked herself into what looked like an unused office, Esther had lain down on the stiff sofa and crossed the veil before her eyes were even entirely shut.

The edges of the forest were closer than ever before, and the strange little creature with the bark-colored skin and twig-like fingers was waiting, its too-big eyes watching her curiously. Esther nodded to it and followed it through the ancient trees, her feet finding their way even as the canopy of leaves blocked out what little light came from the moonless sky. As before, Esther could sense the presence of the Bandia Marbh even before the gentle glow of the light began filtering through the branches. Ceit Robertson stood in the center of the clearing, waiting.

As Esther approached, Ceit turned and motioned for her to follow. Wordlessly, Esther followed. They crossed through more forest, but beneath her feet, Esther detected a narrow path.

Stepping-stones lined the forest; she could see glimpses of deep-red stone. The forest gave way to another sprawling meadow, and beyond that a rocky beach flanked by black ocean waters.

Esther gasped. "It's... it's Venice..."

Ceit nodded, staring out at the sea and its angry waves. "This is where the Society would congregate on the night of the new moon when I was their Matrarc and with Mór Ainsley before me. The elders would sit on this sand and chant the words they believed held reverence to the Night Forest."

"What happened to the Society?" Esther asked softly, staring out at the tide. She jumped slightly at the sight of a scaled and sharpened tail skimming the surface of the water and then disappearing below.

Ceit smiled at her reaction. "The Asrai. They will not harm you. You are my guest here, and it would be rude." She looked back out at the sea. "The Society never should have come to this shore. My great-grandmother had good intentions, but she brought the rot of the old world with her when she boarded that boat back in Cork. She made a deal with a very dangerous demon, a deal she did not entirely understand."

"I think I was very up-front," a smooth male voice intoned from behind Esther.

She jumped again, her heart racing. Behind her stood a tall creature with not entirely human features. His skin was as pale as starlight, his eyes devoid of color. Inside their depths, planets turned and stars were born and died. He wore torn skinny jeans, calf-high chunky Dr. Martens boots, and a "skinny puppy" T-shirt with artful rips to the neckline. Silver chains and leather chokers lined his slender neck. Esther stood stock-still, mesmerized by the sight.

"Amon," Ceit admonished from behind Esther. "You do know how to make an entrance. My apologies, Esther. Amon said he would try to appear as something you would recognize, not this...what is this, Amon?"

"My favorite fashion decade, my liege." He nodded gracefully and stepped toward Esther, taking her hand and planting a kiss on her knuckle. Her skin burned slightly from his lips.

"Things are rather dire out there," Amon said simply, coming to stand beside her to look out at the water.

"You have to stop him," Esther said, looking from Ceit to Amon. "He is going to kill everyone. You have to help me."

Ceit came to stand on the other side of Esther. The three of them gazed out across the inscrutable ocean, watching the Asrai jump and deftly disappear beneath the waves.

"You asked what became of the Society," Ceit spoke softly. Esther noticed a line of bats perched on the tops of the trees closest to the water, as though they were holding audience.

"After I crossed the veil and left behind the destruction my brother had brought upon the cul-de-sac, they died off, as I knew they would. I welcomed them here, and they have long since passed through my world and on to the next. Some went on to live in your world for years. Your grandparents, Meg's mother and father, were quite alive until the Los Angeles tragedy. You never knew them," she said it as fact, not a question.

"My mother told me they had died before I was born," Esther whispered.

"I expect she thought that was true. Your mother was a good soul. I am deeply sorry for the troubles my brother brought her." Ceit turned and took Esther's hand. "I made a grievous error in the time after the tragedy. I did not know it then."

"I wouldn't call it an error. More like a choice," Amon spoke in Esther's ear. His breath smelled of fresh earth.

"It was an error, Amon. I denied my brother passage to the Night Forest. I cast him out to the Sluagh, knowing he would live an eternity walking the planes of your world with the restless and unforgiven souls. His physical form would lose its solidity with every passing decade, until one day he would be no more than a trapped thought, a lost memory. I cursed him to never find the peace of moving to this world. He would be trapped in his misery for eternity." Ceit nodded as she turned her gaze back to the sea. She smiled as an Asrai twisted upward, its barbed spine rolling gracefully back into the water. "I made an error. I thought it best at the time, given what he had done. But he has gone on to cause so much more harm."

"You are still far too sentimental, my liege," Amon spoke. "You see, Esther, to my mind, your world is a fresh hell and this is the paradise. Hastening your arrival to this plane? Your father should be sainted."

Ceit looked at the demon and then at Esther. "It's not senti-mentality. He is destroying the balance, interjecting himself into the natural order. He seeks to sit in my chair. He wants to be the Ceannaire of the Night Forest because he thinks there once was a man who ruled this realm. But he is wrong—it has always been me. No matter how much pain he causes, no matter how many souls he sends me, he cannot rule this world."

"I have to stop him," Esther pleaded. "I have to end it."

"How do you propose to do that, little one?" Amon ran a thin finger through Esther's hair, making gooseflesh rise on the back of her neck.

"I have to kill him," Esther said.

Ceit turned to look at her neice, and a sad smile sat on her lips.

"You cannot kill what is already dead."

ESTHER

ESTHER STOOD STUNNED. HER SKIN FELT CLAMMY. Her heart seemed to stop beating. She stepped away from the two figures and knelt in the waterline, the icy black water rolling up and over her knees. A curious face appeared from the tide. Its eyes were the slanted lines of a fish. Its hair, thick and dark, wrapped around its form. It reached out with a bony arm and claws that held razor talons. Esther stared back at the creature with no fear. Everything was real; nothing was imagined. Nightmares were just the beginning.

"When?" she asked, knowing the answer.

"Alan Robertson died in Los Angeles on November 17, 2012. He was home with your mother and sister. I welcomed them through my gates along with the others, but I barred Alan Robertson's passage to this world." Ceit sat down silently next to Esther.

"He's been dead this whole time?" Esther could feel her blood pounding. "But he has a body. He is in jail. He has flesh and eyes, and he talks and eats."

"Yes," said Amon from behind her. "And he will continue to do so for quite a long time. He will feel cold and hunger. He will feel pain and loneliness. As time passes, he will become less and less substantial. Such is the way of the Sluagh."

"The Sluagh that attacked my mother, that killed Mór Ainsley, were ancient spirits. Your father is young, but those that roam the earth as wisps of dark smoke were also as your father is now for a time. It was my belief he would quietly fade away. But I was wrong." Ceit took Esther's hand. "I cannot help you stop him. What has been set in motion cannot be stopped. I told you to try, but do not fault yourself. You were brave and strong. You are of my blood."

"And mine," Amon said, placing his hands on her shoulders. "You have a family here in the Night Forest, Esther. You will find everything you lack. Stay with us."

Esther turned to look them in their unearthly eyes. "Soon I will. But I have to try."

Ceit nodded. "We will be here. Our arms are open. You have a family—you have a place you belong."

With a tearing sensation to simply melt into the arms of the Night creatures, Esther forced herself back into the waking world. Outside the door, she could hear frantic activity and knew that it would soon be too late to save anyone.

46

COOPER

COOPER SQUINTED AT THE BRIGHT STUDIO LIGHTS and nodded. The CBS crew was nearly done with the setup. Basic lights, rough sound system, and a skeleton crew of producers and production assistants. Bill sat in a rough metal chair, staring at Cooper with weary eyes.

"You have opinions," Cooper said as he adjusted the tiny microphone attached to his collar.

"Yes, I have opinions," Bill said. "You want to hear them?"

"Not particularly," Cooper responded as a PA flashed him a signal that they had fifteen minutes until showtime.

"Too bad, you get 'em anyway," Bill said, standing and rolling his head back and forth, cracking his neck. "I think you need to sleep on this, like actually sleep. You look like shit. That's opinion number one. Number two is while you are sleeping, you need to really ask yourself what the hell you are doing. Have you even turned on the news since that footage from Wyoming hit the air? About three quarters are saying it's some kind of hoax. The rest are building bunkers in their backyards and framing photos of you as the new messiah. And that's not even taking into account all the crank calls we've been getting from people declaring themselves followers of the 'Son of Abraham.' This is a dog whistle, dude, and whether you mean to or not, you are sending a huge flare up for all those crackpots. They *want* to see this guy. They are waiting for it. I should play you some of the recordings. They seemed to know that this interview was happening way before you blew up everyone's phones demanding it."

Cooper took a long look at Bill. "You remember our first broadcast all those years ago? The first shots from Los Angeles?"

Bill shook his head. "You aren't listening to a single word I'm saying, dude."

"I am," Cooper said firmly. "Do you remember that very first broadcast, the first report as soon as we left Lancaster and hit the city limits?"

"Yeah, I remember. Jesus, how would anyone forget?" Bill replied, his voice softer.

"You said the same thing—a dog whistle, a signal to the crazies. You told me to be careful," Cooper said.

"Your point?" Bill replied, but the ice in his voice was gone.

"I'm being careful. You just have to trust me. This guy doesn't need me to be his flare. I have no idea how, but he's way past me. I'm buying time."

"Time for what?" Bill asked.

"I don't know." Cooper sighed. "I suppose I hope that they can evacuate the areas that will be hardest hit. Maybe we can stop Robertson from doing anything at all. Maybe he'll just, Jesus...I don't know."

"You know, they haven't found any evidence of explosives or any human interference whatsoever in Dallas, Utah, or Wyoming.

It's horrible, and unthinkable, and totally fucking natural. I'm seriously questioning your mental health, man. And if I hadn't been your partner for what? A couple of decades? I would be walking the hell away from this." Bill shook his head. Cooper could see the frustration rolling off him in waves.

"I know it doesn't make sense. You have to trust me," Cooper said quietly.

Bill just nodded, a thousand words still unspoken, but Cooper knew he would stay with him, guide him the way he always had.

"Alright, Coop, we're getting ready to roll. We are prepping Robertson. He understands the rules, as do you, I hope." Flagston was hyped on a whole new pot of coffee, his anxiety distracted for the moment by all the activity.

"Yeah, just like the last time, except with better lighting," Cooper quipped.

Flagston gave him a look. "Something like that."

A production assistant with a makeup kit approached, and Cooper turned to her.

"Make me pretty," he said with a grimace.

As the PA brushed powder over the areas most likely to pick up shine, Flagston repeated the directive for visits. Cooper half listened. He knew the deal, and so did Flagston. It was everyone else who thought there was anything routine about this interview.

"Are we good on sound check?" the producer yelled across the room. Cooper watched the activity as the makeup brush disappeared and the last-minute checks were completed. He loved this part—the moment before he went live, the storm before the calm, the last-minute adjustments and checks, the perfectly orchestrated ballet between the cameras and boom mikes, the fluidity of the staff as they executed last-minute tasks. The air was electric. He had started off as a set grip right out of high school, coiling cable, checking connections, running for more of this and that for the senior grips and PAs. He had been seventeen and totally in love with the smell and sound of a studio. Even here, in a dungeon-like cell in the federal holding facility, he felt it. It was, perhaps, even better when he was out in the field. The constant improvisation of materials, making things work, the miracle when it all did. It was his last broadcast, Cooper knew that without a doubt. This was the last time he would stand here in the midst of all this activity and wait for his chance to speak. Even if he survived, if any of them did, he knew this was the end.

"Where's Esther?" Cooper asked abruptly.

"On the way down. She crashed out for a bit—headache," Flagston said. "You ready to do this?"

"Not really." Cooper gave him a half smile. "Can't see as I have a choice though."

Cooper sat in the chair across from where the Son of Abraham would soon join him. In his pocket, a pointed shard of porcelain scraped against his leg. It wasn't ideal, but it was all he had. He'd rolled a coffee cup off a table, offered to clean up the mess himself. Clumsy really, his mistake. Cooper had no idea if it would be enough, but the look in Esther's eyes as the elevator had closed had shaken him to his core. She was right; no one was safe while Alan Robertson lived.

ESTHER

ESTHER STEPPED OFF THE ELEVATOR AND INTO THE chaos of the hastily thrown together broadcast. Cooper stood across the room talking to Flagston. The air held an electrical buzz, the lights artificially bright. Cooper took his seat at the table while production assistants adjusted his microphone and moved lights back and forth. Next to her, she heard the crackle of a headset.

"He's coming down now. I need to clear this path, Ms. Robertson." A young woman in a black T-shirt took her by the arm. Esther allowed herself to be moved out of the path of the elevator and behind the cameras. Cooper caught her eye and gave her a small nod. Esther felt a stab of panic. She needed to tell him.

"I need a sec with Cooper," Esther said loud enough for all the heads in the room to turn in her direction.

"We have to get going. Now—actually five minutes ago. This is live, and we have network hosts killing time waiting for it," a stressed-looking producer behind the camera muttered.

Esther shoved through anyway. Cooper stood. Esther felt arms at her back, trying to pull her away, but she pushed herself forward. Cooper waved the offending crew away.

"It's okay, just one more minute won't make a difference," Cooper said, his eyes locked on hers.

"Coop, don't do it. I learned something you need to know. You can't kill him, you can't." Esther leaned in as close as she could, trying to whisper.

Cooper gently moved her back and looked down at her with a fatherly concern in his eyes. "I hear you, Esther, I do. But you are right. You've been right all along."

Esther shook her head. "You don't understand. There's so much mor—"

She was cut off by a voice behind her. She turned to see her father flanked by four guards, his wrists and ankles bound.

"Hello, daughter. What a surprise," Alan Robertson said smoothly. His eyes were clear and hollow. He was thinner than he had been even a day ago, when she had seen his image in the cabin in Wyoming. He was already beginning to become insubstantial.

Esther ignored him. "Cooper, I have to tell you something—"

"After. Just trust me, Esther. And I'm sorry for being a Grade A asshole. I've treated you poorly. I wish I had really taken the time to know you before. Get on a plane if you can. Go to Boonsboro. I have a cabin out there. You and my daughter would get along."

Esther felt a well of emotion in her throat. "Cooper...I..."

He leaned in and kissed the top of her head. "After. I have to do this."

With that, Cooper turned and sat across from the Son of Abraham. Esther was pulled back into the darkness, and the cameras began rolling.

COOPER

COOPER CLOSED HIS EYES FOR A MOMENT AND LET the familiar confidence fill his veins. He was in charge; he set the tone. When he opened his eyes, Alan Robertson smiled. Cooper stared back for a long moment.

"Thank you for meeting with us. And thank you to the networks for allowing this interruption. I'm Cooper Carlson, and we are here live with the self-proclaimed Son of Abraham, Alan Robertson. Alan, your group has claimed responsibility for the tragedies in Dallas, Utah, and now Wyoming. Is the claim true?"

Alan Robertson grinned. "Cutting right to it, aren't you, Cooper Carlson? Don't you want to talk about my childhood? What made me the way I am?"

Cooper paused. He normally would never allow a subject to direct the interview this way, but the longer Alan Robertson was in his chair talking to him, the longer he had to figure out how to use the shard in his pocket to end this.

"Okay. Let's talk about your childhood. We know your mother was killed when you were a child," Cooper said neutrally. Bill looked up from the camera and shot him a look. He above all the others knew this was out of Cooper's character to follow a subject's lead this way.

"I was a little boy when the Sluagh ate her soul and left her an empty shell, rotting from the inside out. Do you know what the Sluagh are, Cooper Carlson?" Robertson hissed.

"No, I don't. I know the term from your reports. Tell us, Alan." Cooper kept his voice steady.

"Hungry ghosts. Spirits that walk the earth looking for weak souls. They hunt in packs and walk in solitude, bound to the earth for eternity. They were sent for my sister, but they ate my mother instead. You knew my sister, didn't you, Cooper Carlson?" Robertson's voice was metered, rhythmic.

"Tell us what we don't know, Alan. Tell us, how are you responsible for Dallas? For Hill Air Force Base? For a forest fire in Wyoming? How are you responsible for these tragedies?" Cooper forced steel into his voice. He had to get Alan Robertson to lose control, let his guard down.

"Hungry ghosts, Cooper Carlson. Hungry ghosts. You'd be surprised what you are capable of when you walk the border of this world and the next. Turns out my sister wasn't the only one with a little demon blood in her veins. I have just enough to see the veil, but not enough to cross over. So I have to resort to these gaudy shows of attention. You see, Cooper Carlson, I never got enough attention as a child, so I seek it in inappropriate ways now." Alan Robertson laughed, a low, creeping sound.

Cooper cleared his throat. "What are you planning to do next, Alan?"

"How many people died in Dallas?" Robertson asked, his

voice conversational. In Cooper's earpiece the producer's voice quietly rattled off a number and "try not to engage him in this, he's leading the interview, get it back on track." Cooper nodded at her. He knew the crew was internally panicking. He never lost the tail on an interview, never allowed the subject to control the path. He had built a career out of being unforgiving, solid, driven. Cooper knew full well that he looked like he was floundering. It was utterly impossible to explain to any of them that this was exactly what he wanted. He needed Alan Robertson to get comfortable, to feel like he was in charge, to let his guard down just for a moment. Only Esther would understand what he was doing, and her pale face had disappeared from behind the camera. He wished he could see her right now. She was the closest thing he had to his daughter. *Maybe Esther will make it out after all. She could get on a plane right now, make it out to DC. She and Cecily could ride out this thing together.* Cooper knew he wasn't thinking rationally. He could hear how this would sound should he ever put voice to it.

"Well, how many?" Robertson asked again, a curious smile on his lips.

"There were 3,457 casualties, and there are currently over 300 missing." Cooper paused. "How did you cause a sinkhole? How can we possibly take your claim of responsibility for this seriously? You have no power over nature."

"Do you want to know about the first man I killed? How I popped my cherry, so to speak?" Robertson answered with a question.

In his ear, the producer was madly whispering, "We have a report that there's something happening in Yellowstone basin. Some of the networks are cutting your live feed to cover it. I don't understand, but they're saying some kind of human chain is forming, people holding hands. A protest maybe? No word yet. We're staying with you, but you need to find out if this is connected. Quit dancing around."

"Alan, we just got a report that there's a sort of protest forming around the Yellowstone basin. People, lots of people in fact, forming some sort of wall, a human chain? Do you know about this?" Cooper spoke slowly. As he did, he could see Esther move back into his eyeline. She had a panicked look on her face and was mouthing words that Cooper couldn't understand.

Robertson clanged his wrist chains against the metal table. The sound echoed through the small space, making everyone but Cooper jump. "The first man I killed was a homeless drug addict. I was passed out under one of the canals in Venice. Percocet is a motherfucker. Stay off drugs, Cooper. They'll rot your brain. He came at me, I gutted him. Later I stripped off all my clothes and tried to drown myself. I still had a conscience then. I didn't remember any of it until I died. It's true what they say, Cooper Carlson— your life really does flash before your eyes. But not quickly. No it's slow, like the tide rolling in, each wave a new memory, a new regret. Every day of this hell I remember more, a little bit here, a little bit there. I'll be doing this for eternity if my sister has her way. I plan on interfering, taking back my throne. I will be the Ceannaire of the Night Forest. I shall cast Ceit Robertson out to the Asrai, let the beasts rip the flesh from her bones, if she does, indeed, have any flesh left. She left her mortal body behind so many years ago, you see. She left this plane. You always thought I killed her, didn't you? I didn't then, but I will now. I will cast her out as she did me, let her walk the earth until she becomes as insubstantial as the wind, a foul odor on the air."

The producer's voice in his ear was low and urgent. "Coop, there's reports of mass suicide coming from the area. They are trying to contain it, but, Jesus, they're slitting their own throats.

What the actual fuck is going on?"

Cooper felt his entire body starting to go numb, a shock reaction to panic. He knew exactly what was happening, as did Esther and Flagston. They needed to evacuate the area around the blast zone now. Not that it would matter; if Robertson succeeded, it was only a matter of time before the soot and ash killed the world entire. He had to act now. It was the only chance to stop this. Alan Robertson thought to ride in on the blood of hundreds. The power he would carry with him would be beyond reason. Cooper had to act. He had to move his leaden arms and legs. It was the only way.

He stood, the producer shaking her head, her voice rattling in his ear. Cooper tore the earpiece out and threw it on the table. Bill looked up from the camera, his face full of concern and confusion. Esther was screaming something, but Cooper could not hear anything but the pulse of his blood and the mad beating of his heart. Alan Robertson's pale eyes seemed to reflect all the light in the room back at Cooper; the effect was blinding. As Cooper wrapped his hand around the porcelain shard, he felt the edges cut into his skin. The blood was hot against his hand. He pulled the shard from his pocket and lunged forward, his eyes focused on the soft flesh of Alan Robertson's neck, a cry escaping from his lips.

Cooper felt as though he were falling. He saw Cecily wrapped in a blanket, her newborn cheeks red with the furiosity of birth. He saw Caroline's eyes, smelled the vanilla of her hair, felt the skin at the back of her neck where her whole body would shiver if he kissed her just right. He saw Cecily reaching up to be held, the summer sun filtering behind her. Cecily walking the stage in a robe too big for her. It dragged on the ground, and Cooper heard himself laugh and squeeze Caroline's hand. He saw her as a young woman, her eyes clear, her face set with determination. He felt her in his arms, solid and strong. She would always be okay, he knew that. He saw Esther, all those years ago in San Francisco, her lips blue and eyes haunted. He felt exhaustion as he had never felt before flood his body, his legs giving out under him, his eyes closing of their own volition. He fell into blackness and woke in the comfort of the Night Forest.

49

ESTHER

ESTHER'S SCREAM STUCK IN HER THROAT. COOPER had something in his hand. She tried to scream no, tell him to stop, but it was too late. Alan Robertson laughed as the blade scraped his neck, and as the blood sprayed out, the room erupted. Cooper jerked backward. His eyes rolled up in his head, and he plunged the sharpened point into his gut. With inhuman strength, he pulled the blade upward, blood and flesh spilling out onto the metal table. It had taken seconds to occur, and now time seemed to stop. Around her, the crew and agents moved in slow motion. They rushed toward her father and Cooper. Esther was frozen in one spot. Her father turned his gaze on her, and his pale eyes bored into hers. The wound that Cooper had managed to inflict before her father had wrapped himself around his mind was cursory. Cooper was dead before he hit the floor. Alan Robertson died ten years ago, and even the curse of human suffering was not punishment enough.

Already, Esther could see her father becoming less substantial. He was moving into the circle of hundreds, the human sacrifice he needed to garner enough strength from for his final act of cruelty. Esther forced the air out her lungs and ran toward Alan Robertson.

"You're a fool. You will never gain admission to the Night Forest. Ceit will never give you entry."

Alan Robertson gave her a gentle smile and reached out with a hand, as insubstantial as smoke. "Little one, she will, and you will be my voice. Or you will choke to death on the ash of a dying world. Speak for me, and I'll give you a paradise you can only dream of."

With that, Alan Robertson's form dropped to the floor, but Esther knew his spirit was far away, drinking the blood of hundreds. It was too late; the end had begun.

50

ESTHER

THE MAKESHIFT STUDIO WAS IN CHAOS. PRODUCTION crew and agents rushed to Cooper as guards removed Alan Robertson's still form from the room, the chains still tight around his ankles and wrists. He was apparently unconscious, but Esther knew exactly where he was and what was happening. She ran to a shaken producer who was standing apart from the others, staring at the scene as though in shock.

"I need to see what's happening in Yellowstone." Esther tentatively put a hand on the shaken woman's shoulder, trying to snap her out of her fixed gaze. The producer distractedly nodded to a monitor in the corner.

"There...you can see it there," she whispered. "What the hell just happened?" She looked at Esther desperately, struggling to understand. Medics were circling Cooper now, lifting his body onto a stretcher. Esther could hear distant sirens. All of it had played out live. Cooper's cameraman, his friend, was barking orders at the medics, who were ignoring him entirely. The team moved at a hurried but organized pace out of the room and to the elevator.

"He's dead," Esther said softly. "My father killed him."

"I...I can't . . ." The producer slid down the wall and sat with her knees to her chest, staring straight ahead. Esther paused and then crossed to the monitor and put the headset on.

The footage from the handheld camera was shaky. It showed a line of fallen bodies. Blood seeped into the grass, staining the landscape. Esther was hit by a memory of an old news clip of Guyana from 1978, the footage from the helicopters of the hundreds of bodies, lying so quiet and still, side by side. The reporter who was evidently also the camera operator was narrating the scene.

"We have what appears to be a mass suicide here in the Yellowstone basin. No motive has been uncovered, and there is seemingly no political or social rationale. The only connection that has been made as of yet is that many, perhaps all, of the victims here pledged support to the Son of Abraham mass murderer, Alan Robertson. Again, we do not yet know if this is true for all the victims here. A great many, however, have been found to be members of the Son of Abraham cult, which was responsible for the bombing of Los Angeles ten years ago this week. The group has also claimed responsibiltiy for the tragedies that have rocked our nation in the last few days in Dallas, Hill Air Force Base, and the Yellowstone Caldera. What that connection is exactly, this reporter does not know. I can only show you the scene as it unfolds."

At that, the camera fell to the side, the footage still rolling live. Esther leaned forward, waiting for the reporter's voice. The room was still utter chaos. The agents were circling madly and ushering the CBS crew out the door. Agent Flagston motioned to Esther, who shook her head.

"I need to see this," she mouthed at him over the din. He nodded and said something to the other agents, who continued to move the production crew out toward the elevator. The sirens were moving away from the building now, taking Cooper's lifeless form to a hospital where there would be nothing left to be done. Flagston crossed to her, being careful to skirt the perimeter of the room. There was a sea of blood that spread from the table. Cooper's blood. Esther felt her head swim and shifted her focus back to the monitor. Flagston joined her, pulling on a headset. The camera was back on the unsteady shoulder of the reporter. Esther could see fallen trees now and dust in the air. With horror, she saw a crevice had split the land in two, a jagged line divided the area.

"We are experiencing an earthquake, a strong one. You can see how it has split the soil here, and several trees have fallen. I have received word that power lines are down on the main roads, so please, if you are driving right now and you can hear this, pull to the side of the road. Do not attempt to cross the area. Okay, here we go. We have an aftershock coming...It's a powerful one...It—"

The camera fell to the ground again and the footage cut out, going to static and then back to a stunned anchor sitting behind a news desk. Esther pulled off her headset and looked at Flagston.

"It's starting. There's nothing to be done. They need to evacuate," she said urgently.

"There was no early warning. All the signals that would have come through the YVO were knocked out along with the weather satellites routed through Dallas. They had no warning. They should have detected seismic activity forty-eight hours ago at least, had time to try to get the area clear. They have what? Minutes? Hours?" Flagston shook his head. He was pale, and his hands shook.

"My father didn't want them to have any warning. We knew why he destroyed Dallas and Utah and Wyoming—the perfect triangle of attacks if you were going to kill any chance of a warning system," Esther said. She felt numb and suddenly irrepressibly tired.

"It wouldn't matter anyway," Flagston said, his voice hollow. "Evacuations that is. Earthquakes are first stage. It should take months, but something tells me this is different."

"What happens after the earthquakes?" Esther asked, watching the news anchor talk silently on the screen.

"Mount St. Helens took over two months after the initial earthquakes to form a bulge on the north face of the mountain. When it blew, it obliterated everything in an eight-mile radius. A cloud of ash circled the globe within two weeks." Flagston rattled off the facts as though he were reading them from a page.

"What happens if Yellowstone blows?" Esther asked, already knowing the answer.

"Zone one is approximately fifty miles. Everything in that radius will be destroyed immediately and entirely. By the time the ash spreads, which my guess would be about a week, it'll cover the continental United States. In another two weeks, it will block out the sun around the globe," Flagston said softly and then looked apologetically at Esther. "The office in Bozeman sent over a really fun fact sheet after we landed."

"Blocks out the sun," Esther whispered, stunned.

"Nuclear winter without the nuclear part," Flagston said. "Crops die, global temperatures plummet, weather patterns reverse course. We're dead by the end of the year."

On the screen, the shaky handheld camera footage had returned. Both Esther and Flagston pulled their headphones on. The scene was filled with dust and foggy images. The reporter's voice was distant, and in the background a sort of roaring made him barely audible.

"We've had what I counted as four strong tremors. As you can see, the damage is significant. If you are in the surrounding area, please get to safety. I am reporting that there is a dome forming in the area. It is rising steadily. I have been informed that if you are in the emergency evacuation zone, you need to move now. Evacuate the area and get to the safe zone. This is not a hoax. The last eruption of the Yellowstone supervolcano was six hundred forty thousand years ago. There is no way to determine how or why this is happening, and no explanation for its rapid escalation. I'm evacuating now, and we're cutting back to the station."

Flagston turned to Esther, his eyes glazed. "According to the info Bozeman sent, Yellowstone is in a caldera, a sunken hole. It should take years even to rise to a dome before any of this begins. This doesn't make any sense. It doesn't work like this."

The screen flashed to the stunned anchor, who stared into the camera for a moment before she began to speak.

"Thank you, Ted. And as our field reporter Ted Carrington stated, do not delay. If you are in the emergency evacuation zone, you need to leave immediately. This is entirely unprecedented, and without explanation. I have with us the head of the Yellowstone Volcano Observatory, Dr. Wynn Sanders. Dr. Sanders, can you tell us what is happening and what to expect?"

Esther felt a rush of nausea. Cooper's blood smelled metallic and rancid. She retched, and Flagston caught her before she fell from the metal chair.

"Let's get out of here. I can show you exactly what Dr. Wynn Sanders is going to say in my office." Flagston pulled Esther to her feet. She remembered Cooper's arm around her as they exited the airplane, his directive to go to his cabin in Boonsboro. She'd spent most of her adult life hating him, seeing him as an invasive species, a pariah. She had killed him. She had sent him to his death, and hadn't even been able to stop anything from happening. As Flagston pulled her out the door to the elevator, past the remaining officers and agents, Esther knew there was only one entity that could stop this.

"I need to lie down," she said suddenly.

Flagston nodded. "Of course. Let's get you upstairs."

Esther allowed herself to be led. She needed to find Ceit before the entire world was cast into darkness.

51

KERRI

KERRI WRAPPED HER ARMS AROUND HER KNEES AND rocked back and forth, trying to stay silent, as her mother had told her. They had been on the trail on the east side of the basin when they'd seen the first small pocket of people walking across the landscape, off the designated trail, into the off-limits area where the pool of green and blue lay dormant, the remnants of what had once been one of the largest volcanoes in the world.

Kerri's mother had yelled after them, told them to stay on the path, that it wasn't safe. They had ignored her. Kerri had been afraid when one of the men stopped and turned, staring down her mother. "Shut up, bitch," he had said, and Kerri had wanted to cry then too. But she hadn't. She didn't cry all the time, really; just some of it. Mom had taken her hand and led her away, ignoring the man as he turned and followed the group off into the woods.

"I'll call the ranger station," she had said and pulled out her cell phone. Kerri had watched as another group and another walked the same route, off the path, into the land that was dotted with

Do Not Enter signs. Kerri sucked in her breath when she saw that one of the women was carrying what looked like one of the butcher knives they had in their kitchen, but bigger. Kerri pulled on her mother's sleeve and pointed. "Jesus Christ," her mom had muttered and pulled Kerri closer. They had ducked into the bush and out of sight of the groups of people that just kept coming.

Kerri didn't know who her mother was talking to, but her voice was frustrated.

"No, they didn't threaten me, but, yes…yes, he insulted me. But…No, that's not why I called. I don't expect you to respond to an insult. I…They're off trail, and at least one of them has a big knife, like a machete kind of knife…Well no, I don't know for sure it was a machete…I understand, but they are off trail, and there are so many of them. Several groups have walked by, and there's at least five in each group…Me? My daugher and I are on trail. We're out looking at birds…birds. We're birders. No, I don't need help…I mean, maybe. But can you send a ranger out to see what the hell they are doing? I'm sorry for the language. I know…Yes, I know you don't need to hear that.…Can you just send someone?"

Her mom hung up, and Kerri looked up at her. "Jesus Christ, you'd think I asked for the National Guard," she muttered.

"Mom, what's going on?" Kerri asked, feeling a little sick to her stomach.

"I don't know, honey, but I don't want to be involved. Let's go up the trail to the overlook. We can see whatever is happening from a distance up there. We'll be safe." She smoothed Kerri's hair. "Hey, maybe we'll see that flycatcher. You have the binoculars, right?"

Kerri nodded and then trotted after her mother as they ascended up the steeper part of the trail to the overlook. Her mother was a botanist at the community college in Jackson Hole. Kerri went to her classes during the summer, sitting in the back, listening to her mother's voice, watching the college students take notes. She loved those lecture halls with their low theatre lights and dusty smell. But it was the weekends that were the best. They packed up and came here, looking for yellow warblers and buffleheads. This summer, she had promised Kerri they would find a red-breasted merganser. There had been a sighting in this area, and they had come back to the basin every Saturday with the good camera.

As they reached the overlook, Kerri's mom took her hand and pulled her down so they were obscured by the fence. Between the slats, they could see the lake of gold and red and green—the chemical soup, as her mom called it—that made up the basin. Around the perimeter, there were people holding hands, forming a circle. More were joining with each passing minute.

"Mom...what's going on?" Kerri whispered, another sob stuck in her throat.

"Shhhh, baby. Don't let them know we're here. Sound carries from up here. I don't know, baby. I don't know." Mom pulled out her cell phone and pressed the buttons for the ranger station again. Her voice was a frantic whisper, and even Kerri knew she was scared.

"You need to send rangers out to the basin, right off the Overlook Trail. There's something crazy going on out here. No....No. I'm here with my daughter, and we're at the overlook point. I can see, Jesus, maybe a hundred people down below. They're holding hands, in a circle, right at the basin edge....No...right there....Yes, like I said before, they're off trail. Way off trail...Who are they? I don't know. It's men and women. They all seem to be adults, I don't see any kids.... Similarities? I don't see any at all. They're all different ages, races, everything, short, tall. They're just people, lots and lots of people. If they're a group, it's not because they look alike....I don't know…Wait, I don't see anything. I don't see guns, if that's what you mean.…But no, wait…I do see, Jesus, a few more of them look like they have knives, like big ones.…Okay, we'll stay here.…Okay."

She hung up and then pushed the phone back into the pocket of her cargo shorts. "They're sending rangers over. They said to stay here. Honey, I don't know what this is, but just stay down. Whatever they're doing, we don't need to be involved."

"Mom…look…"

A song was drifting up the hill on the wind. The group was singing. Kerri strained to hear. As they sang, each person seemed to sprinkle something behind them, something they took out of their pockets in small bags.

I sing of the fae and the wood and the vine,
And the night that lasts forever.
The ghosts of your loves and the ghosts that are mine,
Will linger there forever.

It sounded like a lullaby song, like the baby songs her mom had sung to Kerri when she was little.

Let's call to the wind, to the sun, and the rain,
And the night that lasts forever.
Out beyond the veil is the blackest of nights,
Your soul gone to the nether.

All the men and women were standing again, clasping hands, their faces tilted toward the sky.

"Momma…" Kerri whispered. She hadn't called her "Momma" since she was a baby—she was a big girl now, and not a baby—but she didn't feel right. She wanted to bury her head in her momma's shoulder and go away from this place. "Momma, I don't like this. Let's go. Let's just go." Below them the song swelled in volume.

The dead never sleep and the night never breaks,
You're alone until forever.
With teeth that can bite and the claws that will tear,
Your soul it will not weather.

Kerri could hear the siren of the ranger vehicle in the distance, but the wind was drowning it out. It had been a clear day, the sky just a little smoggy from the fire that had been contained up north of here. No wind. But now it whipped around Kerri and her mother, making her hair tangle and her eyes sting.

"Yeah, baby, let's go. This is too much," her mom said, pulling Kerri to her feet and back to the path. Just as Kerri started to turn, she saw one of the distant figures put a knife to his throat.

"Mommm…" she half screeched. "Mommmmm!"

In horror, Kerri and her mother stood frozen at the edge of the overlook as the hundreds of men and women below raised knives and daggers and long shards of sharpened metal and glass to their throats. In what felt like slow motion, they drew them across in one synchronized motion. Kerri heard herself scream from a distance. Her head felt disembodied, as though it were floating above her like a carnival balloon. Her mother pulled her back, her voice joining Kerri's in an empty scream.

Bodies dropped to the ground one after another, crumbling onto each other as they fell. Blood poured from their necks. Red-black stained the ground. Kerri stared in horror at a young woman who had fallen faceup. Her dark hair fell across her face, but Kerri could see her eyes were open. Her neck was pulsing, an invisible force spraying more and more across her skin. The smell of iron, of violence, of insanity drifted up on the wind, and Kerri gagged.

"Kerri. We have to run now." Her mother grabbed her hand and pulled her along the path. As she turned, Kerri swore she saw a man standing in the center of the madness, right where the lake of the basin met. *He's walking on water like Jesus did*, she thought absurdly. He looked up and caught Kerri's eye, and she shuddered as it appeared he winked at her. Her mother pulled hard, and they stumbled down the path. They ran back past the point where they had seen the groups crossing into the restricted areas and kept moving. A helicopter circled above in increasingly lower circles. Kerri felt as though her lungs were going to explode. Sirens filled her ears, the sound coming from the road that was impossibly far away.

Suddenly the earth itself shook, and her mom stopped running, standing stock-still.

"Kerri, it's an earthquake. Sit down immediately. If it throws you off your feet, you could be hurt."

Kerri let go of her mother's hand and sat crisscross applesauce on the dirt path. Just as her mom was about to join her, the earth rocked back and forth. Kerry was thrown to her back. The ground underneath her seemed to be rolling. She could see the path behind them rise and fall, the soil splitting, the brush falling down, down. Kerri looked up to see her mother on her back, her form still. Kerri screamed again. This time, the sound was overpowering, deafening in her ears. Again, the earth rolled and split. Dirt spilled into the crevice, which was growing ever wider. Her mom lay motionless, her head and arms hanging off the edge of the crack.

"Momma!" Kerri screamed and tried to scramble forward, but yet another tremor threw her back. She felt a sharp pain on the back of her head, and her vision went all white for a moment. Blind and in pain, she pulled herself forward, trying to grab her mother's leg. Her eyes cleared, and she made out the bottom of her shoe. Kerri breathed with relief as she grabbed her mother's ankle. "Mom! Mom! Wake up!"

The weight pulled her arm taut as another tremor rolled beneath her. Her mother's ankle slipped from her grasp, and she slithered into the hole. Kerri pulled herself to the edge and reached down, desperate to pull her back up, but she was gone. The hole seemed to go on forever. It was sheer darkness filling with the red dirt of the basin. Kerri stared for a moment. *Momma is gone...gone.* She had let go, and her mother was gone.

Another roll of the earth, and Kerri felt herself thrown precariously close to falling in herself. In panic, she scooted back on her butt until she was off the path and under a scrub bush. Her throat was sore and raw, her eyes dry. Kerri pulled her knees to her chest and rocked back and forth. *Stay silent. Don't let the baddies find you. Don't let them find you.* She repeated the words to herself as the din of the helicopters grew closer.

52

ESTHER

FLAGSTON LED ESTHER BACK TO HIS OFFICE.

"I'll take you to a place you can rest in a moment, but I need you for a sec," he said hurriedly. Esther nodded as she took a seat.

Flagston pulled out a thick packet of papers from his desk. "This is the geological report that Bozeman sent over earlier. Everything that is happening right now is basically impossible according to every bit of science I can understand in this thing."

"Not impossible evidently," Esther replied.

"Well yes, it is. It should take years for a dome to rise in the basin, during which time, we would all know that we're basically fucked. But like in those asteroid-hitting-Earth movies, not much we can do about it," Flagston muttered.

"Maybe we should send some oil drillers trained to be geologists down into the lava," Esther said wryly.

"Hilarious. That's hilarious. Really." Flagston rubbed his temples.

"What did you want to talk to me about?" Esther asked.

"Your father caused this. I have no fucking idea how, but he did. Maybe he can stop it. Will you talk to him? I'll take you down there right now, just you outside his cell, none of the pomp and ceremony. Will you do it?" Flagston stared at her, his face desperate.

"It won't help, but yes, I will do it," Esther said. "I know exactly what he is doing. So did Cooper. There's no stopping it. He put a thing in motion, and in motion it will stay."

"Just try, please," Flagston pleaded.

"Take me there. But then I will need some time alone," Esther said firmly.

"Understood."

The FCI was in utter chaos. No one noticed Flagston and Esther in the elevator as Flagston punched in the security code. They descended to the holding cells. As they stepped out from the elevator, Esther shivered. The air was unconscionably cold, and she felt gooseflesh break out across her arms and neck.

"Sorry, cold down here." Flagston took off his suit jacket and hung it around Esther's shoulders. She gratefully accepted it and then looked down the long hallway full of metal-lined doors with thick glass fronts. As they walked, Esther could see mostly empty cells. A man in one looked up curiously and then down again. When they reached the very end of the hallway, Esther turned to see her father lying back on a metal cot with no sheets. His cell held the cot, a metal toilet, and a small metal sink. That was all.

"No sheets, no towels. He was on suicide watch," Flagston explained as he flipped a light on the wall, which illuminated her father's cell.

"Suicide is the least of your worries with him," Esther said.

Flagston ignored her and pressed a call box on the glass front. "Robertson, your daughter is here." He turned to Esther. "He was unconscious when they brought him down, but they told me he woke up a bit when they put him on the bed." Flagston pressed the talk button again. "Robertson, this is the last chance you'll ever have to speak to her."

Esther placed a hand on Flagston's shoulder. "Maybe you could give us a little space." Flagston nodded hesitantly and backed past the next cell.

Esther pressed the talk button. "Dad," she said simply.

At that, Alan Robertson sat up. His face was pale, but his eyes held the same unearthly glow they had always had.

"If you hit the hold button, you don't have to keep pressing talk. Then I can hear you, and you can hear me," he said.

Esther nodded. "I know what you are," she said, her voice level. She was not afraid of this man any longer. Esther realized that even back before Los Angeles, she had always feared him. Feared his anger, his erratic moods. Feared he would leave; feared he would come back. But now she stared at this empty shell, lost and trapped forever in the waking world. She felt no fear or pity, no love or hate. She felt an absence, a void.

"Good," he said, sitting cross-legged on the bed, his spine straight.

"Can you stop it?" Esther asked.

Alan Robertson shook his head. "An object in motion tends to stay in motion."

"She admits she made a mistake in casting you out," Esther said.

Her father chuckled, an oddly human sound. "The great Ceit Robertson admitting she made a mistake. The world really is ending."

"Why did you bomb Los Angeles? Why did you start?" Esther leaned forward and placed both hands on the glass. She could feel Flagston shift uneasily from where he stood.

"Daughter, as we leave this world, as we die, Ceit—the Bandia

Marbh—opens the gate to the world beyond this and ushers those souls into the Night Forest. I brought her an army, an army that would be so full of blood and hate, confusion and pain, that I thought to overthrow her and take my rightful place. The Society did not always have a Matrarc, you see, daughter. They were led by a Ceannaire. And even though I was cursed to be born a boy, I had some of his sight, some of his magick. Not nearly like my sister, and nothing I could control until I was much, much older. But Los Angeles did not happen as I wanted. She opened the gates but locked me out. She cast me out to the Sluagh. I became a hungry ghost, in this body that feels all the mortal slings and arrows but will only die once it rots out from under me. The pain of that is indescribable. I will carry that for eternity.

"So I am bringing another army. In a very short time—hours really—I will have accomplished what six hundred forty thousand years could not do. But this will be different. I planned better this time. No one knew it was coming. The first blast is happening so, so soon, and then the soot and ash will block the sun, and we will all die. I'll send in my first wave, but then the world entire will follow, and I will enter with them, lost in the masses. I will take back what is mine, and you will be my voice, daughter. We can live in such comfort and beauty."

Esther's hands were shaking. "You've never seen the Night Forest. You do not know of what you speak."

"Wrong," Alan Robertson said quietly, rising to his feet. "I saw it for a moment, after I died. I was a child again, sitting on my porch with my big sister. My mother was cooking breakfast inside, and the sun was rising in the sky. I always loved sunrise. Even when I was a little boy I loved it. A new chance, a new start. She denied me. She sent me back to this world in a cursed form."

"Can you stop it?" Esther asked again.

"No," Alan Robertson said and gave Esther a small smile. "The world is ending, daughter. Come with me. Stay with me. I have felt all these years like I didn't have a daughter anymore. Let me be your father again."

"My father is dead. He died ten years ago after he murdered everyone I loved." Esther turned and walked toward Flagston. From the cell, she could hear her father singing.

I sing of the fae and the wood and the vine,
And the night that lasts forever.
The ghosts of your loves and the ghosts that are mine,
Will linger there forever.

53

ESTHER

AT THE ELEVATOR THEY WERE MET BY AN AIDE, WHO hurriedly rushed them on.

"There's been a development. We need you back in your office. The Geological Survey heads are releasing more information."

Flagston just nodded. Esther shifted uncomfortably. "I need to lie down. You don't need me for this, do you?"

Flagston shook his head. "I suppose not. I'll find you a space. Esther, thank you for trying."

Esther felt a wave of resigned sadness wash over her. "It didn't do any good. It's happening anyway."

The elevator door opened, and the aide hurried down the hall. Flagston led Esther back to the little room where she had been before the interview. As he went to leave her, Flagston paused.

"Esther, you know no one could have persuaded Cooper to do anything or stop doing anything. He was bullheaded. It's what made him famous."

Esther nodded. "I know. But I told him to kill my father. I told him that before I knew any better, but still, it was my instruction."

Flagston paused. "Alan Robertson is a murderer. I'm sorry he is your father, but you aren't responsible for him—you weren't in Los Angeles, and you aren't at Yellowstone now. Look, get some rest. I'll come get you if we need you."

The door clicked shut behind Flagston, and Esther stood up and stretched. There was a small mirror hanging on the far wall, and she caught her reflection. Her hair hung in dull, lank clumps. Her face was drawn. Esther tried to remember the last time she had taken a shower or eaten a meal. She suddenly felt exhausted down to her bones. She and Sarai had played a game when they were little girls; it was a game of lasts. What would you eat for your last dinner? What is the last game you would play? How would you spend your last afternoon? What would you wear on your last day of school? Esther always imagined extravagant meals, steak and caviar like she had seen on television shows. She envisioned trips to Paris and riding in a tiny sports car with the top down as she sped through winding European scenery.

Sarai was the opposite. Her last dinner was her mother's croque madame, the fried ham and cheese with a perfect sunny-side up egg on top. Peasant food, Esther had teased her. Esther's perfect afternoon was at the grassy park just off Santa Monica beach, where she could see the Pier and buy mango slices doused in chili spice from the street vendors. Sarai wanted to stay home. She wanted her last night to be quiet and still. Esther was always the one who spun stories of dramatic endings, aliens and invaders from far-off countries. Sarai would listen and smile. Her lasts were born of ordinary things, quiet things.

Esther sank to the floor. What had Sarai's last really been? Had she had her croque madame? Had she been curled up on the couch, their mother close by? Was she scared? Did she blame Esther? Esther was rocked by decade-old grief. She had cried for Sarai and her mother only once and then locked up their memories tight as a drum inside her head. But now they came flooding out, and with them the tears she had never allowed herself to shed. What would Sarai look like today? She had favored their mother. Would her hair have turned dark like hers by now? Would her hazel eyes still take on a deep forest green when she was concentrating? Maybe her mother would have left their father for good, moved away from that little house and all its ugly memories. Maybe she'd have remarried, and have a yard and a dog. Maybe, maybe, maybe. Ceit had told her they had both passed through the Night Forest on that day back in November, ten years ago. Had they forgotten her? Maybe you forget everything as you pass from one world to the next. Maybe you need to. The pain of living is too much to carry.

She didn't deserve to be the last one left. Esther had utterly failed to stop anything. She had killed the world. In a few short hours, days, weeks, all that existed would crumble. Children would freeze in a sunless world. Mothers would starve to death. Sons and fathers and every living thing would close their eyes for the last time, twisted by pain and suffering. Esther had done this. And she knew there was only one absolution for her crime, the crime of getting on that bus a decade ago, the crime of being the one who lived when so many had not.

She pulled herself off the floor and lay down on the stiff sofa. The Night Forest melted into view. The veil was thin, readying itself for the flood of souls to come. Instead of the meadow and the forest, Esther found herself on the night beach, the rocky outcropping jutting into the sea. The Asrai leapt in the distance, sending ripples through the water. Amon stood with his back to her. As she approached, Amon turned his head and offered a gentle smile. He held out his hand, and Esther took it, his flesh cold and inhuman.

"She will be along shortly. There is much to prepare," he said simply.

Together they stood on the shore, watching the black waves roll in and out, waiting in silence for the end to begin.

54

KERRI

THE HELICOPTERS STILL CIRCLED OVERHEAD, BUT THE footsteps that had run back and forth, back and forth had stopped. The earth still shook, but Kerri could stand without being thrown back down. She should have gone with the uniformed men who had been running back and forth on the trail, but she had stayed burrowed in the scrub bush instead. Her binoculars were still around her neck, but her backpack with the bird book and the camera was gone. Kerri pulled herself out of the brush and peered around. Slowly, the crevice that had taken her mother had widened and folded in on itself. Kerri felt numb, as though her entire body was full of static. *It wasn't real, it wasn't real, it wasn't real.* Her mother had to be somewhere around here, somewhere. Maybe she had taken the camera back to the overlook to get some shots of the new landscape. The blue-gold lake of the basin was gone, and in its place it looked like a mountain was growing. Kerri didn't understand. That's not how mountains worked. *Momma will know,* she thought. *She'll explain.*

Kerri struggled to her feet and stepped out onto the path, which was broken in places, but the direction was still clear. She climbed up the hill. It was harder this time; her legs wouldn't stop shaking. As she walked, she sang a song her mother used to sing at night when she was littler. She felt very little right now and hoped her momma would sing it again when she found her.

Oh do you remember a long time ago
Two poor little babes whose name I don't know
Were stolen away, one bright summer day
And left in the woods, so I've heard people say.

Her momma had said it was a song her own mother used to sing to her, and her mother before that. The ground shook again, and Kerri nearly lost her balance, but she grabbed a tree branch at the last minute and steadied herself. Kerri could hear the song of the yellow warbler in the branches overhead. She leaned against the trunk of the tree to try to catch a glimpse. Another tremor hit. It felt as though a wave was rising and falling underground. Her head hurt, and she was suddenly very thirsty. More than anything, Kerri wanted to go home. She wanted to find her momma and go home and forget all the terrible things she had seen. The tremor stopped, and Kerri set out on the path. She had a faint memory that something had happened to her mother and she wouldn't find her at the overlook. Something really bad had happened, but Kerri couldn't quite remember and didn't want to try. She kept walking upward to the overlook, sure that everything would make sense if she got there.

And when it was night
So bleak was their plight

The sun went down, the moon gave no light.
They sobbed and they sighed
And bitterly cried
Till those poor little babes, they lay down and died.

Kerri reached the top of the path and leaned against the wooden rail of the overlook. In the place where the lake of gold and red and blue had been, the growing mountain stood. She squinted, trying to understand what she was seeing. It seemed like all of the land surrounding the mountain as it spread out across the basin was rising up to meet this one impossiby tall spire. Even the dirt under her feet felt as though it were shifting and moving. Trees were being pushed out of the dirt, their roots raw and exposed. All around her, horrible ugly bulges were forming, pulsing in and out. The biggest was on the tallest tower of earth that shot into the sky. The air around Kerri was growing hotter and hotter. It felt like summer when it rained, but so much hotter. Kerri looked around wildly.

"Mommaaaa!!!!" she screamed. The wind around her was whipping her hair into her face, and she remembered that her momma had tried to get her to put her hair in a ponytail before they left, but she'd said no. And now she knew she shouldn't have done that; she should have never said no to her momma. *Where is she, where is she, where is she?*

The bulge on the side of the ugly, terrible mountain began to leak rivers of molten fire. With a cramp of fear, Kerri realized that the entire landscape as far as she could see was pulsing. A spray of fire and smoke shot into the sky. Kerri screamed. The wind was spinning in circles now. The bushes on the side of the overlook were ripped from the ground entirely. Kerri wrapped her arms and legs around the post of the railing and closed her eyes. She heard the sound of the earth ripping apart, and the air turned to fire as the side of the mountain exploded. Another explosion as loud as the first came from a distance. Kerri clung to the post and sang quietly to herself as darkness carried her to the Night Forest.

And when they were dead
The robins so red, took strawberry leaves
And over them spread
And sang them this song, the whole day long
Poor babes in the woods, who ne'r done wrong.

55

ESTHER

"IT'S HAPPENING," A VOICE BEHIND ESTHER SAID quietly. She turned to see Ceit, who walked slowly down the dark beach to stand beside Esther. "The souls of thousands are entering the Night Forest. Most had no idea what was happening. It was an instant in which they went from living to arriving at the gates to my world. They are scared. Their journey will take time."

"Why aren't you there with them?" Esther asked. She felt weary with sadness and futility.

"I am. And I am also here. I am other places too. I am with those who have become trapped in the Night Forest, paralyzed by their fears. I am with those who wish to share their journey, and those who need a guide. I am with the ones who lay dying and feel alone. I am holding their hands so they know they can let go. I am large, I contain multitudes. A poet in your world said that once." Ceit turned to face Esther. Amon had dissipated into a smoky haze that danced on the ocean breeze, and Esther understood his human form was for her benefit entirely, as was Ceit's.

"What happens now?" Esther asked, her voice small and childlike.

"You know what happens," Ceit responded gently. "Your world is dying. Some will die now, others later. In a short time, the ash and soot will circle the globe, blocking out the sun, and they will starve or die of disease or cold. Or perhaps they will kill each other as they fight over what is left. Some may go underground. They will live longer, but there is no life to return to. Your world is scorched earth."

"They will suffer," Esther whispered.

"We all suffer. The mistake is assigning a value to your suffering. Your pain is as great as your joy. Allow yourself to feel every sadness, every bite. Give yourself permission to dive into the depths of your grief, just as you do with love." Ceit reached up and stroked Esther's hair from her face.

"The last time I was happy, my sister and I were at the boardwalk. She got a henna tattoo of a dolphin on her shoulder, and we ate strawberry ice on the sand. I have known only grief since she died." Esther could feel tears on her cheeks. Sarai's face was so vivid before her. She could still remember her hiccuping giggle, the apple scent of her hair.

"You will join her if you wish, or you can stay here in the Night Forest with us. You have a family that loves you, Esther. You have my blood in your veins. You can guide those who are lost. You can revel with the Asrai. You can spend an eternity listening to the songs of the g'nights, and you will never know grief again." Ceit looked up at the swirling cloud that was Amon that moved and pulsated over her head. The smoky haze descended and materialized in human form. Amon gave Esther a small smile and nodded.

"She is right. You can stay here with us, if you choose. You have been alone in the world for so long. Your home is here." Amon dissipated once again and spun in dark circles on the ocean breeze.

"My father says you are the devil," Esther said softly.

Ceit nodded. "I am, and I am god, and goddesses, and all of creation. Just as with your pain, only you can decide what is good or bad. Goodness and evil don't exist in nature, Esther. It is a construct, an idea someone taught you once. Once you allow yourself to be all things, the judgments of the world fall away."

"But my father . . . what he did . . . You punished him. How?" Esther shook her head. She could already feel the ties to the waking world slipping. She could see details in the night her eyes had not been keen enough to make out before.

"I cast him out, this is true. I am imperfect, as are all things in nature. I was angry at his brashness, his disregard. I was wrong. My brother is neither good nor bad either. He is imperfect and sad and broken. He interfered with the path of so, so many all those years ago. He sent them to the Night Forest long before their natural time. And now he has broken the cycle of your world. But he has not done anything that has not been done before. Worlds break. Broken men interfere. It was not my place to cast judgment. He thinks to unseat me, but he does not understand this world beyond the veil. He is powerless here. He always has been. If he were to enter the Night Forest, his pain, his anger, would keep him trapped for perhaps an eternity. If I could undo what I did, I would not interfere with that journey. This is my doing, in truth. I did not cause nature to rise up against its people and I did not cause a disaster to end the world, but I created the monster who did. I failed him, Esther. And for that I am sorry. In truth, I failed him long ago. He was so young when I left your world. He was in so much pain. He wanted love, he wanted to belong, and I left him behind thinking that once he was free of the Society, he would find happiness with your mother, find peace. But I was wrong. He was too broken. And the ties I thought to sever still bound him. He created a new Society, and it was far more deadly than Mór Ainsley ever imagined when she brought her people from Ireland to a new shore."

"How do you make it right?" Esther whispered.

"There is no right—only balance," Ceit responded.

"What of mercy?" Esther asked, turning to watch the Asrai leap into the air and disappear beneath the dark waves.

"What are you asking, Esther?" Ceit said softly.

"The world is dying. I am asking for you to take their pain away. Let them all go softly." Esther turned to meet Ceit's unworldly pale eyes. "I am asking for the end to be gentle."

Ceit's face twisted with concern. "It's not my place."

"It wasn't your place to cast out Alan Robertson either," Esther said. "You said you created the monster who did this. You can restore balance now. Take their pain. Do not let innocent people starve over the course of weeks and months. Do not allow them to live in fear and grief. Take them from that dying world, where they will freeze to death or die of injury and disease alone, scared. Don't let them burn alive when the fire comes raining down on them. Take them now. Let their last moments be gentle." Esther's voice was raw, and she felt tears streaming down her cheeks. She felt how torn Ceit was, and Amon whipped wildly in the space over her head.

"You have your mother's sweet spirit in you. I underestimated her strength, as I know many have underestimated you. Is there anything left in your world that binds you?" Ceit asked gently.

"I want to say goodbye," Esther said softly. "I need to let him go."

Ceit nodded. "Then open your eyes, and when you are ready, come back to us. Your world does not have much time left."

Esther nodded and felt herself falling backward. With a jolt, she awoke on the stiff sofa in the cramped office. On the other side of the door, she could hear utter chaos—footsteps back and forth, frantic voices, the sound of weeping. Esther knew what was happening. With a deep breath to steady herself, she went to find her father.

56

ESTHER

FLAGSTON FLASHED A SECURITY BADGE AT THE PAD IN the elevator, and they descended to the floor where her father was kept in his sterile cell. Flagston had been sitting at his desk with his head in his hands. Wyoming had been leveled in the blast; the loss of life was in the millions. Already, the sky over Denver was black with soot. The sun was gone, and it was eternal night. The ash had spread all the way to Nevada to the west, and Missouri in the east. Winds beyond any meteorological measurings were spreading the poison faster than any scientist had anticipated. The world news was dominated by the disaster.

"The president is evidently in a bunker under Cheyenne Mountain," he said in a stunned voice as the elevator descended.

"It won't save him. Nothing will," Esther replied. "Thank you for trying. You've been so kind." She looked up at Flagston, who was lost in disbelief.

"Nothing worked. I...I...can't understand," he muttered as the door opened to the holding cells.

"I need to see him by myself," Esther said quietly.

Flagston just nodded and stepped to the side of the elevator. "I'll wait here."

Esther steeled herself as she walked to the end of the row of cells. Her father was sitting on his bunk, staring at the wall.

"I knew you would come back," he said, turning to look at her. "At least I hoped you would."

Esther sat on the cold concrete floor. Alan Robertson crossed to the thick glass wall and sat opposite her. For a moment they stared into each other's eyes.

"Do you remember that time you took me to see the horses in Will Rogers Park?" Esther asked quietly.

Her father nodded. "The polo games they used to have up there. We had a picnic on the lawn, remember?"

Esther smiled. "I was so scared. I didn't want to tell you, but I was so scared."

"I knew. But you were trying so hard to be brave," he said with a sad smile on his face.

"I'm not scared anymore," Esther said, placing a hand on the glass. Her father did the same on the other side. She stared at the palm of his hand as she spoke. "I wish I had known you before. I wish I had known the person you were when you were my age. I wish I had known you when you were a child...before..."

"Before I fucked it all up?" her father finished and gave her a sad smile. "I loved your mother, you should know that. She was the first person to really see me, and I remember all the plans we had. If I had followed her to New York like she wanted...If I had...She wanted to run away. She wanted to leave. If I had done that, maybe."

"I need to forgive you," Esther said, staring into her father's eyes.

"No, you don't," he replied gently. "You need to do what you need to do. You can let go of whatever you feel about me without forgiving me. I am exactly where I am supposed to be. Forgiveness is a way to make you feel guilty for your anger. You can be angry. My sister used to tell me that anger was as natural as love, as joy, as sadness. We contain multitudes."

"She said that to me, too," Esther replied, a well of tears threatening to block her throat. "I wish I had you back. I wish I knew you before."

"You will. Talk to your aunt. I live in her memories, and her memories are long. Become what you know you will be. Be kind to yourself," Alan Robertson said gently. It was the voice she remembered from the softest childhood memories, the ones that were more dream than reality.

Esther kept her hand on the glass as she closed her eyes. The veil was so thin, she slipped back through immediately. Ceit and Amon in his nearly human form were waiting for her on the dark sand of the night sea.

"Let's begin," Ceit said softy as Esther took her place.

Night fell quickly. The veil was cast open and wrapped around the world entire. Newborn babies immediately ceased their wailing and grasped with their chubby fingers at the darkness. Tears froze before they fell. The fire-locked pain in dying lungs was cleared. The soot-filled sky, the oppressive heat, the knowledge that the world was broken beyond repair—all these things melted away as every living creature from all continents, all nations and lands found themselves in a perfect green meadow. There was soft green grass under their feet, and an ancient woods bordered the perimeter. A few brave souls set off immediately. Some stayed. Time was not as it had been, so maybe it was years, days, months. They stayed until they were ready to journey through the dark and twisted trees. Some met nightmares and demons. Some were guided by strange creatures with overlarge eyes and skin the color of the birch and maple.

Esther stood on the shore with Ceit and Amon and watched as every living creature down to the smallest insect crossed the veil to the Night Forest. Eternity and no time at all passed as she stood with the Bandia Marbh and her demon. Esther's mind became unbound, and she could see the souls that trudged through the dark growth. Some had suffered greatly, but a great many more had passed through the veil as though it were a dream, a blink of the eye that was met with peace.

Esther saw a little girl lost and hunched at the base of a great oak tree. She flew to her side. The child was cowering and whimpering, singing a strange little song to herself.

"Come, love. Let me help you find your way," Esther said gently.

"I want my momma," the child whispered, her voice choked with grief.

"She is here, looking for you. I can take you to her. Will you follow?" Esther asked in a lilting voice.

The little girl nodded and took her hand. They walked through the forest, whose paths were now clear and bright to Esther's eyes. There was a woman in the next clearing—a woman who had been pulled into the earth by an earthquake, a woman who had taught her daughter the strange little song. As the two souls met again, they embraced, already less substantial than they were a moment before. They were ready to leave the Night Forest and go on to what lay beyond.

"Will you come?" the child asked Esther.

Esther shook her head gently. "No, my place is here."

EPILOGUE

CEIT COULD SMELL PANCAKES AND SUGAR IN THE AIR. The rising sun was creating streaks of gold across the cloudless blue sky. She sat on the steps of the little house on Sinder Avenue and watched the day begin.

Alan sat on the step below her. He had a Matchbox car that he was running back and forth along the wooden plank. Ceit reached out and stroked his hair. It would grow coarse and thick when he was older, but now it was silky, and it caught the morning light in its radiance. He looked up at her and grinned.

"You said you'd never see me again," he said, his little boy voice cross.

"Never is a long time," Ceit said softly.

"I'll be okay," he said.

"I have to say goodbye now," Ceit said and pulled his thin but solid little form up to her step and wrapped her arms around him.

"What will happen to me?" he asked, his small hands twined in her hair.

"I don't know. You have to stay in your world, and I in mine," she replied softly, kissing the top of his small head.

"It's a spirit world now. I will starve there." Alan looked up at her, his eyes wide and full of understanding.

"I know," she said simply.

"Maybe, a very long time from now, even the hungry ghosts that have to stay behind will die. Maybe then," Alan said hopefully.

"Maybe then," Ceit said. "Goodbye, Alan."

The sun rose over the rooftops of the little bungalows, and Alan's hand in hers became as insubstantial as the breeze. Ceit stood as the smell of home and the steps beneath her feet faded away. She was once again on the shore with the Night Forest to her back. Her niece, her blood, was in the forest guiding lost souls as Amon twisted and writhed through the treetops, keeping watch. They were a family, and the world was once again whole.

ACKNOWLEDGMENTS

ANYTHING AND EVERYTHING I WRITE ONLY EXISTS because of the love that surrounds me. Thank you to my husband, who has been made to muse about interesting ways the world could end for a couple of years now, and he still hasn't changed the locks. My son, whose endless creativity amazes me every single day.

Thank you to the team at Turner Publishing, who took a chance on a crazy trilogy about a devil-girl and made it real. Thank you to my agents at Paradigm Talent for your encouragement and support.

The Son of Abraham enters the world in an interesting time. A book about the end of the world as we know it in a time when we are working to start a new way of living. Hope is the purest of things, perhaps the most fragile, but still it persists.

ABOUT THE AUTHOR

KATHLEEN KAUFMAN'S prose has been praised by *Kirkus Reviews* as "crisp, elegant" and "genuinely chilling" by *Booklist*. She is the author of the Diabhal Trilogy, featuring *Diabhal* and *Sinder*, with *The Son of Abraham* being the third and final installment. Her novel *The Lairdbalor* will soon be a feature film with Screen Australia and director Nicholas Verso. She is also the author of acclaimed historical horror *Hag*, and sci-fi thriller *The Tree Museum*. When not writing, she can be found teaching liter-ature and composition at Santa Monica College or hanging out with a good book. Kathleen Kaufman is a native Coloradan and lives in Los Angeles with her husband, son, hound, and a pack of cats.